Vivian Conroy is a mu... ...th
25+ contracted titles. A... ...g,
crafting and spending ... ...rs
can connect with her u...

Also by Vivian Conroy

Miss Ashford Investigates Mysteries
Death on the Rhine
Last Dance in Salzburg
A Fatal Encounter in Tuscany
Last Seen in Santorini
Mystery in Provence

Cornish Castle Mysteries
Rubies in the Roses
Death Plays a Part

Country Gift Shop Mysteries
Written into the Grave
Grand Prize: Murder!
Dead to Begin With

Lady Alkmene Callender Mysteries
Fatal Masquerade
Deadly Treasures
Diamonds of Death
A Proposal to Die For

Merriweather and Royston Mysteries
Death Comes to Dartmoor
The Butterfly Conspiracy

Murder Will Follow Mysteries
An Exhibition of Murder
Under the Guise of Death
Honeymoon With Death
A Testament to Murder

DEATH ON THE RHINE

Miss Ashford Investigates

VIVIAN CONROY

One More Chapter

a division of HarperCollins*Publishers* Ltd

1 London Bridge Street

London SE1 9GF

www.harpercollins.co.uk

HarperCollinsPublishers

Macken House, 39/40 Mayor Street Upper,

Dublin 1, Ireland, D01 C9W8

This paperback edition 2025

1

First published in Great Britain in ebook format
by HarperCollinsPublishers 2025

A catalogue record of this book is available from the British Library

ISBN: 978-0-00-873707-8

Printed and bound in the UK using 100% Renewable Electricity
by CPI Group (UK) Ltd

Chapter One

Bonn, April 1931

Miss Atalanta Ashford crossed the street and stood looking up at the façade of the house on Bonngasse. It was impressive with its large front door of shiny painted wood, tall windows, and white stone elements, but many buildings in this beautiful German city exuded such splendour. It was the particular history contained in this house that had drawn Atalanta here. For many years she had taught music at an exclusive Swiss boarding school and one of the composers whose work she had often taught her pupils was Beethoven. She had read about his life and knew he had been born in Bonn, but she had never imagined herself being able to visit the house of his birth. After all, her salary from teaching had been sent to England to pay her late father's debts and she hadn't had much left for herself, let alone to indulge in travel.

Still, she had often dreamed about seeing faraway places and had kept a large collection of magazine clippings and postcards her pupils sent her. Those fortunate young girls had seen a lot more of the world than Atalanta had, and although she had fought the feeling, she had sometimes felt more than a little jealousy at their position in life. She herself had been the daughter of a titled man, born into privilege, but her father had spurned his birthright, determined to forge his own path in life. He had often tried to prove himself or made decisions in order to spite his father and these had not all turned out well. Atalanta sometimes felt sorry that her father's life had been so much of a struggle and it could have been easier if he had focused less on the past and looked ahead to the future. Or perhaps if he had come to terms with his position and returned home to his father… She would have so liked to have known her grandfather.

Now, both her father and grandfather had passed away and she was the only heir to all her grandfather had left: houses, cars, stocks, and a sleuthing business for the elite of Europe. The latter had brought her to many places she had never seen before: the lush lavender fields of Provence, the red cliffs of volcanic Santorini and the picturesque countryside of Italy with its charming cities like Venice and Milan. She had often travelled somewhere on assignment, mixing the pleasure of seeing amazing sights with the unpleasant business of hunting a clever killer. So far she had enjoyed enough success to keep clients coming to her door. But she also wished from time to time to travel for her own enjoyment, and with her birthday a few days away it had seemed appropriate to plan a little trip.

Renard, her invaluable butler, had taken care of all the arrangements, promising her a fabulous stay with plenty of history. He had not revealed too much about the actual plans in order to surprise her, and as she stood now and surveyed the house where such a musical genius had been born, she felt a surge of energy at the idea that this was but the beginning.

It was a pity though that Renard had not been able to come himself to explore the streets of Bonn. He had muttered something about following up with a contact in a case she was still working on. It had proven to be a difficult matter of retrieving an heirloom that had disappeared with a runaway son and been sold off for travelling money. The inquiries had to be made with the utmost discretion and so far she didn't have much progress to report.

I wonder, it flashed through her mind, *whether Monsieur Gispot would have solved it already.*

A few weeks ago, the morning paper Renard always put ready for her on the breakfast table had sported a conspicuous large advertisement offering the services of a new detective. This man, who claimed to have worked for the crowned heads of Europe, had established himself on one of the most prestigious streets of Paris and Atalanta, fuelled by curiosity, had gone that very day to see his house. It had looked spectacular, with people rushing in and out:

servants with parcels, telegram boys, and two well-to-do ladies with a hushed air about them, suggesting they were there to consult the detective. As she had stood on the other side of the street watching the bustle, she had wondered what Gispot's arrival might mean for her own detecting. Would he steal all her potential clients? Or would people who had known her grandfather and relied on his wisdom still come to her?

Perhaps she was coming to a hasty conclusion as it had only been a few weeks, but she had most certainly already lost business to him. It had been decidedly quiet and apart from the pesky case to recover the heirloom, not much had come her way. She should be happy perhaps and enjoy her birthday celebrations but somehow the idea that this man had come to draw all of Paris to him and leave her out in the cold bothered her more than she cared to admit. Who was he? Why had he come to Paris? Was he really any good or just good at making people pay for inferior services?

She had asked Renard to look into the man's past and background but Renard had reported back to her that his usual contacts were loath to say much about Gispot. Apparently they all feared him because he seemed to know everything that happened, every whisper on the streets, and he could be vengeful when he felt he was being crossed. Renard had said it might be better to just leave Gispot be and trust that after the novelty of his advertisements wore off people would return to her. After all, she had her grandfather's long and established reputation to rely on.

A ray of sunshine brushed across the year carved into the house's front. 1770. How much had happened in this street. What changes this house had witnessed since the days of Beethoven when there had been just carts and carriages in the street via the arrival of the steam tram and electric tram, then motorcars. The nearby river Rhine had originally transported cargo and troops, had been used as a line of defence, and to collect a toll from ships travelling from Switzerland further into Germany and eventually all the way to the North Sea. The elegant castles and impressive strongholds erected along the stream had started to draw tourists and then boats were also used to transport these eager travellers to the region who would then follow the river along majestic cities and charming villages, past lush vineyards producing prize wines, and the towering stone formation of the Loreley, celebrated by poets and painters alike. Everything here seemed steeped in history and have some story to tell.

She was very much looking forward to seeing more of it.

"Fräulein Ashford?" a voice asked. She looked down to see a small boy standing by her side. He smiled up at her and gestured with his hand for her to follow him. She had no idea what he wanted of her even though she asked him in fluent German. He didn't seem to understand for he just kept gesturing. She thought it could not hurt to walk along and see where he wanted to take her.

Casting a last look at the house of Beethoven's birth, she followed the boy across the pavement. He seemed headed for a nearby coffee house. She could smell the scent of spices on the air. It was a spring day with a brisk wind and her cheeks and hands were chilly. Perhaps it could not hurt to venture inside and see if the coffee was as good as the scents promised it to be. They might also serve some kind of delicious *Torte* for her to try. German pastry was among her favourite sweet treats and she couldn't wait to try the local specialties.

As she entered, the light was dimmer than the bright sunshine outside, momentarily making her pause to allow her eyes to adjust. As she regained focus, she saw a tall figure standing by the hearth. He turned to her and smiled widely. She blinked to clear her vision. Dark hair, broad shoulders, self-confident stance with his feet planted apart... But it could not be...

Or could it?

"Raoul!" She started towards him and he met her halfway, catching her hands in his.

"Atalanta! Happy Birthday! I know it's not for a few days yet but on the date I have a race I really have to attend. I thought I could come early and surprise you."

She kept smiling even though her heart sank a little at his immediate mention of a race. He was a race car driver – a passionate one, a good one, a true champion. He lived for his racing, as he often emphasised. To her mind it was a dangerous profession, but who was she to say so to him when she herself hunted killers? But it was more than just knowing his life was in constant danger. It was the way in which racing consumed him. It always came first in his life;

she came second.

Or perhaps third or fourth?

She didn't even know. When they were together, there was a special pull – a feeling that they were connected and somehow meant to be together. But when they were apart and he didn't write because he hated writing letters and he didn't call because he never had the time, she wondered how much she really meant to him and whether it would in fact be better to accept that they would always be friends but nothing more than that.

Raoul had often made it clear that he didn't want to marry for feelings. That if he ever married at all it would be for gain – to promote his career and have money for his racing. On impulse, she had once offered him her fortune to start his own team and offered to join him in this venture, to give up sleuthing to marry him. Raoul had refused.

Her rational mind told her that he had done the right thing, as he was a proud man who would have difficulty living out of her pocket. He might not mind if the relationship were distant and without feelings, but with her and Raoul the trouble was that there were always too many feelings; an inexplicable but very real attraction and the inevitable bitter disappointment that it wasn't big enough to overcome the things that separated them.

"You look very serious," Raoul said as he studied her features. "Is this competitor still bothering you?"

She had written to him about Monsieur Gispot and even included one of his advertisements torn from the paper.

Raoul had called to tell her she need not worry and the novelty would wear off soon.

But it had not.

Not yet.

Perhaps it never would.

She shook her head to dismiss the thoughts.

"It doesn't really matter now. You are here. That is what is important. Did Renard know you were coming? Did you agree on this with him?"

"Yes. I made him keep me informed of when you planned to arrive and what you would be doing. I also told him to make up some excuse to make himself scarce." Raoul beamed at her. "Now we have time to explore the city together."

Atalanta nodded with an enthusiasm she didn't truly feel. Her happiness to see Raoul and be able to spend time with him was marred by his casual dismissal of Renard. Her butler was so good to her and had helped her with so many things. It felt callous to send him on a petty errand when privacy was wanted.

And why did Raoul resent his presence anyway?

Because, she realised, when he was there, he wanted the limelight to himself. He didn't like to share her, not even with a faithful servant. The faithful servant who had to do all the work and take care of her in lonely times when Raoul wasn't around. It felt almost like he could attract people to him and push them away at will, however he liked. She loathed that character trait in others but with Raoul she always found some excuse for his behaviour.

Wasn't she much like a puppet dancing to his tune? As soon as he had time for her, she obliged him by being ready to join him for any idea he came up with. She tried to fit into the empty spaces in his busy schedule. She travelled sometimes to meet him for a few hours between races. She was always happy to see him, but was this really how she had imagined a relationship to be?

Did they even have a relationship?

Raoul had said she had too little experience with men to know if she was truly in love with him. If she wanted to be with him. That she needed time to explore her own feelings and see more of life. It was sound advice and yet it also felt a little like an easy escape route for himself. Because he was nowhere near ready to commit to her.

Perhaps he would never be.

Would she just keep waiting for him? Following him around like a little dog?

It was her birthday soon and he had no time on the day itself because his racing was more important to him. She was supposed to be delighted by this sudden surprise arrival and the prospect of spending time together in beautiful Bonn, but was she really? Or did it also feel like he was giving her the scraps and never the real thing?

"Let us sit down and have coffee with cake," Raoul urged. "I arranged for them to have various kinds ready to offer us. I know how you enjoy a good slice of cake while abroad."

"It's always nice to try the local speciality," Atalanta agreed.

She sat down and Raoul took a seat opposite her. He leaned his suntanned hands on the table edge and the fingers of his right hand started playing almost nervously with something attached to his left wrist. As she looked closer, she saw it was a gold link bracelet with a charm on it of a bird in flight.

"I don't think I ever saw that before," she said, nodding at it.

Raoul glanced down as if he didn't know to what she was referring. Then he withdrew his right hand quickly and said, "After we have coffee, I have arranged for us to go and see the zoological museum. It is said to have an excellent collection of dead beetles. I can imagine doing more pleasant things on a spring afternoon in Bonn than looking at dead beetles but I know you love all those kinds of things."

It seemed to underline the differences between them. Here he was sitting with her having snatched a few hours away from his precious racing and they weren't even going to do something he enjoyed.

She swallowed, then said, "We need not go to the zoological museum if you would rather do something else. We could take a walk along the river and just … enjoy each other's company."

Raoul seemed to recoil at the suggestion. He sat up straight and said quickly, "No, I arranged for tickets and for the conservator to be present to explain a few things. It would be very impolite not to show up."

"I see."

The waiter came with coffee and a tray full of plates with slices of cakes. Some were prepared with chocolate and nuts; others had crumble on top and a filling of fruit such as apple and rhubarb. There was a sponge cake with lots of little black dots in it, and the waiter explained it was *Mohn* – poppy seed – and that it was very delicious. She decided to try that one first.

Raoul chose the rhubarb crumble cake and they ate in silence for a few moments. Atalanta chewed the deliciously light cake and watched Raoul sitting across from her, his strong profile outlined against the coffee house's classic interior. This trip had everything she loved – beautiful architecture, delicious treats, and the best company in the world – and still she didn't feel totally happy. There were too many questions going through her head.

For instance, why he hadn't answered her question about the bracelet.

Her heart raced at the idea that it was a gift from a female admirer. There were many rich, middle-aged ladies following sports and trying to get into contact with the sportsmen. Just a few weeks previously, the papers had been full of news about the scandalous affair of a widow in her fifties and a thirty-year-old jockey who rode her late husband's horses. She had actually married the man, much to the dismay of her children who feared that their inheritance would be squandered. They were even seeking legal advice to prove that their mother had been lured into the marriage with false promises or that she had been of unsound mind when she made the decision to marry someone so far beneath her station.

Atalanta wondered if there was a rich woman somewhere right now who was smiling to herself at the idea that the interesting, attractive race car driver Raoul Lemont was wearing her gift and would soon be her husband … or just her lover. Atalanta didn't know which would be worse. To have to share Raoul in casual affairs with women who could promote his career while he didn't marry because he was shy of commitment. Or losing him forever once he was married and bound to the woman he might not love but had promised his future to.

She shook her head impatiently. He had not even told her who the bracelet was from. It could be from…

Yes, from whom? What lie could she tell herself to keep believing that she and Raoul could be together some day?

Raoul looked at her over the rim of his coffee cup. "Renard told me you were out of sorts and he was right. I have never seen you look so glum."

Atalanta felt a flush creep up her neck. "When did you speak to Renard?"

"When I made the plan with him to lure you here for the surprise. I just mentioned it. You really are distracted." He frowned, his deep brown eyes filling with concern. "Is this new detective such a huge problem for you?"

"No, not at all," she lied hurriedly. "I mean, he is not what I am thinking about."

"Can you share?" Raoul reached across the table and put his hand on hers. "I know I should have written more letters. You asked me to, over Christmas and on New Year's Eve and in early March when we met in Rome."

Atalanta flushed even deeper. He made it sound like she was constantly begging for his attention. But she wasn't. Not really. She had just wanted him to write more often so she could get to know him better from his letters. She might know a few things about him but she didn't feel like she really knew him inside; what he loved or loathed, what he dreamed of, what kept him awake at night. She wanted to know something more personal that could tell her whether they could bridge their differences and connect in a deeper way.

But with him sabotaging the plan by never writing more than a few hurried lines about trivial matters, she had made no progress at all.

"I am just busy." Raoul shrugged as he withdrew his hand from hers. "I often have engagements in the evening and I don't feel like sitting down to write a letter at one in the morning. I sleep in late to keep my health strong and then I have to run after more engagements."

"How is the situation with the team?" she asked. When they had met in Salzburg in November of last year, she had discovered that his team had doubts about his future with them and were thinking of releasing him. It had hurt that he had not shared this with her and she had found out by accident. But she had also realised that she didn't show enough interest in his career and should be more active about it.

Raoul didn't seem happy with the question. He plucked at the bracelet again and said, "We're getting there."

It was a cryptic reply. "So you will still be racing for them this season?"

"I'm keeping all options open. I might even start my own team."

"I'm glad to hear that." Where would he get the money for that? She knew he liked to live well and spend most of what he earned. And his parents didn't support his career so he couldn't expect any funds from that direction.

She couldn't help herself casting new suspicious looks at the bracelet. The more she thought of it, the more its links reminded her of a dog collar. Had some wealthy widow put a collar on Raoul by offering him money for his own team if he spent time with her?

Raoul stared past her. He seemed to see something interesting behind her back, but when she glanced over her shoulder, she realised he was merely checking the time on the beautiful old clock standing there. It had wooden carving depicting birds and flowers. They had been painted in vivid colours, the artist taking the time to add the smallest details.

"I should get a clock for my home," she said. "Do you know a good shop here that sells them? Perhaps you can help me pick it?"

"I don't know much about such things." Raoul finished his coffee. "I think your butler would be more up to the task. He seems to know something about everything."

That sounded like Renard had said something to Raoul

that had ruffled his feathers. She didn't know what it might have been. Had Renard felt like Raoul seemed to be usurping the birthday party trip for his own purposes? Had her faithful butler tried to clarify to Raoul that he wasn't *his* servant and would not simply do anything he asked?

She had to find out more about that. Later today or tomorrow.

"Once you're done with your cake, we must be on our way," Raoul said. "We don't want to keep the conservator waiting." He got up. "I'll pay the bill."

Atalanta watched him as he walked away with a confident stride. She never failed to see how handsome he was and think she was lucky to be by his side. But how did he feel? Why had he planned the tour at the museum in such quick succession to this stop at the cafe that they barely had a chance to try all the cakes laid out for them? It felt like they were in a constant rush towards something.

Or was Raoul running away from something?

Raoul was waiting at the bar to pay the bill when he caught sight of his own face in the reflection of the mirror behind the counter. He saw the tension in his jaw, the caution in his eyes. Did Atalanta see it too? She was, after all, a detective.

He clenched his teeth as the memories assaulted him of too many nights sitting at the desk in another hotel room, his hand holding the pen hovering over the paper as he tried to write a letter to her. Such a letter she so badly wanted to have from him. A deep heartfelt letter full of things that could connect them.

But all that came to mind when he sat there was: *I am tired of it, Atalanta. Tired of having to live up to expectations I cannot meet – the team's, my parents', and yours too. I am not that wonderfully romantic man you want me to be. I am a cynic. I go through life with careless abandon, never thinking too much about tomorrow. I cannot do otherwise or I would never get into a race car again. I know I look death in the eye every time I race and still I have to get back in. It is like an addiction. I cannot stop doing it. I have to keep racing. Even if it costs me everything. My pride. My honour.*

He closed his eyes a moment. He had gone too far already accepting the bracelet. It was bound to get him into trouble. But he had had no choice. His future was at stake. Oh, he could have gone to her, he supposed. He could have told her the truth and she would have helped him.

But he didn't want her help. He wanted her admiration, her smile, her affection.

He did not dare call it love. It wasn't that; it couldn't be. Not for him. He wasn't the type for that. *She* wanted that, and it divided them. It was so easy to see when you took a moment to analyse. Which was why it was so frustrating that she, a world-class detective who had solved difficult murder cases, could not see it.

She did not *want* to see it. That had to be it. That was the only explanation really. She ignored what she knew deep down inside because the conclusion was unwelcome to her.

She wanted to float on the feeling of being in love with him. Of wanting to be with him.

But she was only hurting herself. He could not give her what she wanted. He could not be the man she needed for herself. He had to be the wise one, the sensible one, the one who … walked away?

If he knew that, then why was he here to celebrate her birthday? Why was he taking her to see dead beetles merely to stare at her face as she looked in all those glass cases muttering the Latin names that were far beyond him. She seemed to enjoy those strange lifeless things more than any other gift. So why did he feel the need to be with her when he knew it could only end in heartbreak between them?

Her heartbreak of course. Not his. He didn't have a heart that could be broken.

He paid the bill and turned to the table where she was getting herself ready to leave. He looked at her face, her lips, her nose, her temple; the interest in her eyes as she looked at some little detail in a painting on the wall. There was life inside her. In everything she did. He wanted part of that life. It had to flow from her into him, into the deepest darkness inside him, to light it up. To make everything easier. But Atalanta was too good for such a one-sided relationship. She could not keep on giving to him while he never gave in return. She wanted intimacy, sharing, closeness, connection. He could offer none of that.

And with the bracelet that was like a cuff around his wrist, a dead weight on his arm, he had taken a step that would alienate them even more. She would never understand his choice. But for him it was about survival.

Their gazes met across the room and he felt that jolt of electricity he always felt when she was near. When he realised that they were somehow connected beyond what he could reason about. He could tell himself all these pretty words about being sensible and letting her go, but he could never bring himself to actually do it. He could never walk away.

This time you will have to, he urged himself. *Or the lies will come to light and she will lose all faith in you. You have to act or else…*

Atalanta stared at Raoul as he stood there. There was something in his eyes, something restless and almost anxious. As if he were waiting for a trap to spring close. As if he were desperately searching for a way out. An escape route. The moment was brief, the emotion in his features there one heartbeat and gone the next. She was not even certain she had not imagined it because she herself felt so tense. What were they doing to each other? This was simply a beautiful day in Bonn, with plenty of opportunities to talk and enjoy each other's company. They had to stop acting like there was something major at stake. They were not deciding their future together right here and now.

But as he walked over to her and offered her his arm, she felt perhaps they were. Or rather, they already had. That he had. That in the brief moments during which he had crossed the room to her, a door had closed and it would be like it had been when they first met in Provence: he would be a charming, slightly superficial, handsome man who took her on a tour because she was new; someone she might like but would never love. Because it was dangerous to fall for someone you could never be with.

And as she linked her arm with his and they walked outside, she knew they could pretend to be a couple but deep inside they both knew it would never – could never – work.

Chapter Two

"I wonder how many dead beetles one can collect," Raoul said as they wandered the large exhibition room to yet another glass cabinet holding specimens. "To me they all look alike."

"I know you are not serious. They have very different colours and patterns on their wings."

"They remain what they are: rather ugly little crawling creatures that everyone abhors. I might have liked it if there had been a mounted snow leopard here or another majestic animal. But this is really a waste of time."

"If you feel that way, why did you even come?" Atalanta asked him without anger in her voice. Just a hint of sadness. "Did you feel obliged because my birthday coincides with one of your races and to make up you offer me this little trip to the museum?"

Raoul seemed to want to respond. There was a flash of defiance in his eyes and she really believed that for once he would pour out some heartfelt words instead of statements that he could use with anyone to keep them at arm's length. But then the fire died and he said, "I'm sorry. I will look at all their different patterns." He leaned over a cabinet and peered in with a frown.

Atalanta felt an odd sense of disappointment. She had hoped for more of a response, a fight even. It might ruin the visit to the museum but it could save their friendship. Right now it felt like it was all the same to him whatever he said to her. As long as she didn't question him further.

She turned and walked quickly into another room. A sign over the entrance read *ornithology*. She knew that the man who had started the museum had studied birds and she was really looking forward to seeing this part of the collection. Despite Raoul's certainty that she was so fond of beetles, she also enjoyed other species. Especially if they were rare.

Looking to her left at a display with mounted seagulls, she wasn't watching where she was going and collided with another visitor. She almost lost her balance and cried out.

"*Entschuldigung*," a male voice said as a strong hand grabbed her arm and prevented her from falling over. "My fault. I was not watching where I was going."

"No, it was my fault…" She automatically spoke German like he did. She looked up into his face, into concerned blue eyes. The blond hair that hung in a thick lock over his forehead seemed somehow familiar and…

"Otto?" she asked, tilting her head.

"Atalanta?" He seemed as surprised as she was,

surveying her from her hat to her shoes. Then he burst out laughing. "What a coincidence that we should bump into each other in Bonn. I was certain you were still teaching."

"Did Gertrude not write to you that I left the school?" Atalanta asked.

As she put it into words, she realised that she was making a mistake. Otto Rabenhorst was a man from a wealthy family. His youngest sister might have been teaching at the boarding school but that had been a punishment from her grandmother because she had been seeing a man of whom the family did not approve. She had been sent away from home to learn how to behave better and then she could come back. But it didn't mean that the family in general associated with schoolteachers. Atalanta's question had been born from the fond memories she had of Gertrude, who had been the closest thing to a friend to her back at the school. Spending time together had been discouraged by the stern head of the school, but they had somehow found moments to enjoy a cup of tea and share a few stories.

And one day Otto had come to pick up his sister for a short break and he had stood opposite Atalanta in the school's large garden. He had talked to her as he had waited for Gertrude to get ready. She was hopeless at packing bags and always late. They had walked past the sensationally blossoming flower beds. The air had been full of scents and butterflies. They had talked about history and music. He had shared some childhood memories that had made her laugh.

Atalanta felt slightly breathless as she recalled that half hour that had seemed to be so different from the rest of her life at the school. In Otto's company she had felt like an equal. He had invited her opinion, and she had felt seen and appreciated. Her sense of shame at having to work there to pay off debts had been completely absent from her mind. She had felt that perhaps … he liked her.

Her cheeks grew hot.

Otto smiled down on her. "Gertrude may have written about it to Grandmother but she never told me. Neither of them mentioned it. Do you have a teaching position here now, in Bonn? Or perhaps you work here at the museum? I remember you telling me how you love museums. Especially zoological ones. You knew the names of all the butterflies we saw in the garden."

It amazed her that he remembered that. It was years ago.

She flushed deeper. She should now tell him about her inheritance, being a wealthy woman and a detective to boot. But she suddenly ached for the acceptance he had shown her when she had just been that teacher. She had not had to prove a thing with him.

"I am on a short vacation," she said. "I wanted to come here to celebrate my birthday."

"Your birthday? Is it today?"

He already seemed to want to congratulate her and she rushed to say, "No, it is in four days. But I came early to see the city and the Rhine."

"The river is lovely this time of year." Otto smiled again. "Grandmother ordered all of us to come here to go on a river cruise. We are leaving tomorrow. Tonight we have a private dinner at our hotel. You must come and join us."

Atalanta's mouth fell open in shock. Otto still took her for a teacher. How could he invite her to such an occasion? His family stood above her.

"No objections," Otto said. "I'm sure Gertrude will love to see you. She was always a firm friend of yours. Besides, I want to hear more about your life after we last met. I…" He frowned a moment. "I did think back on our conversation quite often."

Atalanta felt even more overtaken. That sunny half hour in the school's garden mattered to her because it had been a highlight in an otherwise unremarkable existence of duties and obligations, but why would he have ever thought about it again? He was an important man with a full social calendar. Had he not been merely polite to her, passing the time while his sister got ready to leave?

She took a deep breath. "I don't know if I can intrude on a private dinner. I don't know your grandmother at all." Gertrude had mentioned her a few times and it had seemed from those stories she was quite a force to be reckoned with. She was the family matriarch as Gertrude's parents had died in an accident when she and her older brother Otto had been little. Their grandmother had raised them at her home, providing for them and steering them on in life. Gertrude had always spoken of her with a mix of fondness and awe.

Otto said, "I insist." He pulled a card from his pocket

and wrote something on it. "Here is the address and the time. I will be waiting for you."

He pushed the card into her hand and made a bow. "I have to go now. My daughter is waiting for me."

"Your daughter?" Atalanta breathed as he turned away. She had never known he had a child. But maybe he had married after they met?

Perhaps he had even been married at the time? She had checked his hands for a wedding ring and there had been none, but … some men didn't like to wear one.

She had checked his hands.

She had found him attractive.

In fact, after their meeting she had entertained wishful fantasies that he would come back under some pretence and they could meet again. Spend time together, and talk.

She had had a dream one night in which he had arrived at the school, walked into her classroom during class and had simply said, *"Come away with me."* And while the pupils all stared at them, she had taken his hand and walked out of the classroom past a shocked head of the school who asked her what on earth she was thinking.

Yes, what had she been thinking? Had she been in love with Otto Rabenhorst? After a half-hour conversation? Was that not a bit sad? Testimony to the lonely life she had led there?

Everything was different now. She was a rich heiress who travelled and met people. Who would never have to pine for a man to come and take her away from it all.

But with Otto it had been more than just a good time

and a silly hope to escape her dreary existence. They shared so many interests – history, music, architecture.

In fact, all things she didn't share with Raoul.

She saw him standing there watching Otto walk away. There was a frown over his eyes. A sort of suppressed anger in his stance.

Atalanta went to meet him and said lightly, "Wouldn't you know what can happen in Bonn? I had never thought I'd see him again. He is the brother of a girl who taught with me at the school. We only met once, years ago, and talked for half an hour."

"But he gave you his card. He wants to see you again. I bet he is only interested now because he heard you came into money."

Atalanta didn't know whether to feel offended or amused that Raoul seemed to be a little jealous. Putting the card away in her purse she said, "I do want to reconnect with his sister. I hope you don't mind that I can't have dinner with you tonight then?"

"Why not?"

"Because Otto just invited me to his family's dinner party. It has to be tonight because they are leaving Bonn tomorrow to go on a river cruise."

"I see." Raoul seemed to hesitate a moment. "If they are leaving, of course you can't postpone it. You have to meet them tonight." He waited a moment. "I suppose you can bring a friend?"

Atalanta eyed him. "As in you?"

"Yes. I came over to spend time with you. I am not going

to sit in my hotel room feeling glum, while you party with some man who is pursuing you."

"Otto is not pursuing me." Atalanta waited a moment. If Raoul was coming with her, he had to know. "He doesn't know I came into money. I only said I was on a short vacation here to celebrate my birthday. I am sure he assumed I am still a teacher."

Raoul hitched a brow. "Why did you do that?"

"Because I never felt he looked down on me for having to work for money. That was nice. Different from how other people acted at the time. I just wanted to…"

"Keep him in that illusion?" Raoul pursed his lips. "I guess if he is leaving town tomorrow and there is just this one little dinner tonight, it can't hurt."

Atalanta clenched her purse strap. She felt as if she had to defend her decision to Raoul, which was silly. She could see whomever she liked. With or without him. In fact, it would be easier going without him. How would she explain what their relationship was?

"If you want to come with me," she said, "you must tell them what we are to each other." Her heart skipped a beat hoping he would say something to alleviate her doubts and reinforce their bond.

Raoul shrugged. "Just friends having a good time in a nice city."

Her heart sank. Her mouth went dry and she had to swallow to be able to speak again. "Just friends? I thought we were trying to build more of a—"

"I *am* trying Atalanta, but that is never good enough for

you. You want letters and phone calls and all kinds of things I cannot provide." He said it brusquely, turning away from her so she couldn't see his face very well. "I don't like feeling inadequate."

"I'm not making demands. I just think it is good to exchange more personal information to become closer."

"Yes, and the fact that I am not able to do any of that should tell you something." He formed his hand into a fist by his side. "I can't be the man you want me to be. I can't keep playing a part."

"You never played a part. You were yourself and I … loved you for it." She said it breathlessly.

Raoul looked at her, weariness in his eyes. "I don't feel like you know me at all, Atalanta. And if you did…" He fell silent. She saw the tension quiver across his features. She so wanted to reach out and hold him and tell him that regardless of what he was now thinking, she would be there for him.

But she disliked the times when he just disappeared and did not answer calls or letters, hated not being able to reach him when she needed to hear an encouraging word. Perhaps it was true that she wanted more from him than he could offer.

Raoul forced a smile. "Let us not argue about it. We are here to celebrate your birthday. We will dress up and go to that dinner party tonight. Then you can reconnect with old friends."

Atalanta nodded and they walked side by side through the room. Her heart was racing. She was putting pressure on their bond, and now Otto had reappeared in her life. A man who was totally different from Raoul but who had also touched her in a special way. Why was this happening? Was this what Raoul had meant when he said she needed to have more experiences with men? That she did not know her own mind and would make a mistake committing to him in haste?

He often frustrated her but in this respect he might see more than she did. After all, he was a man of the world.

Chapter Three

When Atalanta arrived at Otto Rabenhorst's hotel that evening, she stood a moment regarding the building with awe. It was a large structure of brown stone with pale yellow decorative elements. It was three storeys tall but its most striking feature was its two wings that stood slightly forward from the main building. It could easily have been a former residence of some prince or other member of a noble family. Otto had told her that his grandmother had requested use of part of their hotel so they also had enough space for the dinner party but, looking at it now, Atalanta realised that to be able to afford use of part of this prestigious project the family had to be wealthy indeed.

She tried to recall whether Gertrude had ever told her what her brother did exactly but perhaps he didn't have to do anything as he had inherited enough to make his way through the world. Still, many people from the high classes were involved in some kind of trade, if only to earn money to sustain their large properties which by nature required funds in their upkeep. With the advance of time, as progress was knocking on the doors of even the most conservative houses, amenities needed to be modernised and staff were demanding better pay. Having access to a well-filled money coffer became more and more vital for survival of the family estate.

Raoul had said he would join her at the hotel but she didn't see him yet. As it was rather chilly outside now that the darkness closed in, she decided to go inside without him.

A man in luxurious gold-adorned livery showed her through the large revolving glass doors and directed her with a gesture of his immaculate white-gloved hand towards the reception desk. Atalanta explained she was invited to dine with the Rabenhorst family and with a short, subdued ding of the gleaming bell on the desk a bell boy in dark red with shining gold buttons was summoned to lead the way.

He looked like he was but fourteen but beamed at his own importance as he strode ahead of her, holding his head with the dark red cap high. He opened a large, decorated door and showed her into a room. Stepping from the lobby with its lamps along the walls into this room with a large chandelier dripping light from overhead, Atalanta stood a moment, blinking. She didn't know where to look first: at the stuccoed wall opposite depicting life-size figures of a man inviting a woman to dance; or at the long table with its white damask tablecloth, tall candles, large fruit baskets, and exquisite flower arrangements in pink, purple, and white; or at the fireplace with gold trimmed edges over which a large oil painting offered a glorious view of the Rhine.

That same river flowed outside the window since the hotel was built on its embankment. The fading light didn't offer a good view, but Atalanta understood that in daylight it would be spectacular. This was a place of constant wonder for those fortunate enough to stay here.

"Fräulein Ashford!" Otto appeared by her side and offered her his hand. He smiled at her as he said, "May I call you Atalanta? It is such a lovely name, with a classic ring to it. You are most welcome here. Most of the family members are not yet ready for dinner so we have a few moments to ourselves."

Atalanta's heart skipped a beat. After the sudden meeting this afternoon she had told herself that her interest in Otto Rabenhorst had only been the result of her confined life and the lack of any excitement while she had been teaching. That she had naturally fantasised about the only interesting man she ever met and that she had not really wanted his company, only a chance to escape the drudgery of everyday life. It was not as if she had been violently in love with him or anything that should make her uncomfortable in meeting him again. No, she could only smile in fondness at the memory of what her life had been like and feel gratitude at the knowledge of what it was today. She had moved up in the world and though the status of her new position didn't necessarily mean a lot to her, she did enjoy the travel opportunities she would not have otherwise had. She wasn't a person who needed to be rich and important, but it certainly helped her get to places of which she could otherwise only dream.

However, as she stood there and Otto held her hand just a moment too long, she wondered if her feelings back then had perhaps been a little more than merely a response to the welcome break in her treadmill existence. They had talked about many things they had in common. Had forged a bond during the short time they had spent together.

"I have to say…" He hesitated a moment, as if torn between wanting to adhere to propriety and making a heartfelt confession. "I have thought back on our meeting quite a few times. I mean, that time when we walked in the garden and you talked about music in a way I never heard anyone discuss it before. With such … passion and insight."

"I know what you mean," she rushed to assure him. "It was a very special conversation. I remember thinking to myself I had never before met someone with whom I had so many interests in common. History, music…"

"Yes, here in Bonn one can certainly dive into both," he said, perusing her with an earnest intention. "You chose a very beautiful city for your holiday. But you still have not told me where you are teaching now. Or if you are even still teaching. For at the time I already wondered why someone with so many talents and such a zeal for life would confine herself to such a … restrictive environment."

Atalanta flushed.

He rushed to add, "I do not mean to criticise your choice of profession. I admire teachers, for it is not easy to engage the minds of young people in subjects that will be important only later in life. Often they balk at having to make an effort and… Well, as a widower raising a daughter, I know how hard it can be to achieve results."

So he was a widower. She hadn't known at the time. That did explain the lack of a wedding ring. "How old is your daughter?" she inquired.

"Eleven. She is very mature for her age – the result of having been raised among adults without any siblings. Grandmother insisted I employ private tutors for her and she is allowed very few friends."

"She is *allowed*…?" Atalanta resisted the urge to question him too directly and thus sound critical in the process. She knew nothing about his life and therefore should feel her way into it gently. She said, "Your grandmother plays a large role in your life? I remember Gertrude mentioning that your parents died in an accident when you were still little."

"Gertrude was little at the time – only two years old – but I was eight." Otto stared ahead a moment as if he recalled when the terrible news had been broken to him that his parents had gone and would never be back. "I am grateful that Grandmother took it upon herself to care for us. Not all children who lose their parents end up with a family member who cares and can provide for them."

"That is certainly true." Atalanta looked a moment at the stuccoed wall on the other side of the room, the gallantly held out hand of the male figure while the female rose from a curtsey, her skirts wide around her. A true artisan had created that panel.

"I suppose," Otto said softly, "that because Grandmother took such good care of us after the tragedy with our parents, I have always felt indebted to her. I allowed her to guide my choice of studies and career and … even with whom I associated." A frown formed over his clear blue eyes. "I relied on her too much perhaps. Also with regard to raising Lisl."

"What a sweet name."

He winced a moment. "Grandmother insists we all call her by her full name – Clara Annalise – but to me it's much too formal. She is not some princess from Bayern, although my grandmother likes to think of her as such. She is training her for something grand in life."

"A good marriage, I suppose," Atalanta retorted. "That is often the case in well-to-do families. Women are merely seen as assets or pawns that can be manipulated to advance the family's interests."

She asked herself instantly if this was too forward, but he held his head back and laughed. "I remember that you were not afraid to speak your mind and I liked you for that. I see you haven't changed. Fortunately." He became serious in an instant and leaned over to her. "For now that we have met, I think I need your help."

"My help?" Atalanta echoed, overtaken by the sudden change in him. He looked so grave and there was genuine concern in his eyes – something of fear almost, as he glanced around to ensure no one was near enough to overhear the next words.

"It is a very delicate matter. I cannot discuss it with anyone within the family. That would be too—" Before he could fit a word to it, a loud scream resounded from the next room. It echoed against the ceiling and bounced back to them. It felt like even the windows rattled at the sudden sound.

Otto's eyes widened. "Lisl!" he cried.

He left Atalanta standing and rushed to a door to the left. Judging by the grandeur of the entire room it was rather inconspicuous and obviously only meant as a way through into another room, not the main entryway. Atalanta hurried after him.

The adjoining room was much smaller but still elegantly furnished. A desk of carved wood with ivory inlay stood against the far wall. The chair that sat before it to allow letter writing and other pursuits had fallen over and beside it stood a girl with a delicate face and high blonde hair that flowed freely over her shoulders. She wore a dark purple evening gown and sparkling jewellery as if she were much older than her age. But her hands were clenched into fists and she stamped her foot as she cried out to the elderly lady who surveyed her from a few feet away, "You always do this. You always destroy everything! You are a monster. You should be dead."

Having been a teacher, Atalanta was well acquainted with the overly dramatic behaviour of frustrated girls and didn't take the words too seriously, but she observed how the expression of the elderly lady set in disgust and she inched back as if she found herself close to something repellent.

Or dangerous?

Otto closed in and said, "Lisl, I don't want you to take such a tone with your great-grandmother. She is only trying to—"

"Look what she did!" Lisl pointed at something on the floor. Atalanta peered closely to see what it was. It appeared to be shreds of paper, as if someone had torn up a letter, perhaps.

"I made a whole fairytale world from paper," Lisl said in a strange, thin voice, as if she were trying to swallow her tears. "I worked on it for many hours. I had kept it here in the desk to look at before I have to do something hard. When I opened the box it was in, I found this. Someone shredded it into a thousand pieces. Everything I worked on, gone."

Her expression tightened as if she fought against total despair. Then fire lit in her eyes and she glowered at her great-grandmother. "*She* did it. I know she did. She never liked me being creative. I am never allowed to make anything. Remember I made a painting and it was suddenly stained? And I made something out of clay and it fell off the table and was broken? She is always destroying what I make. You know why? Because she wants to destroy *me*. The side of me she doesn't like. What I cannot be because I have to be what she chooses for me."

"You are a very uncivilised young lady." The elderly

lady spoke in a deep, melodious voice that belonged on stage performing Shakespeare. "You never think about your last name and what it entails to be born into this family. I am only trying to show you how you can adjust to your destiny as a Rabenhorst."

"My destiny?" Lisl was now red with anger. "I will run away. I will!" She looked at her father as she shouted the latter threat. "I won't stay here one hour longer."

"Don't be silly," her great-grandmother barked. "You are a child. You cannot go out alone. You have no money and no place to stay. You would only make a fool of yourself and have to come back like a dog with its tail between its legs." She held the girl's gaze. "You don't like to be humiliated, do you?"

The words seemed to hold a subtle warning. Atalanta was conscious of the intense strain in the room, as though everything was crackling with tension. These people were obviously caught in a power struggle that had started long before this night. A fight neither could win without harming the other profoundly. It shocked her, and at the same time there seemed to be a sadness inside of her that perhaps such struggles were the result of caring too much and she wondered if anyone in her life had ever cared too much for her.

Otto said, "Lisl, please go to your room for a moment to calm down. Wash your face and then come back for dinner. We are having guests tonight."

The elderly lady now looked past him at Atalanta. Her gaze was cool and assessing. Frau Rabenhorst wasn't tall but her straight stance made her imposing nevertheless. Her dark green dress was simple but refined, her jewellery kept modest with just one large emerald in a pendant around her neck and smaller ones in the same cut set in drop earrings. She wore no bracelets or rings but she didn't need to show off her wealth or her pedigree. She was a commanding figure in her own right.

Otto said, "Grandmother, I'd like to introduce Fräulein Ashford. She is a friend of Gertrude's and of mine. We met in Switzerland when Gertrude was teaching there."

"Gertrude never brought you home before." The elderly lady gave Atalanta a disdainful look. "You cannot be much of a friend. And as for you, Otto—"

Otto stepped back and said, "We must get ready for dinner. The staff are standing by to serve the first course."

"Very well." The voice of the elderly lady held a slight hint of amusement as if his immediate retreat in response to her attack gave her deep satisfaction. She went over to Atalanta and said, "You may sit beside me so I can speak with you."

"That is impossible, Grandmother," Otto said quickly. "You will have Gertrude's fiancé on your right and Herr Kaufmann on your left. If you change the order now, they will feel insulted."

She huffed but did not protest. She passed Atalanta and went to the door leading into the dining room. She stopped a moment in the doorway and said without turning around, "I will speak to her later. I want to get to know her."

"Yes, Grandmother." Otto bowed his head briefly, as if an empress were leaving the room.

Lisl laughed loud and bitterly. "You never say anything to defend me. You never confront her with what she is doing. Look at my paper creations! She cut them up." She knelt down to gather the scraps of paper.

Otto said sharply, "I told you to go to your room and wash your face before dinner. Why don't you do as I ask?"

"Because no one is doing what you ask anyway." Lisl kept picking up small white pieces.

Atalanta said, "Let me help you." She bent down to gather some shreds that had floated away across the shiny floorboards.

Otto sighed and said, "I will go and greet the others." He left the room quickly, the scent of his cologne floating back to Atalanta. Part of her was sorry for not taking a different position and keeping his goodwill but she felt a certainty inside that this girl needed someone to choose her side and to acknowledge that her pastimes were important and her creations worthwhile.

She said to Lisl, "I am sorry I can't see what you made. I love those paper worlds. I have several books at home about the art of creating them with beautiful illustrations."

"You only say that because Father told you to be nice to me." Lisl huffed. "Every female acquaintance he brings home is always nice to me because they think it will help them win his heart so he will marry them. Do you also want to marry my father?"

It was said in anger, but Atalanta flushed nevertheless.

She was glad it could be ascribed to her bent over position as she kept gathering paper pieces. "I hardly know your father," she said honestly. "We met once, many years ago. He was coming to pick up your aunt Gertrude."

"Then why are you here now? This trip is very important, Great-grandmother says. She keeps saying that to anyone who wants to hear. Or doesn't want to hear," Lisl scoffed. "She only invited people for whom she has plans. So I assume she also has a plan for you. She must think you are the first one to be worthy of marrying my father. The other ones were never good enough."

It sounded like there had been a whole parade of them. Invited by the grandmother? Brought by Otto himself and then found inadequate and dismissed? How should she interpret this information?

Did it matter since she was not going on their travels?

She said softly, "You misunderstand. I am only here for the dinner party. Tomorrow you will all go on a boat to cruise the Rhine and I will be staying here in Bonn to explore the city. It was a birthday present to me."

"From whom?"

"From myself." Atalanta stood up and looked at the scraps in her palm. "I am an independent woman. I have my own means and I can do what I like."

Lisl stood up too and eyed her with interest. "I did not know that was even possible. I thought a woman always has to have a husband to look after her. Or a brother or a father or … some man to make sure that she is not doing anything scandalous or forbidden. Great-grandmother always makes me feel so very … stupid."

"I am certain that is not her intention. She only wants to protect you."

"You don't even know her. How can you tell?"

"Because that is what families are about. Protecting each other."

"Not ours." Lisl sounded convinced. "Our family is about making prisoners of one another. With secrets."

Atalanta stared at the girl as she arranged the scraps of paper on the desk and tried to piece them back together. Her expression was tense and her lips trembled but she was not hysterical. She meant what she said.

What secrets?

"Ah, there you are." Raoul came into the room and smiled at Atalanta. "I am sorry I am late. I received a telephone call I simply had to accept."

From the woman who had given him the gold bracelet with the bird charm? Atalanta swallowed hard before she could force a smile. "It doesn't matter. You are here now. I would like you to meet Otto's daughter. Lisl."

"Only Father calls me that." Lisl's eyes flashed. "My name is Clara Annalise Rabenhorst." She stuck her nose in the air.

Atalanta feared that Raoul would laugh and drive the girl into another tantrum. But Raoul took her hand in his and kissed it gallantly. "I don't get to meet such noble persons often," he said. "It is my pleasure. I am Raoul Lemont."

Lisl's mouth fell open. "The race car driver? I have seen your picture in the papers. Is it really you?"

She looked at Atalanta. "Is he teasing me?"

"Oh no, he is really *the* Raoul Lemont." Atalanta was glad for this diversion that seemed to cheer Lisl up immediately. "He is very famous. He has to hand out autographs wherever he goes."

"I don't want an autograph." Lisl smiled up at Raoul. "I will make a sportscar paper cut for you sometime, if you would like that."

"Naturally. No one has ever done that for me before." Raoul offered her his arm. "May I escort you in to dinner?"

When Lisl accepted and beamed as he guided her to the door, Raoul quickly met Atalanta's eyes. He seemed to understand instinctively that he had to take this girl seriously and do something to lighten her mood. He even refrained from winking at Atalanta in case Lisl caught the look.

Atalanta followed the pair with a sense of relief. Raoul's company and exciting stories would ensure that Lisl was amused and would not seek another confrontation with either her great-grandmother or her father. It promised to be a light-hearted and pleasant dinner party after all.

But still Atalanta's mind played with the words the girl had said right before Raoul had come in. That in her family it wasn't about protecting each other, but about making prisoners of one another. It was an interesting way to put it. She could have said: *It is about controlling one another*. Or *confining each other*. Or *not allowing someone any freedom*.

But she had used the word *prisoners* and she had also specified the method by which these prisoners were made.

Secrets.

Having investigated several murders in her brief career as a detective, Atalanta knew just how much power a dangerous secret could wield. It could keep people captive in relationships; it could push them to make rash decisions. It could even induce them to … take another's life.

Secrets were potentially explosive, and as she came to the table and looked around at the well-dressed, smiling people who took their seats, she wondered if below the surface lay a ticking bomb and she had come at just the right moment to witness it explode.

Chapter Four

"I can't believe Otto simply bumped into you at the zoological museum," Gertrude said after dinner as they were retreating for coffee with cakes and chocolates. The men were gathering in another room to play billiards and to smoke. There seemed to be no end of elegant spaces in this hotel wing, each one even more refined than the next, and all at the disposal of this single wealthy family.

Judging by all this available room, Atalanta had perhaps expected their party to consist of thirty or more people but it had been only eight. At the head of the table the matron, Frau Rabenhorst, had been flanked by two men who couldn't have been more different. One of them was Gertrude's fiancé – young and attractive with quick nervous smiles at the imposing lady, obviously eager to win her favour – and the other at least sixty with a well-trimmed beard, moustache, and long sideburns, intelligent, watchful eyes and the demeanour of someone who is assured in his surroundings and doesn't need to earn anything anymore. That had to be the Herr Kaufmann Otto had mentioned. His relationship to the family wasn't clear to Atalanta and his profession or the reasons for his presence had not been touched upon in conversation.

Then there had been Gertrude seated beside her fiancé, with Raoul on her other side and Lisl beside him eyeing him full of admiration. Atalanta had sat between Herr Kaufmann and Otto, who looked across the table with a worried look every time Lisl laughed too loud at one of Raoul's stories.

"Your friend is very dashing," Gertrude said, taking Atalanta's arm and leaning closer to speak softly. "Are you…?"

"Merely friends," Atalanta rushed to say. "Very good friends but still… I am not sure I want to commit at this moment in my life."

"I understand. You have so many opportunities now. I wish I were in your shoes." Gertrude released a dramatic sigh. Although she was, if Atalanta calculated correctly, thirty, she behaved like a schoolgirl, flirting with every man at the table and even serving at the table. Her dress had a daringly lowcut neckline and her ostentatious jewellery featuring both diamonds and rubies seemed chosen to emphasise her wealthy background.

Now that she leaned closer, Atalanta could smell the alcohol on her breath. "You have no idea what my life entails," she said, a little more sharply than she meant to.

"Of course not. All those parties, all the socialising. It

must be so difficult." Gertrude laughed. "Then again, you do deserve it. You were always nice to me back at school. I'm so glad I'm no longer teaching there. It was just like a prison."

Interestingly, her niece had just compared their family to a prison, or rather its members to prisoners. Would Gertrude ever feel that way? Or was it just the over dramatic impression of a girl who felt the others allowed her no freedom to pursue her artistic hobbies?

Atalanta said, "I never knew Otto had a daughter."

"Little Lisl?" Gertrude shrugged. "Yes, unfortunately. I don't mean to be rude but … it does hamper his chances of remarrying. I mean, it must be that. He has been alone for so many years now."

"Perhaps he still misses his wife?" Atalanta ventured, her heart beating fast at what the reply might be.

Gertrude laughed again. "He was only married to her for two years and during that time they barely saw each other. He was tending the family estate and she was traveling for her exhibitions."

"Exhibitions?" Atalanta queried.

"Yes, she was a sculptor. Very scandalous to my grandmother's mind. She never wanted the marriage. Oddly, it was the only thing Otto ever did in which he went against her. He usually followed her instructions to the letter, but it was different with this woman. I suppose he was just blinded by her beauty and thought he couldn't live without her or something. It was very strange as I never thought my brother was the emotional type who wastes away for love, like the poets say. Remember those horribly long poems we had to teach the girls? Once I left that school, I never touched a poetry book again."

Atalanta quite liked poetry and had even brought some books to read during her birthday trip. This region, and especially the Rhine, had always drawn writers who found their inspiration in the beautiful but wild landscapes on the riverbanks.

Gertrude stared ahead a moment as if recalling all those unwanted poetry lessons, then shrugged. "Anyway, Otto had better not push through against Grandmother's wishes. She was very sour about it for a long time. She cut him off, and to make matters worse, the marriage was a bad one. His wife only cared for her own pastimes and ducked all social engagements. People started to whisper because they were never seen together. Otto kept saying they were happy but we never believed it. They were just too different to ever be able to be happy together."

Like Raoul and me, Atalanta wondered.

Gertrude said, "Then she was shot to death."

Atalanta blinked, not having expected something so dramatic. "That sounds rather violent," she observed.

"Yes, well, she was at some bar where all the artists meet and then there was a painter who was angry at another painter for stealing his model or something and he carried a gun on his person and fired some random shots and she was hit by accident and died on the spot. The gunman was apprehended and sent to prison for ten years. Otto thought the sentence wasn't heavy enough, but once in prison the man contracted a lung disease and he died. Grandmother believed that the matter would now be cast from our minds quickly and Otto would remarry. She already had a few candidates in mind who would suit Otto much better than his late wife. Or should I say, suit her own interests much better?"

Atalanta took a moment to let these revelations sink in. She was sorry for Otto that the marriage for which he had risked his grandmother's wrath had taken such a tragic turn. Had he felt like it proved that his grandmother had been right? Had it infused him with a new urge to follow her directions for his life? "But he did not remarry," she said softly, almost more to herself than to Gertrude.

"No. I guess he learned his lesson the first time. He may have been infatuated with her but they were never happy together. She hardly cared for her child either, always going to these artist meetings. But"—Gertrude made a dismissive gesture—"let's not talk about Otto. His life is boring. I want to know all about yours. The places you go, the people you meet. Raoul Lemont is simply … magnificent."

The intensity in her eyes as she said it struck an unpleasant chord with Atalanta. She said sharply, "But you are engaged."

"Yes, merely to end Grandmother's nagging. According to her I am at an age now where I should have been married for five years and be a mother of three already." Gertrude shivered. "I am engaged now so she doesn't nag that much and, well, it is a pleasant arrangement for both Erol and me. He can do what he wants and so can I, as long as we are discreet about it and no one finds out."

Atalanta blinked at the idea of such an arrangement. "But you will have to get married."

"Some time in the future. In my mind, it is still a long way off and a lot can happen. For instance, perhaps he betrays me, word gets out, and I am heartbroken. Then I get engaged to someone else." Gertrude waved her hand in the air again. "I can certainly keep that up for a few years. And Grandmother will not live forever you know. Some day we will all be free."

It was an interesting echo of Lisl's observation. Atalanta asked, "This Rhine cruise you are going to go on together, is there a special occasion for it? A birthday, anniversary, or…"

"Well, actually Grandmother said something about changing her will." Gertrude frowned hard as if trying to recall what exactly had been said. "That is why that dry old Herr Kaufmann is coming with us. I always look at him and wonder if he is anything but a human calculating machine. There does not seem to be much life behind his eyes. He has been Grandmother's trusted lawyer for many years now. He takes care of the business accounts, both for the family estate and all the companies the Rabenhorsts own, as well as Grandmother's personal affairs. He knows all her secrets."

Atalanta shifted her weight as the latter word was mentioned. This was all rather … curious. "And what does she intend to change?" she asked. "I mean, is Otto in any danger of losing his position as heir to the family estate?"

Gertrude eyed her a moment. "No, of course not. He already inherited everything when our parents died. He is the male, the heir, the most important thing in the world." She said it with disdain but also a hint of bitterness. "Grandmother has money and assets of her own and she will have to dispose of those. I guess it is about that. I don't know for certain." She leaned in and added, "Are you worried that Otto will become less valuable? I didn't know you were hunting for a rich husband, Atalanta."

Atalanta felt a flush come up. She wanted to defend herself but Gertrude was already speaking again. "Don't apologise to me if you are. I am not going to object. I just told you that I am not very serious about ever getting married to Erol or to any other man for that matter. If you feel like marrying my stuffy brother while you are having an affair with this delicious race car driver, I will be the first to applaud you."

Atalanta blinked. "Would you not feel hurt if I betrayed your own brother?"

"When Otto was married before, he did not mind being betrayed. I mean, the woman was always around all these artistic types. They let women model for them with barely any clothes on. She may have been a sculptress but she also started out as a model for the painters in her little group. Do you really think she was faithful to my brother? In fact, there have been ugly rumours that Lisl is not even my brother's child."

Gertrude waited a moment to let the weight of that revelation sink in. "That is probably why Grandmother hates her so much. At first I thought it was because she never supported the marriage and she could not stand Otto going against her and wedding someone inferior, but now I think she is convinced that Lisl is not a Rabenhorst. That she is an outsider, a danger to our family."

Atalanta held her breath. Was that the reason why she had destroyed Lisl's artwork? Because she felt it was proof that this girl was not a member of the family, but a young cuckoo?

If that intensely unhappy girl with the sharp insight into people around her understood why her great-grandmother acted the way she did, that it wasn't merely out of spite but betrayed a conviction that Lisl was an alien who could never have a rightful place among them, how would she respond? What deep-seated emotion was behind her words that she hated her great-grandmother and wanted her dead?

Atalanta wet her lips a moment. The intensity of Lisl's utterances had shocked her earlier when she had believed it was a mere response to the violation of her carefully crafted paper world, but now it all took on a more sinister meaning. A really unpleasant and potentially explosive question came to mind. She should not ask it – it was overstepping every social boundary – but since Gertrude had obviously drunk a little too much wine at the dinner table and was free with her confidences, she might as well try. "Has your grandmother ever … suffered a strange accident? Something that you could not explain?"

Gertrude frowned. "What do you mean? She does not drive her own car. How could she ever be in an accident?"

"Well, people do have little accidents at home. They slip or…"

"Oh, you mean with the lamp?" Gertrude pointed a finger at her to underline that she now understood the point. "The cable was frayed and that was why there were sparks. She could have felt a shock, I suppose, but she was fine. Her heart condition has been much better since she started taking those drops. They are made from a plant. What is it called? Digi something."

"Digitalis?" Atalanta suggested.

"Something like that. She has a nurse who reminds her to take them, else she would probably never touch them. The nurse has to stay with her until she actually drinks the concoction. I know she used to pour medication down the drain or empty her glass in a plant pot if she didn't like it. She loathes her doctor and thinks he invents things that are wrong with her to ask for more money."

Gertrude laughed loudly and her grandmother looked their way. Atalanta was again struck by the presence this woman exuded. She was controlling the room even from a distance. It was almost like she had listened in on every word they had said and was thinking about what she would do to make them pay for damaging the renowned Rabenhorst family name by their gossiping.

Atalanta rolled back her shoulders. She was getting a little nervous because of the strained family relations. But she only had to spend time with them tonight, make a little polite conversation, and then in the morning they would board their river cruise and she would continue her exploration of the wonderful city of Bonn. She was already dreaming about the sights she would see and the exciting new things she would discover…

"Fräulein Ashford," the elderly lady called out to her. "Come to us. You are the only person in the present company whom we do not know so you must fascinate us with some story." Her blue eyes had a mocking gleam. She knew of course that Atalanta had worked with Gertrude at the school and probably thought she had nothing worthwhile to tell. Nothing that would interest people such as them.

Atalanta knew she should resist the challenge. That she should stick to her role of being the humble schoolteacher that Otto Rabenhorst had once met. That there was no need to prove herself. That it was in fact contrary to her usual behaviour to show off her money and status. That when others did it she always found them a bit pitiful.

Lisl said, "I believe you do have something interesting to tell. All people have some story. A story about their life that is special."

Frau Rabenhorst huffed. "You always want to be special, Clara Annalise. But you must keep something in mind. We are all just human beings. We are born, we live, and we die. That is the way of life. Some of us live and die in better circumstances than others. But we are, none of us, that special."

"How odd of you to say so." Lisl stood straight, her feet

planted apart, her chin up. "*You* always act like you think yourself very special. Like you are a queen and everyone should bow to your wishes."

The elderly woman smiled softly. The girl's indignation seemed to give her pleasure. "I have the advantage of you, young lady. I am older. Old age deserves reverence even if you have never learned that lesson. Your father raises you too freely."

Gertrude said sharply, "He barely gets a chance to raise her with you interfering all the time. If you feel Lisl's upbringing is in any way lacking, it is yourself you should blame."

Her grandmother's eyes shot sparks at her. "We will speak again when you have a child of your own and can experience first-hand what a task it is to shape someone's personality."

"My personality needs no shaping," Lisl said. "It is already shaped the way I like it."

"You are merely a child who knows nothing. You need someone—"

"I would certainly not want," Lisl continued, cutting across her grandmother's voice, "to be shaped by you. You would ruin me completely for you only create very ugly things."

Gertrude burst out laughing. "It is so amusing to hear this little girl say this to you, Grandmother, and to realise it is strangely true." The exuberance in her expression turned to something colder when she added, "You do only create ugly things."

The look on her grandmother's face became stern. "You have been drinking."

"I only took the wine served over dinner. If it was too much then you offered too much."

"Blame me for everything. You two are mindless children who don't see reason. I must explain everything, chew it out for you so you finally understand. Understand what it means to be born a Rabenhorst."

"I am thirty," Gertrude countered, now red in the face and swaying on her legs. "I am not a mindless child. Neither is Otto. He knows what he wants. And if what he wants is Atalanta, then he will get her."

Atalanta stood motionless. Her mind swam at the suggestion. The idea that Otto Rabenhorst had designs on her and that he would have shared these plans with his sister. Who was admittedly misbehaving grandly tonight.

"You said you hardly knew my father," Lisl spat to Atalanta. "You are all lying to me."

"Because you are a child and no one tells children the truth," the elderly lady said. "They cannot handle it."

"I can handle it. You could have said you liked him. Or he liked you. I am not little anymore. I am eleven. I want to know things. I don't want to be kept out of everything!" Lisl ran out of the room and slammed the door.

Frau Rabenhorst let out her breath in a rush. "She acts like a toddler. I must speak to Otto about this."

"About what?" Otto asked as he walked in. A scent of cigarette smoke wafted inside with him. "The others are still playing billiards but I wanted to show Atalanta the conservatory of the hotel. She told me she loves orchids and that her late mother grew them."

Atalanta's heart grew warm as she realised she had told him that during their brief conversation all those years ago. He remembered. That was so special.

She went over to him. His grandmother said sharply, "You cannot stay away too long. It would be impolite to the other guests."

"Your trusted lawyer and Gertrude's fiancé hardly count as guests."

"I am not asking you for an opinion, Otto."

Atalanta saw the muscles in Otto's jaw work. He was a grown man, father to an eleven-year-old girl, and his grandmother was commanding him like he was an irresponsible little boy who had to be reminded of his duties.

Once outside the room she said, "You must not blame your grandmother for urging you to spend as little time as possible with me. It was something Gertrude said."

Otto slowed his steps and surveyed her. "What did she say?"

Atalanta was already sorry she was steering in this direction, yet she wanted to know. "Gertrude suggested that … you invited me because you … like me."

Otto laughed softly. "Gertrude can only see affairs all around. There is nothing in her head but thoughts of romance." It sounded bitter. "But in truth there is little romance in the world. Too little romance and too much sense of obligation."

"Your daughter said to me that in your family everyone is a prisoner," Atalanta blurted.

He stopped and stared at her. "Did she say that?"

"When we were picking up the ruined paper cut. She was upset but she also seemed to mean it."

He nodded briefly. "I guess she must feel that way. My grandmother is very stern. That can feel confining."

"She was not only speaking of herself. She said everyone in the family."

"Gertrude talks to her too much about being forced to marry when she wants to do other things with her life. She loves Lisl but she is not always a good influence on her." He sighed. "I am sorry if her remark made you feel uncomfortable. I can assure you she only says such things to rile my grandmother."

"Because in truth you could never be with someone in as lowly a position as I am. A schoolteacher with no prospect of ever getting on in life." Atalanta said it to dare him.

He held her gaze. "I never cared much for position in life. I married my first wife even though she was an artist and my family abhorred the alliance."

"You say your first wife." Atalanta stood feeling slightly breathless. "Does that mean you intend to marry again?"

"What if I do? A man cannot always be alone."

"Of course not." She broke their eye contact and looked along the corridor. "Shall we go and see that conservatory?" Her heart pounded painfully and she didn't know whether she felt glad or disappointed.

He gestured ahead. "That way." As they began to walk

again, he glanced at her. "You seem to have listened very closely to my daughter. Not dismissing her concerns as mere obstinate talk."

"I have worked with girls for years, I know their ways. I know when they are overreacting and when they mean it. Your daughter is really upset with your grandmother's behaviour."

Otto halted again as he asked sharply, "Upset enough to take action?"

"What kind of action?"

He held her gaze, searching in her expression with urgency. Then he said, "I am probably worrying for nothing."

"What are you worried about?" Atalanta wanted to give him space to unfold his thoughts with care but deep down inside she already knew what he was going to say. If she, a perfect stranger who just joined them for the night, already sensed such tension, how could he have failed to see it and feel concern about it?

He waited a moment and then said, "That my daughter will someday harm my grandmother. That she will push her in an argument and cause a fall or something. That she will die and Lisl will be blamed. That her entire life will be ruined. Shredded like those paper figures she so loves to create."

Atalanta's throat tightened at the idea that a girl that age would be accused of murder and imprisoned. There might be circumstances that would drive her to act but it would never be enough to acquit her. People who didn't understand the desperation of Lisl's position as scorned and unwanted all her life, would only see the fact that a child had caused another person's death, not by accident but deliberately. They would be horrified and would judge Lisl harshly.

"Why would you conclude she is ready to do something drastic? There is still a great separation between saying things, thinking about them, and actually acting."

"I agree but pressure has been building for a long time, and some day it must go wrong. It is as inevitable as boiling water. As long as the source of heat is not removed from under the kettle, the kettle will continue to heat up and the water inside will start to boil. And then it will boil over." He wrung his hands together. "It must. I can feel it."

He looked around him quickly and urged her to continue walking. In a low voice he said, "I did not want to take Lisl on this trip, Atalanta. On that boat she has nowhere to go. She will be forced to spend more time with my grandmother than usual. She will be expected to perform to even higher standards than at home. My grandmother wants her to jump through hoops like a little trained poodle. And Lisl is at an age where she doesn't want to do it anymore. When she was younger, she tried to please my grandmother by learning poems and reading books to her and hiding her more artistic interests at my request. But now she is becoming rebellious. She wants to break free and … I am very afraid it will land her in trouble."

They entered through a heavy oak door into a

conservatory with many bright blossoming tropical plants and potted palms reaching all the way up to the ceiling. Despite their serious conversation, Atalanta felt a little surge of happiness inside her as she breathed the scent of wet earth with relish. "I love travelling but I always miss my plants at home." She prevented herself from mentioning Paris. Otto was unaware of her new position in life and especially now that he shared these worries with her, she ought to be careful what she revealed to him.

Otto nodded. "I knew you would like this. Your story at the time painted this touching image of a young girl helping her mother with the orchids. There was so much love in your voice, so much tenderness. I … just couldn't forget it."

She stared up into his handsome face and saw the warmth in his eyes. He had brought her here to honour that memory. That was so special.

Otto said softly, "That afternoon you gave me a little insight into your heart, Atalanta. I feel like I only shared light-hearted childhood memories of using my slingshot and building tree houses, while you were far more serious and absolutely frank. I was so surprised that it could be that way; that in such a short time I got to know you better than I knew other people whom I had met dozens of times. I saw someone who is sensitive, creative, intelligent, fiercely independent, but also loyal and faithful and … I need you." He grasped both her hands in his.

Atalanta's breath caught. This was so sudden. So unexpected. Was this what she wanted? What about Raoul and all she felt for him?

Otto said, holding her hands firmly, "I need your help. With my daughter. Lisl is drifting away from me and I cannot reach her anymore. I am so worried it will end in disaster. I have not been a very good father. I was often at a loss as to what to tell her when she cried for her mother and suffered from Grandmother's demands, but I do love her and … I cannot let her be broken. Please help me save her. Please."

Atalanta flushed as she became aware of his true intentions. This was hardly an expression of deep personal feelings, but a desperate plea for help from an overburdened father.

She pulled her hands from his grasp and said, "Otto, I agree that we had a wonderful meaningful conversation that day. We found we had much in common, even though we hardly knew each other. That is indeed rare. But apart from that, nothing connects us. How could I help your daughter? She doesn't trust me. She thinks I am … somehow close to you and she doesn't want me to be."

"That is all Gertrude's fault. She will be sober in the morning and can tell Lisl she was only joking. You can tell Lisl that you are not in any way…" He searched for words. "I thought you and the race car driver…"

"We are friends. Very good friends, and admittedly we did entertain the thought of being more than that, but it is so complicated and … I am not sure it will ever work between us."

Otto sighed. "Relationships are just … impossible to get right. That is my experience anyway." He lowered his head.

"I apologise for inviting you to the dinner party and taking you away from the group to see this. I genuinely wanted you to see this because you talked to me about your mother and…" He swallowed hard. "I know what it is like to lose your parents at a young age. To feel alone and wish they could come back to you. To know everything would have been different if they had not been swept away."

Atalanta touched his arm. "You need not apologise, Otto. Not for any of it. I do see the position you are in. A man on his own, trying to do the best for his daughter. Your grandmother is so domineering and Gertrude is not much of a help."

He laughed softly. "That is true. I had once hoped that as an aunt she could steer Lisl in the right direction, but I do not want my daughter influenced by someone who drinks too much and is always having some new affair, sometimes with married men. What kind of an example is that? I need someone solid and steady. Someone I can rely on. I know you are on holiday here and I am imposing on your time, but please … come with us on the river cruise. Try and talk some sense into Lisl. I don't know what to do anymore. If something happens to my grandmother and Lisl is blamed…"

Atalanta wanted to repeat that she was not in a position to help but maybe she was? Gertrude had mentioned changes to a will and a frayed cable causing a lamp to almost hurt Frau Rabenhorst. If the cable had been frayed on purpose, the first step towards murder had already been taken before this family trip.

She said slowly, "You are worried Lisl will hurt her grandmother in an argument by giving her a wild shove or something like that. But do you also believe her capable of something more subtle?"

Otto stared at her. "Subtle?" he repeated.

"Yes. Something like … sabotaging a lamp to electrocute her and then having everyone think it was an accident."

He turned red in the face. "That is a monstrous suggestion."

Atalanta rushed to explain. "Gertrude told me that your grandmother is changing her will. It struck me as a moment in time where … it might be pertinent for people to get in her good graces or ensure that…"

"The will does not get changed? I will not listen to such nonsense!" He was shouting now. "I wanted you to *help* my daughter, not imply horrible things about her. You are casting a net of suspicion around her and—" His words died away and he stood suddenly ashen, staring into the distance.

Atalanta's heart was heavy when she understood what emotion this was. Not anger at her, not indignation or frustration. No. It was despair. The despair of a man who knows that…

She put her hand on his arm. She had to swallow before she could put it into words. "You also suspected Lisl of being behind the frayed cable."

He released his breath slowly. "Two days before the incident I saw her coming from her great-grandmother's bedroom. She had a pair of scissors in her hand. I thought nothing of it as Lisl is always carrying some tool for her paper cutting. I merely thought she had created a little something to leave for my grandmother. She does not appreciate what Lisl makes but the girl tries to persuade her anyway. She can be very stubborn in that respect. I guess she inherited that trait from me." He smiled sadly. "When the accident happened and Grandmother was almost hurt, I remember Lisl coming out of the bedroom and my heart grew cold. I refused to believe that a girl her age would do anything to truly harm someone but … part of me cannot deny that there is so much pent-up anger inside Lisl. She feels her great-grandmother does not value her or love her. That she is unseen and unheard. She feels that I—"

He had to clear his throat before he could go on.

"That I only do what is expected of me and I never take her side. In short, the whole world is against her and everything would be better if…"

"Your grandmother were no longer alive." Atalanta concluded it with a chill inside.

"Exactly." Otto looked at her again. "I feel terrible, Atalanta, thinking something like that of my own daughter. I do not want it to be true. I am desperate for some other explanation. For it to be merely a coincidence."

"Which it might have been."

"No. I looked at the lamp's cable and the fraying was intentionally created. It was done with a sharp tool, like a pair of scissors." He sighed. "I cannot ask Lisl directly why she was in the room with the scissors. Should she even get a hint that I am somehow suspecting her of anything, she will never forgive me. Never. I am not ready to lose her."

"Otto…" Atalanta raised a hand to calm him down. "Your grandmother is such a strong personality that she must have annoyed other people aside from your daughter. Anyone in the household could have tampered with the lamp."

"I know. I told myself it might have been Gertrude, or that fiancé of hers, Erol, with his smooth smile and confident ways. Or even a disgruntled servant or… I tried to think of a reason why Herr Kaufmann would want my grandmother dead because he was also staying with us that weekend when the accident with the lamp happened." He made a throwaway gesture. "I was accusing everyone, in turn and at will, to clear my daughter."

"A natural thing. And it is certainly possible several people had a motive and the opportunity to get to the lamp in question."

"Motive, opportunity? You sound like a detective."

Atalanta took a deep breath before she said it. "Otto, I *am* a detective."

Chapter Five

Otto stared at her.

"What did you say?"

"I am a detective. I mean, I inherited my grandfather's detective work. That is why I quit teaching at the boarding school. I have a house in Paris now and I work for many high-placed people. I solved three murders at the estate of the Comte de Surmonne in Provence, two murders in Santorini, and I even got an invitation to a murder on the Orient Express."

Otto Rabenhorst blinked. "You cannot be serious. Is this some kind of joke? It is not amusing. I am very serious about this lamp. I am not making it up and accusing people at will, least of all my own child!"

She took his arm. "I am not joking. It is true. My grandfather was Clarence Ashford, a detective for the elite. He never advertised his services but people who needed him found him by word of mouth, on the strength of his reputation. He helped many people. I inherited all he owned on the condition I would continue to help people who would ask for my advice. As you are asking for my help, I will help you. I will take the case and look into the question of who tried to kill your grandmother with the lamp. In the meantime, I hope they do not try again."

Her heart was heavy as she stood there.

"In Santorini I was looking into a suspicious death when another murder occurred. It was the same killer. I am still asking myself whether I could have prevented that murder. I still wonder if the victim could have been saved." She eyed him earnestly. "I can try to find out who is after your grandmother but I cannot guarantee that she will not die. You just said that you suspected others of involvement beyond Lisl. Gertrude, her fiancé, and Herr Kaufmann. All three of them are coming on this river cruise. If they want to try again there will be plenty of opportunity."

He shook his head. "I tried to convince myself that they were suspects because I could not bear Lisl to be involved. In reality, they have no reason to want my grandmother dead. I mean, I would not know why…" His voice faltered and he fell silent.

Atalanta nodded. "You do see it, though, do you not? They could very well have a reason to want her dead. We cannot discard anything in advance. I have to look closer at everyone and… That is, if you can take me on this cruise."

Otto sucked in air. "I already invited you, but I do realise I need a compelling reason for you to be there. And I can't reveal you are a detective."

"Nobody knows. Not even Gertrude. She does know I came into some money and can afford to travel now, but she doesn't know about my sleuthing. I keep that to myself as much as possible."

He nodded. "That is good but doesn't help us with the reason why I would... Unless..." He waited a moment and then said, "Gertrude did suggest I was interested in you, did she not?"

Atalanta nodded, her cheeks warm again.

"We can tell my grandmother I am thinking about marrying you. She will hate you for it and try to sabotage our relationship at every turn, which is good, because once you have found out that Lisl had nothing to do with the lamp and you have persuaded her to let go of her anger and not hurt her own interests, we can say we are not fit to be together anyway and go our separate ways."

Atalanta shook her head in disbelief. "I am not going to pretend that we... That you... That..." She shifted her weight uncomfortably. "How would that look? I mean, Raoul..."

Otto hitched a brow. "You can tell him the truth, if you want. Just as long as he doesn't give anything away."

"And can I bring my butler Renard? He is a very knowledgeable man who has useful contacts to help with my sleuthing. You can rely on him to be very discreet."

"Of course." Otto grasped her shoulders and beamed at her. "Atalanta, this is wonderful. I could not have asked for a better solution. Not only will my daughter be cleared but we can also find out if anyone is truly after my grandmother. She can be hard to live with but that does not mean I want her to die." He leaned over and kissed her on the cheek. "Thank you."

Raoul stood at the door of the conservatory and watched as the tall blond German who had so suddenly inserted himself into Atalanta's birthday party here in Bonn leaned in to kiss her – on the cheek, not on the lips, so it could just be a friendship, but still…

It hurt. It made Raoul angry that he had allowed her to come here tonight. That he had once said to her that she needed to have more experience with men. That she should not just fall in love with him.

Why had he not accepted her feelings? Why had he not taken advantage of the situation in Salzburg and her willingness to drop everything to come with him and be with him?

It was not like her to be so impulsive. She was always sensible and practical. He had feared she would regret her decision later on and … it would have hurt to realise she was drifting away from him. He would rather push her away before she got too close than take her into his arms first and then lose her later.

She turned away from the man and saw him standing there. Her eyes widened and her cheeks turned red. "Raoul, I…"

"I am going back to the others," Otto Rabenhorst said

with a smug smile. "Until later." He passed Raoul without making eye contact, but Raoul could feel his satisfaction like light radiating from him. What had he talked about with her? Why had he taken her here, in private, away from the rest of the party?

He looked about him, noticing all the various tropical plants. He saw there were orchids, which she loved. He knew that, had gifted her one on the Orient Express. It seemed like ten years ago. Then they had still been friends with an attraction, travelling to explore Tuscany together. It had all been light-hearted and pleasant. Now his feelings for her were one big tangle which he feared he may never undo again.

Atalanta said, "Raoul, you must understand that… Otto just told me of a most pressing matter. His young daughter is suspected of a serious crime and… It is very harmful for a father to have such doubts about his own daughter. I must look into it. For his sake, for the girl's sake. She is only eleven. And I was friends with Gertrude when we taught at that boarding school. I feel I owe the family…"

He waved a hand. "You do not need so many reasons, Atalanta. You are free to do whatever you want. I am not your husband nor your fiancé. I have no right to a say in your life. I am only here for the day to celebrate your birthday. Tomorrow I am going back to train for a new race. I have a full agenda. I can never give you the time you feel you deserve. So why not go with this family and do a good thing by clearing this girl's name? It is all part of your profession. Your vocation even. Your destiny in life."

"Are you being cynical now?" She eyed him earnestly. "I want you to understand."

"Oh, I do." He nodded with a heavy heart. "We decided in Salzburg that we needed to get to know each other better before we could ever make a commitment to each other. We were to write letters and … develop a deeper connection than this mere attraction we are feeling. We tried but it is not working."

"It is far too early to conclude that," she said hurriedly. He saw the panic in her eyes as she sensed what he was about to say.

He felt the same panic and also an urge to shy away from this; to postpone it until later. But he steeled himself and pushed on. "Atalanta, I have failed you on all accounts. You want someone who shares your interests and your plans for the future. I am too different. I cannot write all those wonderful letters you are always waiting for. I have neither the time nor the patience to sit down to write them. That should tell you something. If you really meant that much to me, I would make the time, do you not think?"

He saw the pain in her eyes and he hated himself for it. But that cold part of him, the ice at his centre, made him go on. "I would make the time to be with you instead of carving out a few hours only to rush back to what is more important to me – my career, the racing. Playing with my life, as you see it."

She wanted to protest but he stopped her.

"We tried and we found out it will not work. That is

regrettable, but it is better to be honest now than to be miserable later."

"I am miserable right now," she said as tears began to flow down her cheeks.

His hands ached to reach for her and hold her close to him and tell her the truth about what he had done. But he could not.

He should not. He would have to depend on her willingness to understand. And how much could he expect anyone to understand? To forgive also.

No, it was all much too late. He had made his choice, risky or not, and he now had to live with the consequences. With the pain of losing her, before she ended up entangled in the same mess he was in.

He took a deep breath. "I am sorry, Atalanta. I wish it could have been different. For your sake. Because you always had this beautiful romantic image of the two of us…"

"That is not fair," she said clenching her hands into fists. "You know I have always been realistic. I knew that it might not work. But I wanted to try. I invested in it."

"And I never did." He said it in a definite, almost aggressive tone. "Because I cannot become someone I am not. You simply fell for the man you thought I was, not for who I really am." And with those words a door shut. He could hear it bang to a close, locking her in, locking him out. The pain was unbearable, but he had to do this.

He turned away.

"Goodbye, Atalanta. Take care."

Atalanta watched as Raoul walked away. His words made her reel. The coldness with which he severed their bond! On the eve of her birthday party too… How could he do this to her? How could he hurt her so badly?

She wiped at the tears that kept rolling down her cheeks. She wanted to run after him and beg him not to leave her like this. But the last remainder of her pride kept her rooted to the spot. She was not going to make a fool of herself. She had to keep some dignity. She had to…

She hid her face in her hands and sobbed.

Chapter Six

The next morning, Atalanta stood in her hotel room and threw garments into an open suitcase on the bed. She had slept badly, lying there tossing and turning, thinking about how things might have been different if only she had not let Otto take her aside…

But she knew it would not have made much of a difference. She had sensed that Raoul was drifting away from her long before this. He had only used the situation to distance himself from her, to blame it all on Otto's request to her and her profession in life while he himself didn't take responsibility for any of it.

She tore so hard at the fabric of a silk blouse she heard a ripping sound. Her sadness from last night had turned to anger and right now she wanted to go to Raoul and scream reproaches at him. But she must not sink to such behaviour. He would not yield anyway. If she accused him, he would only get mad at her and…

And what? Everything was lost anyway. Their bond was broken. He was gone.

She suppressed a new sob. She would not cry again. She would not.

A brief knock sounded at the door. She recognised the discreet signal at once. She took a deep breath to be able to call out calmly, "*Entrez.*"

Her butler Renard entered carrying a tray with her breakfast. He had arranged for her to breakfast in her room so she would have some privacy to read her correspondence, which had been forwarded to her, and to dive into her books and maps to make plans for the day.

When he saw her standing at the bed with the suitcase, a look of surprise crossed his face. It was brief, since he was trained to be very discreet and hide his own feelings at all times. He put the tray down on a beautiful little table in the corner and said in a neutral tone, "Are you looking for a garment you cannot find, mademoiselle? I thought I had unpacked everything the other day and placed it in the wardrobe to your satisfaction."

She eyed him with tilted head. "You are very observant, Renard. You have noticed, at once, that I am not looking for any garment because, as you have just confirmed yourself, you unpacked the other day. I am putting these things back in the suitcase because I am leaving Bonn today."

Now Renard had obviously prepared himself to hear something unexpected for there was no visible response in his features. He turned to the breakfast tray and rearranged the egg beside her plate then straightened the spoon to align with the coffee cup.

Finally, he spoke. "It is of course your prerogative to change your plans, but I thought you were enjoying your visit here. Does it"—he waited a moment as if he wondered whether he could even ask this—"have to do with some new plan you have made with Monsieur Lemont?"

Atalanta had been well aware for some time that Renard did not approve of Raoul's influence on her. He did not feel that Raoul was stable enough to be a suitable companion to her and although he would never question her choices, his discomfort whenever she undertook things with Raoul was clearly felt. His immediate assumption that it was Raoul taking her away from Bonn, when Renard felt she should stay longer, made new anger course through her veins.

"No, it has nothing to do with Monsieur Lemont. Contrary to what you seem to think, I am capable of making a plan of my own."

Renard blinked a moment. He averted his eyes from her to look at the window. Walking over, he made sure that the folds in the long lace curtain were all the same distance apart. She assumed he was thinking about an appropriate reply. Servants should not cross their masters and after her clear words he should refrain from asking anything. He had served her breakfast and he should retreat now.

But her relationship with Renard was not like that with just any servant. He had been her grandfather's trusted valet, his confidant in the detective work. He had also helped her many times. She owed him more than this curt retort.

She took a deep breath and said, "The situation is complicated. It involves people I think deserve my attention. Even though I haven't been in touch with them for a long time."

Renard waited for her to continue.

Atalanta said, "You know I went to dine last night with the Rabenhorst family. I worked at the boarding school with Gertrude Rabenhorst and on one occasion in particular I also became acquainted with her brother Otto. At the time I had no idea of his personal situation, but he made a favourable impression on me, being an intelligent man with an interest in many subjects that also interest me." She waited a moment before adding, "When I met him yesterday at the zoological museum, I was surprised to see him but also glad. I wanted to reconnect. That is why I accepted his invitation to dine with his family before they were to leave on their Rhine cruise today. He mentioned having a daughter whom I looked forward to meeting."

Renard's eyes flickered a heartbeat when she mentioned the daughter. She wondered if he had readily assumed she was romantically interested in Otto Rabenhorst and whether the mention of a daughter, and by deduction possibly a wife, changed his mind about that possibility.

She continued, "Last night I met the girl and … the circumstances were not ideal. Right before I entered the room, her great-grandmother, Otto's grandmother, who raised him and still has a great deal of influence on his life, had destroyed something the girl had created with painstaking care. At least that is what the girl assumed. They had an argument which grew ugly. In fact, the girl said she wanted her great-grandmother to die."

Renard nodded slowly. "Children get overexcited when they feel injustice is done to them and they use big words to express their feelings."

"I know that. I worked with girls for years. But this was different. There was tension and … the elderly lady has a very dominant personality. She won't give others any freedom. She dictates their choices and the way they should live. It becomes smothering, to a point where one *must* rebel."

Renard nodded again. "I understand your concern for this girl's position, but you were only invited to dine with them. A polite invitation when one meets abroad. I understand you have not seen these people or spoken to them in many years. Why would you care for what their family relations are?"

"I felt sorry for the girl. Her full name is Clara Annalise, but Otto calls her Lisl. She is both very young and innocent looking but at the same time very mature, as she has obviously been raised among adults and been forced to behave like one prematurely. The dress she wore, the jewellery … it did not feel entirely appropriate for a girl her age. But she has no mother and…"

"Did her mother pass away?" Renard asked. She assumed that he was now going to tell her it was logical she felt sorry for the girl because she recognised something of herself in her, having lost her own mother at a young age.

"Her mother was killed when a bar fight went wrong and the bullet meant for a rival hit her instead."

She watched his expression as the words sank in. He was always able to keep his emotions in check. She saw nothing in his eyes even though she found this backstory immensely tragic. But perhaps she had so little experience with clients yet that she wasn't aware most people had tragic events in their past?

She continued, "This girl has never known much feminine support in her life. Her great-grandmother is too demanding and her aunt, Gertrude, doesn't really care for her; she is only interested in having an adventurous life herself."

"And now you feel compelled to be a benign influence on her?" Renard asked softly. He was not questioning her in any impolite manner and still she felt an immediate need to defend herself and her choice.

"I haven't told you everything yet. The girl uttered harsh words against her great-grandmother, wishing her dead. When we were together and I helped her gather the pieces of her ruined art project, she told me that in her family people are like prisoners. Captive by secrets. I felt it was somehow ... the truth. Gertrude, for instance, has become engaged to a man she does not love so she can have freedom to have affairs with those men of whom her grandmother does not approve of. And Otto ... I am not sure but I don't think he feels really free to make his own choices and forge his own path."

Renard watched her carefully. "I still have not heard a clear reason why you must interfere with these people. You are here to explore the city and enjoy some time away from sleuthing. It is a birthday gift to you."

"I know you took the trouble to arrange it all. I know that Raoul also contributed with his coffee and cake party and the tickets he bought to the museum."

Renard cleared his throat. He did not have to say anything for her to all of a sudden understand. Renard had arranged all of it and Raoul had waltzed in as he usually did and taken over, acting like it had all been his doing. She disliked him for not telling her honestly and pretending he had set it up, and at the same time she could not get angry because her heart was so sore.

She quickly averted her eyes and pushed on. "The point is that I did enjoy the things arranged for me until I met Otto and got drawn into his family affairs. It is not just that I met his daughter at a moment of conflict with her great-grandmother. I might have looked past that. But Otto also told me things…" She bit her lip. "He asked me for help. Did not my grandfather stipulate that I have to help the people who ask me for advice, that that is part of my new life? I can't simply stay here tracing the footsteps of Beethoven while I know that such a troubled young girl is leaving the city without having been helped."

"Who says you can even help her?" Renard said. It was

logical that he asked but in her unstable state of mind Atalanta immediately sensed some distrust in her abilities.

"I *can* help her," she said sharper than she meant, "because I am good at what I do. Detecting killers."

"Is there a killer involved here? The girl merely said she wished her great-grandmother dead. It may be unpleasant to hear and it may reflect badly on their relationship, but I see no actual crime."

"And how does the fact strike you that before this trip was made a lamp in the elderly lady's bedroom was sabotaged when someone intentionally frayed the cable in order to electrocute her?"

Renard hitched a brow. "And this girl is supposed to have done this?"

"Her own father suspects her because he saw her coming from the bedroom with a pair of scissors in her hand." Atalanta gestured wildly. "I assume he is not accusing his only child lightly. This suspicion has gnawed at him for some time. I can feel it. I have to help him to see if something substantial lies at the heart of this matter."

Renard bowed his head. "If you have taken the case, there is nothing I can do to dissuade you from it. It is not my place to do so and, may I add, not within my abilities to judge whether the case merits your interest or not, as I have never met this girl nor the rest of the family and I cannot judge their relationships or the strain these might be under."

"Exactly. Which is why you are coming with me on this

river cruise. You will be present everywhere, silently going about your business but in reality observing them all and reporting back to me what you see and hear. Four eyes are better than two."

Renard seemed reluctant to agree to her suggestion. She straightened up and asked, "Do you not wish to help me?"

A smile touched his lips as if he found her reaction amusing. "It is not for me to wish anything. You are my mistress. I will follow your orders."

"For someone who is merely following my orders you take a long time to actually start following then. All this conversation is taking away from my time to pack the suitcases. We have a timetable to follow if we are to meet the ship on time."

Renard came over at once. "Then let me pack your suitcases for I am much faster than you are. I also do not tear the seams of silk blouses."

She flushed as she realised he had immediately spotted the maltreated garment.

"Eat your breakfast," Renard said. "Your egg will now not be as warm as you like it but inside that silver coffee pot the coffee should still be hot and strong. You need a good start to the day."

A good start? When she realized Raoul had left her, she was about to cry. She seated herself and forced herself to peel the egg and start eating. Renard was busy packing her suitcases without saying another word as to the situation. Finally as he was done, placing her beauty case with the other cases at the door, he turned to her and asked, "Will Monsieur Lemont be joining us on this river cruise?"

"No. He wasn't invited and besides, he has other things to do. His agenda is very full."

Her stomach squeezed when she repeated the words he had used to dismiss her, their bond, the feelings they had both acknowledged. She pushed her plate away and rose.

"Please ring for the luggage to be moved downstairs. We will need transportation to the dock. I will write down the address for you." She went to the writing desk where her mail was waiting for her. She quickly gathered the envelopes without looking at them closely and put them in her purse, then provided Renard with the address he needed. He had already rung for the bellboy.

At the door, waiting for the hotel staff to knock, he turned to her and said, "I hope you do not begrudge me my interest in your choices. I sometimes feel like…" He looked for words. "Your grandfather would have wanted me to watch over you."

He lifted a hand to stop her from responding right away.

"Not because you cannot take care of yourself. I know you are independent, resourceful and growing in your role as detective. But because … it can be useful to have someone reliable around." Worry shadowed his eyes. "If your assessment is correct and this family is hiding dark secrets that affect its members deeply, your interference with those secrets might put you in danger. Should you require any help, I would like to be on hand to provide it."

Atalanta felt relief that he wasn't angry at her. Relief also that despite feeling so lonely she had someone left who stood by her and was there for her. She smiled at him and said softly, "That is exactly why I am taking you along. To be my eyes and ears, yes, but foremost to be there to help me should I need your assistance in any way. Because I know I can rely on you."

Warmth infused his features. A knock at the door broke the moment and the bellboy bustled in to get the cases. But Atalanta knew as she left the room to go on her new adventure that whatever she had lost here in Bonn, she had not lost the support of the man who had stood by her from the very beginning and who had guided her into her new life with a hand that was both firm and kind. He never let go of her, not even when she gave him cause to back away from her. That was what loyalty truly was.

A sharp pain shot through her as she realised that this kind of loyalty was what she had hoped for in a romantic relationship, but it didn't seem like Raoul could provide it.

Had he not merely been honest with her when he had pointed out the deficiencies in their relationship? Had he not touched a sore point when he had emphasized that she expected more of him than he could offer? It was true. She wanted more than she ever got. And to deny that would be to deny the very heart of her.

If he knew that, was it not only right that he let go of her? Had he done it not only for himself, but also for her? Because he knew, by experience, that she had to live by a code of honour, by her own convictions that couldn't be watered down? If she settled for less now, she would regret it later.

Oh Raoul. You know me so well. And still I feel like I don't know you at all.

Chapter Seven

When the taxi halted at the dock, a bright spring sun illuminated everything with a sharp glow. The ship that lay ready, the staff carrying many cases and parcels on board, the captain with his uniform of gold tresses standing watching the proceedings. And Otto, coming over to her at once, with outstretched hands.

"Atalanta! I am so glad you came." He leaned over to her and said in a low voice, "After last night I was worried you would have too much time to think it over and decide that our family is too difficult to get involved with. I would not blame you if you had decided this morning to write me a polite note to say that you would rather stay here and enjoy Bonn than come with us on this trip down a river that stirs darkly."

Atalanta eyed him with surprise. "The Rhine? It looks so friendly and calm on this beautiful morning."

"But it's surrounded with tales of legend and folklore.

The castles on the bank testify to a past of warfare and dispute. Ships are lost on the river just as easily as they are lost at sea. Water is never safe."

Atalanta shivered involuntarily. An elderly woman whose life was under threat was going on a river cruise during which she would be on, or in any case near, water all the time. Would it not be easy to bring about a fatal accident?

Nonsense, she told herself, *the ship is very safe. Passengers don't just fall overboard. And Otto and I will watch her closely. We can do it together. Even with the three of us if I also count Renard.*

She gave Otto a pat on the arm.

"You mustn't let yourself be influenced by tales. I have been to many places where folklore and superstition were rife but I have always managed to find out the truth, which was grounded in very human behaviour."

"I am not afraid of supernatural things," Otto said with a grave expression. "I am well aware that humans can do enough damage." He looked at the ship and its large glass windows behind which shadows moved. "This morning everyone was acting friendly to each other, playing the part of a happy family going on a cruise. My grandmother is all smiles, Gertrude supports her, and Lisl was even singing. It almost felt like … my dark thoughts of last night were nothing but a nightmare, wiped away when day breaks."

"But…" Atalanta leaned closer and spoke softly. "The frayed cable of a lamp is not a nightmare. It is not imagined but real. And we must take care of the matter. Face the questions head-on and save you from doubts about your own child. I know how you love her."

Otto sighed. "I fear that I never loved her enough. I've been away too much, leaving her with servants and ultimately at the mercy of this cruel old woman who…" He stopped himself and forced a calmer tone. "I made mistakes and now I regret them. I can only hope it is not too late."

"I will do everything within my power to clear things up." Atalanta smiled up at him. "Now, shall we go on board and have a look around?"

He led the way and soon they found themselves in the large salon on deck with glass windows all around offering breathtaking views of the riverbanks. It would be delightful to sit here during the journey and be able to see the river's beauty all around. But the salon itself was also worth looking at, with its luxurious carpets, sofas and chairs, and a buffet in the corner where drinks could be served. A bookcase offered reading material and there was even a record player with music. Lisl was already looking through the recordings to see what she could find there. Atalanta went over to say hello to her while Otto informed his grandmother and Gertrude that they were about to disembark.

Lisl looked up at Atalanta when she came to stand beside her. "My father told me this morning that you were coming. I think he wants us to be friends. He always wants me to make friends with people but I am not like the others. I have very special tastes."

"Well, why can we not be friends just because we are not alike? Then we have interesting things to tell each other."

She had thought it could be that way with Raoul. That they would complement each other: his talent for improvising and her foresight; his boldness and her carefulness; his Mediterranean sunniness and her English practicality. She had wanted it to work. She had hoped for it. She had even thought there must be some truth to the saying that opposites attract.

But attraction did not mean they could make a relationship work long-term. Her standing here was proof of that. She was alone. Yes, Renard might be on the ship helping her with the case but personally she felt alone.

Lisl said, "You look sad. Do you not want to leave Bonn?"

"I did not get a chance to see much of it. I had wanted to learn more about Beethoven. I often play his pieces."

"I don't like the piano. I want to sing. But Great-grandmother says singing is common. That it debases people." Lisl snorted. "There are many important people in history who were great singers."

Without waiting for a reply she added, "But if you like Beethoven, you can also follow him outside of Bonn. We are going to Koblenz and I believe his mother was born there. Perhaps we can see her house? People like to see where important people were born. They come to stare at the front of the house as though there is some wonder hidden inside or as though they can sense something special by standing there."

"Do you never sense a connection to the past?"

Lisl nodded earnestly. "I often do. When I read stories, like fairytales and folktales or myths and legends. They inspire me to create my paper worlds."

"I love myths. I heard my first Greek and Roman myths when I was just a little girl and my mother read them to me. I am even named after a heroine from Greek mythology. Atalanta."

"I wish I were named after a Greek heroine. I am named after some family member. Because Great-grandmother wants me to be like everyone else in the family who came before. But I am not like them. I am different."

"Nobody expects you to be a copy of somebody else," Atalanta said softly.

But Lisl's expression turned grim. "But they do. They all have expectations of me and nobody asks what I want. Where I want to go or what I want to do."

"Perhaps on this trip you can tell me what you would like to do and I can suggest that we go and do it. Since I am a guest of your family, they may want to accommodate my wishes."

Lisl burst out laughing. She hastily suppressed the emotion and looked askance to where her great-grandmother was sitting. She said in a whisper, "They don't accommodate others. They only do what they themselves want. She … is a tyrant."

Atalanta decided that this was not the time nor the place to address these concerns and asked instead about the record Lisl was playing. Although the girl was obviously reluctant to take part in pleasant small talk, she did answer the question and after a few minutes they were chatting animatedly about music and the festival Atalanta had attended on Santorini where there had been musicians playing traditional instruments and women in costumes folk dancing.

Gertrude came to stand by them and asked whether Lisl wanted to see the ship's control room from where the captain directed its course. Lisl immediately agreed and went with her. Atalanta remained by the record player as it wound down after the last notes. She automatically stopped it and turned to the room. Frau Rabenhorst was watching her with a heavy frown over her eyes.

"What were you talking about to the poor girl?"

"Is Lisl a poor girl?" Atalanta asked as she closed the distance between them. The elderly lady didn't invite her to sit so she remained standing. She felt a little like a pupil called in to explain some bad grade or other form of misbehaviour.

Frau Rabenhorst stared past her with a stern expression. "My great-granddaughter is an impressionable girl who believes anything told to her. Therefore I would appreciate it if you do not regale her with made-up stories."

"What made-up stories do you mean?"

"Your visit to Santorini." The woman's pale blue eyes flashed with indignation. "You are a schoolteacher. You earn little money. You cannot possibly have travelled to a Greek island. And the gall to mention a *burg*, a castle, where you allegedly stayed. This is too much. I already have to endure a chronic liar in our midst. I will not have another one added to it."

Atalanta blinked. She hadn't expected the elderly lady to be able to overhear what was being said between Lisl and her. Or this vehement response.

"I can assure you," she said, "that I have indeed been to Santorini. I worked there, temporarily, as a companion. I was recommended to the family after their companion had a fatal accident. She fell off some cliffs."

The elderly lady winced. For a moment her eyes carried something akin to ... fear? Then the mask of stern reproval was again firmly fixed to her features. She said slowly, "I don't think, Fräulein Ashford, that I want to hear any more about your trip to Santorini. You will not mention it again. Not to me nor indeed to anyone else in the family. Do you understand?"

"But surely," Atalanta protested, "it is not for you to dictate what I am allowed to talk about. I am a free woman."

The elderly lady snorted. "I would hardly call a teacher who has to jump at everyone's beck and call a free woman. You may wish you were one, just like you may wish you were a worthy prospect for my grandson. But you are not. I only want to warn you not to overreach. You see, Otto is a very sensible man. I think he will soon see that certain alliances are not to be made."

"I can assure you," Atalanta said, hating the flush that rose in her cheeks, "that I am not here to seek any alliance of the sort to which you refer."

Again the elderly lady let out this low derogatory sound. "You may tell yourself lies, Fräulein Ashford, but you cannot deceive me. You intend to marry and marry well in order to be able to give up teaching and live in luxury. Then you may travel to Santorini or anywhere else in the world, at your husband's expense."

Atalanta felt anger rush through her chest and had to steel herself not to burst out and tell this woman how wrong she was. What wealth she possessed and how she was in no need of any man who would throw her a pittance. But she knew it would not serve the purpose for which she was here. She had accepted Otto's plea to join his family and see what she could do to find out more about the strained relationship between his daughter and his grandmother. Whether there was really a risk of the elderly lady being murdered. Perhaps it was in her own interest, and in the interest of the case, to play along?

She straightened up and said, "I did visit Santorini, even though it was to work and not as a tourist. You may look down on hard work but it is all I have ever known." She caught the flash of triumph in the old woman's eyes.

Good. Think you have bested me. Believe in your victory, for it may cause you to grow careless and let something slip.

She pushed on. "I'm not ashamed of my position in life. There are far more people who must work for a living than people who can afford to do nothing and live off their family fortune."

"*My* family," Frau Rabenhorst said with emphasis, "hardly does nothing. We have a lot of enterprises all around the world which provide us with income. We have built an empire of sorts and we intend to make it even greater. Otto has worked hard for this because he believes in protecting the family name and all it stands for. This is also why I am cautious as to whom I allow to come near him."

"I do see your point." Atalanta acknowledged it with the intention of leading the elderly lady further into believing she had broken her resistance. "I think you have the wrong view of the situation. Otto may have pretended to invite me as a guest and friend of the family, but in reality he is paying me to accompany you on this trip. He wants me to keep an eye on Lisl as she has been so ... difficult lately."

"He is paying you?" As expected, this added extra glee to the old lady. Surely, a man with some self-worth would not start a relationship with someone in his employ. He would certainly not marry that woman. With every revelation Atalanta became less of a threat to the old lady's mind, and that was exactly her intention.

She nodded solemnly. "I can use the extra money. I came to Bonn to holiday with little money on me. Frankly, I also have some uncovered expenses."

"I see. Does Otto know this?"

"When he mentioned to me that he is having difficulties with his daughter, I suggested we could both benefit from this arrangement." Atalanta held her head down as if it were hard for her to confess this. "I told him we should not tell anyone else as it is quite ... embarrassing for me. But I should have known better than to try to hide it from a woman of your astute insight into human character. You immediately sensed that something was not right here." Atalanta halted, afraid to overdo it and make the other woman suspicious of her again. In her experience, people who were confident in their own abilities to steer and command others rarely thought they were being duped because they were so certain they would immediately detect this. They expected deference so when they got it, it was no cause for extra scrutiny. But she didn't know this woman well yet and it was difficult to gauge what she was really thinking.

"I'm sorry if you had the wrong impression."

"I'm only sorry Otto did not discuss it with me first. I could have told him that there are many women among my acquaintances whom I could have invited on this trip to make friends with Lisl and better the situation."

Atalanta was reminded of Lisl's words that everyone always wanted to make friends with her and wondered if Frau Rabenhorst had attempted before to find a new wife for Otto by inviting female acquaintances to get closer to Lisl.

"It is too late now," Frau Rabenhorst said with resignation in her voice. "The ship is about to disembark so you will have to accompany us."

The door opened and a tall woman entered. She had a young, round face with a healthy flush and wide green eyes. Her dark brown hair was tucked away neatly under a fashionable hat. She came over with confident strides. "Frau Rabenhorst. How are you today? Have you not exerted yourself too much? You must think of your heart."

The elderly lady sighed. "I hired you as a companion to fetch for me, not fuss over me and make me feel even older than I already am." She glanced at Atalanta and said, "Fräulein Ashford here also worked as a companion, she was just telling me. On Santorini."

"Oh, I wish I had the opportunity to be there," the woman gushed. "I love the sunshine and the warm climate. Everything is so grey and chilly here." She shivered.

Frau Rabenhorst said sharply, "Don't be silly. The German climate is perfectly balanced. The winters are not too cold and the summers are not too hot. Why would you want to go somewhere where you can get a heat stroke?"

The woman extended her hand to Atalanta and said, "I am Sabine Freund. I work for Herr Rabenhorst as companion to his grandmother but I am actually a qualified nurse. I am here to look after her and ensure she takes care of herself. She is on heart medication and must rest regularly. In fact, I will take you to your cabin now to rest." The latter words were directed to Frau Rabenhorst again.

Atalanta had seen the glint in the elderly lady's eyes when the companion had mentioned, subtly, that she was not working for her elderly charge but that she was actually in the employ of Otto. Was she also taking her orders from him? Was she a force who could actually stand up to the elderly lady's tyranny? She looked efficient enough, brisk and optimistic.

Atalanta said, "I look forward to talking to you later and getting to know each other better. I think we may find we have things in common."

Sabine Freund nodded at her. "I look forward to it also. But now we must go and rest."

"You can go and rest all you want, I want to stay here," Frau Rabenhorst protested. But the young woman simply wrapped an arm around her and helped her to her feet. Talking kindly to her, she led her away. As the two left the room, Otto entered. He looked after the nurse and her charge a moment before turning to Atalanta to say, "How are you this morning?" He added with a wink, "Do you already regret your impulse decision to come along?"

"I did a few minutes ago." She hurriedly told him how his grandmother had confronted her and what she had thought of to defend herself. "So I am officially in your employ now and taking your money to pay my bills. It immediately made her feel more confident that she can avoid any—" She fell silent and felt hot again.

Otto said, "Attachment between the two of us?" He held her gaze. "Atalanta, when we met in Switzerland, I already realised you are unlike any woman I have ever met. You are practical and full of common sense, yet you are also passionate and energetic. You have a wonderful knowledge of music and history and I enjoy immensely talking with you and hearing your opinions. I invited you along for Lisl's sake but also … to have the pleasure of your company for myself."

Atalanta's cheeks were burning. She took a deep breath. "Otto, you must know—"

He stopped her by placing his hand on her arm. "I realise how I am intruding in your life with my problems.

That I am a complication you could do without. You have everything you wish for now and you certainly do not need me to take you places or show you things. But… while you work on my request, could we not … spend some time together and enjoy our journey? We need not be anything but friends – companions with a common desire to help Lisl and to find out what is happening in the family." He held her gaze. "What do you think? Can we do that?"

She smiled involuntarily. His plea was heartfelt and resonated with her.

"We can certainly try."

Chapter Eight

The magnificent ship that carried them smoothly across the river's deep dark waters only took a day to reach the beautiful city of Koblenz. It had been visible in the distance for some time before they were actually docking, and Atalanta had had time to find a book in the bookcase describing some of the highlights of this historic place which had been so important throughout history both for defence and trade.

"There are a lot of churches," Lisl observed as she looked at the many towers protruding towards the blue spring sky. "I hope we will not have to see all of them. I often feel one is a lot like the other. I am much more interested in that." She pointed to the other riverbank where a large fort sat on top of a hill. "It looks adventurous. I would rather go exploring there."

"I read here that it has been a strategic place of defence for many centuries. Even in the recent war it was still in use." Atalanta read quickly through the detailed account of the various armies that had used the fort for their purposes. "I don't know if we are able to visit it. It could be closed off to the general public."

"Besides," Otto's voice said by her side, "it will be difficult to navigate for Grandmother."

"Why can't she go and do something she likes, with Sabine?" Lisl looked up at her father with a pleading expression. "Why can't we go and see the fort? Just the three of us."

Atalanta felt a little tug at her heartstrings at the girl's suggestion. She would love to spend some time with Otto, away from his family. There was too much tension and unwanted questions put to her or just raging in her own mind. She needed a break from it all.

Otto shook his head. "We would not want to disappoint Grandmother."

"*You* would not want to disappoint Grandmother," Lisl said with a break in her voice. "I have already disappointed her many times and I don't care!" She ran away, probably back to her cabin.

Otto sighed. "More than one person warned me that it would be much more difficult to raise her once she reached this age. I laughed at them. I thought she would always be a sweet, obedient, little girl. But now... I often don't know what to do or say. All I want from her is a little cooperation. A little understanding that Grandmother is a frail, old woman who cannot go traipsing around an old fort."

"What are you whispering about?" a sharp voice

demanded behind them. Frau Rabenhorst stood stiffly, regally attired in a dark blue coat with white fur trimmings. Her hat was decorated with beautiful feathers and she carried an elegant dark blue leather purse. "I am all ready to explore this city. I want to see the sights and I am not yet too old or too weak to walk about."

"But Grandmother—" Otto protested.

She raised a hand to cut him off. "I have not paid so much money for this trip to be abandoned in a tearoom while you see all the interesting places. What were you talking about?"

Wordlessly Otto pointed a finger at the fort on the other side of the river. "But we are not going there," he added feebly. "It is much more convenient to—"

"Nonsense." His grandmother cut him off. "If that is an interesting place of historic significance then we must see it. I observe you hold a book about Koblenz, Fräulein Ashford. You are a teacher. Do carry it along and teach us something." She turned on her heel and marched off. The nurse who had waited a few feet away followed her hurriedly. The large bag she carried probably held items needed to support the elderly lady during the day.

Otto rolled his eyes. "She is always like that. She sees and hears everything. She wants us to do exactly what she wants." Frustration raged in his features.

Atalanta said, "It is not so bad. At least Lisl will have her way. Perhaps it will lighten her mood."

Otto said, "You do not understand, Atalanta." He

seemed to want to add something but refrained. "I will go and get Lisl. We must not keep Grandmother waiting."

Atalanta stopped a moment to catch her breath. They had walked uphill to reach the fort and now once inside they had to climb stairs to reach a vantage point. She wanted to see the sights across the river – actually, across two rivers as the Moselle joined the Rhine here. The day was bright and sunny, promising unhampered views into the distance where they might discern landmarks that were up to thirty kilometres away. She looked forward to standing there and enjoying the scenery but getting there was a bit of a challenge.

Moments before, Lisl and Otto had been with her but suddenly she found herself quite alone. She strained up the last few steps and grabbed the metal railing, forcing herself to draw breath through her nose and exhale as slowly as she could. If her breathing was too rapid, she might get dizzy and that could be dangerous as the vantage point was very open. In fact, it was a good thing she did not suffer from vertigo for it was possible to look straight down and the depths were overwhelming. It had struck her before, for instance on Santorini, how the human brain seemed to feel an instinctive fear of edges and used unpleasant sensations to force the body away from them. But in a place like this it seemed illogical and even foolish not to reward all the exertion one had endured with a little look around.

She tightened her grip on the railing and steadied her breathing with every inhale and exhale. The sweat on her brow began to dry in the cool breeze as she cast her eye across the panorama unfolding in front of her. The riverbanks were mainly forested with the church towers of villages peeping out from among the trees. Birds soared high above and in the distance she saw little boats navigating the river. There was such tranquillity in the view that she drank it all in, her hands relaxing and her heart filling with gratitude that she was here; that her grandfather's inheritance had enabled her to come here; that everything he had entrusted to her had put her on a path from which she could explore the world beyond the images she had previously collected from magazines and postcards.

A sharp shriek pierced the air. It came from below her, to the left. There was also a sound. Quite dull. Like a thud. Atalanta stood motionless a moment, then as concerned voices began to cry out she turned away from the beautiful view and rushed down the steps. Her heart beat fast and new sweat dripped down her face as she hurried to see what had happened. Dread pounded in her ears that something terrible had occurred. Would she come upon the scene of ... a murder?

Had she not learned from Otto that someone wanted his grandmother dead? Ought she not to have realised that a place like this with the many differences in height was ideal for an ambush?

When she reached the courtyard with the towering walls

all around, she saw Frau Rabenhorst sitting on the ground, looking quite dazed. The nurse was leaning over her and talking to her. Otto stood beside them, a concerned expression on his face. Gertrude held Lisl who cried that she did not want to look because she could not stand blood.

When Atalanta closed in, she did not see any blood but as the nurse was busy with a cloth, she might have already wiped it away.

"What happened?" she asked Otto. He looked at her with a grave expression. "Grandmother had a dizzy spell and fell. I warned her the exertion would be too much for her weak heart but she never does listen to me." His hands were clenched into fists by his side. The nurse said, "Can someone steady her while I pour a glass of sherry for her?"

Once Otto had his arm around his grandmother, the nurse pulled a silver flask from the large bag she carried and unscrewed the top. It functioned as a small cup and she poured the brownish liquid into it then she offered it to her charge. As soon as the elderly lady smelled the alcohol, her expression turned more cheerful and she quickly swallowed the cup's contents.

"More!" she demanded.

The nurse looked at Otto who gave her a quick nod. She filled the cup and helped Frau Rabenhorst drink it. This time she swallowed it down with such gusto she choked and burst out coughing. Otto gently patted her back.

"You must learn to do things slowly and with care, Grandmother."

"I am not old. I do not need help." She tried to push him

away. "I did not get dizzy and fall. I was pushed over. I clearly felt a sharp nudge between my shoulder blades. That made me lose my balance and fall."

There was a sudden shocked silence.

Then Otto said, "But Grandmother, who would do such a thing?"

"I do not know. But I do know that I saw a shadow and I heard a voice whisper at my ear that I had to die."

Otto turned pale under his tan. He seemed to struggle to find words to dismiss his grandmother's fancy.

The nurse said, "This courtyard has such tall walls that every little sound echoes all around. You must have mistaken voices from further away as speaking to you."

"Saying I had to die?" the elderly lady asked sharply.

"Echoes change words." The nurse stood there with her fresh young face tilted up, her feet planted apart, clearly convinced it was her duty to dispel the patient's bizarre notion at once. "Listen." She held her head back and called out, "Today we dance."

It came back as "*Ey ee ance*". The nurse nodded with satisfaction. "You see? Vowels stay clear, but consonants are often lost. You could have heard the echo of someone saying any other word ending in 'ie'. Anything but die." She leaned over and said, "I understand that once one gets to a certain age, the concept of death is more prominent on one's mind, and your heart has not been strong lately. The medication, however, has been doing a lot of good and you must not be morose and dwell too much on the possibility of dying. You came on this trip to have a good time with your beloved family."

Gertrude made a sound as if she were smothering laughter. Otto threw her a warning look. He said to his grandmother, "Now you listen to your nurse, Grandmother. Take it easy and sit here for a while. We will have a look around and then we will leave. We will go and do something different for the rest of the day. Something that doesn't require much exertion."

"We are young," Lisl said with defiance in her voice. "We can do what we want. We do not need to take it easy. Only for her. She always ruins everything." With that, she ran off towards the vantage point on which Atalanta had been standing when she heard Frau Rabenhorst call out.

Otto wanted to go after her then thought better of it. He released his breath in a deep sigh. His grandmother looked up at him and shook her head. "She is just like her mother. Irresponsible and wild. It would have been better if—"

Otto cut her off by saying loudly to the nurse, "Sabine, you take care of Grandmother while we take a quick look around." He stalked away after his daughter.

Gertrude drew Atalanta to the side. She said softly so her grandmother could not overhear, "I think she just let herself fall."

"Why would you think so?" Atalanta was confused. "She looked genuinely shaken."

"She is very good at playing a part. She cannot enjoy herself when she is not the centre of attention. She felt neglected and played this trick on us." Gertrude sounded angry. "She has done it before. She cannot stand being ignored." She took a deep breath. "I feel sorry for us though. We all thought something terrible had happened and came rushing to see what was wrong."

"Was no one with her when it happened?" Atalanta asked. "Where was Sabine?"

"I can only imagine she was with Otto." Gertrude leaned closer and whispered, "It has been very clear to me from the start that she fancies him but he will not be drawn into a relationship with an employee. Grandmother would have his hide if he even looked at her in that manner."

"Why does she not dismiss the nurse if she believes she is after her grandson?"

"I don't think Grandmother notices."

Atalanta eyed Gertrude with scepticism. "Your grandmother listens in on every conversation and interferes with everything she sees – or thinks she sees. Why would she not see this?"

"Because she believes that she has a firm hold on Otto. She controls part of the money and if he misbehaves in any way, she threatens to cut him off. She thinks he is too afraid of her power to take one step outside the trodden path."

"But did you not say he married his first wife without her consent?"

"That was years ago. Things are different now. He had money of his own but that has been blown away. Bad investments, the stock markets taking such hits…" Gertrude shook her head. "Otto has had to deal with one blow after another. I think he is pretty desperate by now."

Desperate enough to harm his own grandmother to get control of the family money?

The small voice inside Atalanta's head would never stay silent. It always suggested unwelcome possibilities. Her common sense told her she could not dismiss Otto as a suspect just because she liked him. But there was more than that. He was worried his daughter was behind the attacks on his grandmother. Would he suspect her, or pretend that he did, if he himself was out to take her life? Surely, there were more desirable people on whom to cast suspicion? People who were not close to him and whom he could easily blame. His plea for help with Lisl had seemed genuine.

Still, Atalanta knew what despair could do to a person. She did not want to believe it, but she had to keep the possibility in her mind that Otto himself could be involved in the accidents that were happening to his grandmother.

She suddenly felt as though the weight of the world rested on her shoulders. Here she was, in a beautiful place, on a perfect spring day, and again she was caught up in the unsavoury business of murder – or rather, attempted murder.

One could argue that pushing over an old lady was hardly an attempt on her life. The culprit should have tried to shove her over an edge to ensure the fall would indeed be fatal. And why add the sinister words that she had to die? Was it really an attempt to kill or just to frighten? Was it part of something else? A campaign against the Rabenhorst matriarch to terrorise her? To weaken her and cause her to be suspicious of everyone around her?

It could be part of a wilful campaign to alienate her from her loved ones. Did it have to do with the will? Was it possible that someone who knew what Frau Rabenhorst wanted to change was turning her against her family members in order to prevent the changes? But who would know what she was planning?

Herr Kaufmann probably.

How much did the family members themselves know or suspect? Had she already alluded to the changes? To try and strike fear into them, so they would dance to her tune? Such behaviour would be in line with her unpleasant character. But all this was speculation. Atalanta knew nothing about the current will or the one she intended to make. Given Gertrude's suggestion that her grandmother had feigned having fallen in order to get attention, perhaps there might not even have been any attempt at either killing or scaring her. There was nothing substantial to go on.

Still, as Atalanta stood there and considered the old woman who looked fragile as she sat there, there was one thing that was very real to her mind: the sense of menace that hung around them. She could feel a sort of heaviness in the air. It had been tangible even when they had gathered in Bonn for the dinner party. Even before she had known of any family troubles she had sensed that things were not running smoothly.

And what about the past? Tragedy seemed to strike again and again. Otto's parents had died in an accident. His wife had been shot in a bar fight. It seemed like death haunted the family and that it was determined to claim another victim. But where the other deaths had been the result of chance or fate or whatever one wanted to call it, these attempts on the life of Frau Rabenhorst did seem to be intentional. She claimed to have been pushed. Her lamp cord had been frayed with a sharp blade. Otto had seen it himself and had shared his concerns with her.

Atalanta rubbed her hands together. Despite the sunshine, she was cold.

She had been drawn into a family with secrets. Secrets that, according to Lisl, kept people prisoner.

Were they also secrets to kill for?

Chapter Nine

"Look at these beautiful flowers!"

Lisl pointed at the large yellow blooms that hung down over the narrow path. They had entered one of the greenhouses of the botanical gardens of Koblenz and were exploring the tropical plants that grew around them, some reaching all the way to the high glass panels overhead. The air was heavy with the smell of dampness and earth and Atalanta almost felt at home. This was so much like her conservatory in Paris, only there were even more flowers to enjoy.

Lisl stopped and looked at her. "Are you worried about Great-grandmother?" she asked.

Atalanta did not know how to respond. Why had Lisl concluded that she was worried at all? To her knowledge she was walking around with a smile on her face. At least, she was trying to look happy and unconcerned. But apparently this sensitive girl saw right through her pretences.

"I never knew my own great-grandparents," she said softly. "Not even my grandparents either. My mother died when I was little and my father is also no longer alive. I suppose I am often a little jealous of people who do have family, because it is not easy to always be alone."

Lisl nodded with a serious expression. "I am told often I should be grateful that I have a father who loves me very much and a great-grandmother who cares for me. But I don't feel like they understand me or care about what *I* want in life."

Perhaps it was a little amusing to hear a young girl say such a thing, but Atalanta was well aware how serious Lisl was and did not think it helped to belittle her feelings. "What do you want in life?" she asked. "It is always good to dream about things you want to achieve, places you want to go, or experiences you would like to have."

"I wish," Lisl said, "to become so good at creating my paper worlds that they are exhibited all around the world. I would travel to see them in Japan or Brazil, and people will love them and admire them and … admire me for making them." She swung her arms with a forlorn expression. "Everyone calls it just a pastime. They don't take it seriously."

"I think you are very talented."

Atalanta said it because she meant it, but Lisl immediately shot back, "You've never seen any of my work.

How would you know? You are only saying that to make me feel better."

"I do think—" Atalanta protested but Lisl turned away from her.

"Nobody understands me. They all push me to become what they want me to be, but I only want to be myself."

She disappeared down a path running behind a large purple flowering bush. Atalanta took a deep breath. She had experience with girls and their mood swings, but here she felt like she had to take an exam and was not passing it. She had offered Otto her help but she had so far been unable to help in any way. Lisl was convinced everyone was her enemy and that if someone was nice to her, they had an ulterior motive.

Which of course Atalanta actually had.

She sighed. There was a shadow behind her and she turned quickly, her hands tensing as if she had to defend herself. Renard stood beside her. He had come along on this excursion to photograph plants for her that she wanted to buy for her own collection. In reality, she expected him to keep an eye out for anything unusual which might shed more light on the strange happenings in the family.

He leaned over to her and spoke in French, "The nurse has left the old lady in the care of Gertrude and her fiancé. She met someone. A man. They stood talking for a few minutes and she gave him money."

"Does the man work here? Can she have arranged something? Refreshments later perhaps?" Atalanta tried to think of some innocent reason for the nurse's behaviour.

Renard said, "Possibly. But I thought you should know."

"Yes, thank you."

"After the man walked away, she stood by herself and looked very pleased. She even took out the silver flask with alcohol for her mistress and treated herself to a little drink."

Atalanta huffed. "She obviously feels like she is part of the family. I am not certain whether her self-important air is due to her character or her role as nurse. I feel like people who are constantly in charge of others often act with more confidence or become a little commanding because they are used to playing that part. It need not mean she has anything evil in mind."

"I agree." Renard adjusted the strap on the heavy camera he was carrying. "But I wanted to let you know." He added after a few moments, "I took the liberty of calling a few contacts and asking for information about the family members. All of them."

Including Otto, he meant, Atalanta realised. She flushed. "That is very good of you. I am curious what we will learn."

"I told him not to contact me. I said I would call him again from our next stop. I think we should be very careful in all our movements." Renard looked around him as if he expected someone to be spying on them, listening in on their conversation. But there didn't seem to be anyone nearby. The greenhouse was very large, and there were sounds of dripping water and the caged birds near the entrance to drown out what they said. Speaking in French was an extra precaution, even though Atalanta suspected that a well-bred girl like Lisl would have learned the language from an early age. Gertrude had always claimed she despised it and could never master much of it. Otto, however…

Atalanta wished she could discuss the case in more detail with Renard but the risk of attracting attention to themselves was too great. She said more loudly, "That is very good. Keep going. I want to have photographs of all the important plants. And take notes of the names and how to tend to them. If you could also interview a worker here, learn something about how they get the plants to produce so many flowers that would be marvellous."

Renard nodded and walked away in the direction Lisl had taken.

Atalanta stood by herself, drawing breath slowly. In a hot, damp environment like this, breathing was more difficult than in the crisp air outside. She liked greenhouses but the atmosphere in here was positively stifling. She raised a hand to wipe sweat from her forehead. The birds at the entrance were chirping, their sounds shrill in her ears. It seemed like they grew louder, the notes echoing against the glass all around her. The flowers she was looking at – large orange ones with brown smudges on their petals – faded into a blur. She blinked quickly and they came back into focus.

Again she dabbed her forehead. Had she not drunk enough water? Or was it because their lunch seemed like ages ago?

"You look tired," a voice said and Lisl stood before her again, eyeing her with a worried frown. "Here, have a toffee." She held out her hand with a light brown sweet in it, and when Atalanta took it and brought it to her mouth, she smelled caramel and butter. "They are delicious," Lisl said, as she crinkled the red and yellow wrapper that had been around it and put it in her pocket. "I could eat them all day long. Don't tell my father I have them for he thinks I eat too many of them. He does not like sweet things."

"But I do," Atalanta said. The sugar made her feel instantly better and she smiled at Lisl. "It is just too hot in here for me. I am going back outside. Are you coming with me?"

"Yes. I have seen what I wanted to see. These plants are all very special. The people who live in the rainforest use them to make medicines. Medicines are often made from plants. Did you know that? My great-grandmother's heart medication contains digitalis. That is also a plant. But not a tropical one. It grows everywhere. I wonder if you can simply make medicine from the plant."

"By yourself, you mean?" Atalanta asked.

"Yes. Does it require a factory, or a laboratory? Or can anyone do it? In the Middle Ages they also made medicines from plants and they did not have the factories we have now. They did it themselves, in a cooking pot. I read about it. I think the Middle Ages are fascinating. I wish I lived back then."

"So you can contract the plague?" a teasing voice said. Gertrude appeared beside them. She wagged a finger at Lisl. "You should not idealise a time when people all died young, either because of disease or war or ... unjust trials.

With such talk about medicinal plants, they would take you for a witch and burn you at the stake."

Lisl did not seem perturbed. "Then I would simply grow wings and fly away."

Gertrude huffed. "You read too many fairytales. You think everything is pretty and idyllic."

Atalanta was looking at Lisl's expression as Gertrude spoke and she saw something there she could not quite put a name to. Was it rebellion? Was it the secret satisfaction of a child indulging in a fantasy that is hers and hers alone? Some children retreated to a safe place of their own where no one could reach them, touch them, or hurt them. Was Lisl simply using her imagination to keep the darker sides of life away from her? It might be logical in her situation. After all, her mother had died a violent death.

Gertrude said, "I think we have seen enough greenery for one day. I want to do something exciting. Shall we go to a casino or something tonight? I have to ask Otto. He knows all such places."

Atalanta was surprised and it must have shown for Gertrude burst out laughing. She touched her arm and whispered, "You think too well of my brother. He likes the good things in life as much as I do. He is a little more discreet about it, I suppose. This morning he was asking Great-grandmother for money because he wanted to invest in some stocks his broker had recommended to him but I know for a fact he is using it to pay his gambling debts."

She cast a quick look at Lisl who had stopped at a sign outlining details of the rose garden. As she was certain the girl was not listening to anything they said, she continued, "Otto is the male in the family, the one on whom all of our hopes are riding. At least, that is how Grandmother feels. I think she refuses to see his bad side. But sooner or later, his spending will come to light and she will have to see him for who he really is – a lot weaker than she always thought."

Atalanta realised with a shiver that this was another motive for Otto to want his grandmother dead. If she were no longer alive, she could not make unpleasant discoveries. She could not ask hard questions, express disappointment, or take measures to cut him from her will.

If he had incurred debts by gambling, he might also be addicted to the act of gambling itself and be desperate to keep access to money to facilitate it.

Yes, her case against Otto was building nicely. The only problem was that she did not want to believe he was guilty.

She asked Gertrude, "This morning, when your grandmother was pushed over, where were you then? I mean, the fort offered so many vantage points. Did you happen to look down and see anyone near her? Do you have any clue as to who would want to harm her?"

Gertrude shrugged. "I told you I think she pretended to have fallen to get attention. Or perhaps she was unsteady on her feet. We all know she drinks too much. Fräulein Freund makes certain there is always alcohol at hand. Sometimes I think she does it on purpose. It gives her pleasure to know my grandmother is in her power."

Atalanta blinked. "But your grandmother takes heart medication. Is it safe to combine it with alcohol?"

"I have no idea. Even if her doctor advised against it, my grandmother does what she wants. She does not want to believe she is ill. I wonder if she takes her medication at all or simply pours it away when no one is looking."

Atalanta frowned. "You said Sabine Freund enjoys having power over your grandmother. What do you mean?"

"I can't quite explain but ... sometimes when she leans over her to straighten her collar or help her with something, I could swear she says something to her, very softly, and it makes her afraid."

"She is afraid of her own nurse? If so, why not dismiss her and find another?"

"I could not say. I can only suppose that Fräulein Freund has some hold on her that ensures she is not dismissed." Gertrude held Atalanta's gaze. "I also expect she will get a mention in the new will."

Atalanta blinked rapidly. "You think your grandmother will leave money to an employee?"

"It would not surprise me if she did." Gertrude straightened her cuff. "In the old will, she had already settled sums of money on her chauffeur and maid who served her faithfully decades ago when my parents were still alive. They accompanied her everywhere and were very supportive when my parents had their accident."

"I do not think you ever told me what kind of accident they had," Atalanta said, thinking this was as good an opportunity as any to learn a little more about the family's troubled history.

Gertrude sighed. "It happened on holiday, in Bayern. They were staying at a hotel in the mountains. My grandmother was taking care of Otto and me while my parents went for a walk together. They were caught in the mist and must have lost the path. They fell into a ravine and died. It took days to find the bodies. They had to use dogs and all." She fell silent and for a moment Atalanta saw genuine pain and shock in the features of her usually light-hearted former colleague.

"I am so sorry," she said softly, squeezing Gertrude's arm.

She took a deep breath. "I was only two at the time so I do not remember anything of that day, only what I was told later. But it is quite shocking to think of how they died. I often wonder whether they knew what was going to happen. I wonder whether they died instantly or whether they survived for some time, calling for help while nobody came to their rescue." She was pale now and shivered. "I still hate mountains, which is why I detested Grandmother so much for sending me to Switzerland to teach. But Grandmother has never cared for traumas. She thinks it is nonsense that the past influences people. She herself has a heart of stone."

There was so much suppressed anger in Gertrude's voice that Atalanta wondered if she had pushed her grandmother with those whispered words you have to die. If she had frayed the lamp cable not knowing if it would actually lead to her death but just wanting to put fear in her. Make her afraid while she always claimed to know no fear?

Gertrude said, "Just don't mention the accident again. I don't like to talk about it. And Otto doesn't either."

"He was older so he must have more memories of it," Atalanta mused to herself.

Gertrude said, "No, the odd thing is he remembers next to nothing. The family doctor said later that it's possible to suppress memories that are unwelcome. That the mind does that to prevent shock."

Atalanta nodded. She had heard something much like that before.

"There you are." Otto came over to them. "Have you seen the greenhouse? You love orchids so you must see that."

Atalanta assured him she already had. The sweetness of Lisl's candy and the conversation with Gertrude had revived her. Her mind was agile again and trying to piece together all the separate bits of information she was collecting about these people. An image was building: a stern matriarch who suffered a devastating blow when her son and his wife died in the mountains; who raised her grandchildren with little emotion thinking they needed to be tough to survive in life; who put a stamp on their upbringing, leading both of them to find ways to let off steam. There was Gertrude with her romantic adventures and Otto with his gambling – things the matriarch despised and could not forgive. So either of them could fear that someday the life of luxury would end if the old lady cut them off from the family fortune.

Otto had the additional pressure of having to raise his

daughter alone and her not being what his grandmother wanted either. He watched Lisl grow more distant and become more wrapped up in a fantasy world which was on the one hand idyllic and beautiful but which also held hints of suppressed violence that she found fascinating. Her words about the Middle Ages, her interest in poisonous plants…

Otto was clearly worried about her, especially since she had said, out loud, that she wanted her great-grandmother to die.

Atalanta took a deep breath. Ideally, she would like to know a lot more about facts. What the old will said. What the new one would entail. Whether Otto's debts were so substantial that his grandmother would cut him off. And she would also like more information on Gertrude's fiancé Erol Müller. Why had he chosen her for this business arrangement in which they were both free to do what they wanted while they pretended to the outside world to be in love? Merely because it was convenient? Or did he have a hidden agenda?

Fortunately, Renard had said he had tapped into his contacts to get information about the family members. He would receive this information at their next stop. She had to hope that whatever he learned would shed new light on the situation.

Chapter Ten

The next morning, Atalanta awoke with a sense of urgency. She recalled this feeling from her time at the boarding school where she had always lived by the clock and been obliged to follow a schedule set by others. Being late was not acceptable – could even become disastrous. She had to keep her job or she would lose the only chance to pay her late father's debts.

She lay on her back, willing herself to breathe slowly. Her heartrate had to come down again. She was no longer teaching. There were no more debts to pay.

She assumed that the idea of debts and the sense of dread associated with them had re-entered her brain after Gertrude's mention of Otto's position. She found it very hard to believe that a calm and collected man, such as he appeared to be, would be addicted to the thrill of gambling and yet, somehow, it also seemed a terrifyingly understandable possibility.

After all, Otto was under a lot of pressure to do what everyone wanted of him and he might need some way to relax. If he did gamble, she could not blame him, even if she found the memories of her father's debts and the way in which these had influenced her childhood rather daunting. Now, in her new life, she tried hard to avoid those recollections.

Was she perhaps running from her past? From the sense of loneliness that had always accompanied her because she hadn't had any siblings, no mother to confide in, no father to lean on when things got hard? Her father had shied away from responsibility letting her handle debt collectors in order to provoke pity in them. It had been a difficult childhood, though she had never thought of it that way at the time because she had not known anything else. She had been taught obligation and duty from the very start. But the weight of it had become heavier over the years, and now that she had a totally different position and could travel where she wanted and buy whatever her heart desired, she still felt alone. Under pressure to perform, as well. For though she may no longer be teaching, and she need not respond to the call of an alarm clock, she was not merely holidaying here either. She was on a case, accepted from someone she cared for. She wanted Otto to find out what was happening with his grandmother and how he could reach his daughter again.

But perhaps it was asking too much of her? She was an outsider, not a close family friend. And so far there was only a series of strange events and nothing substantial to go on.

There was a soft knock at her door. She slipped into her dressing gown and went over to it and called out, "Who is there?"

"It is me, Otto. You have to come and see the Loreley."

Atalanta's heart leapt at the mention of this famous rock formation. When deciding to go on this Rhine cruise with the Rabenhorst family she had already been looking forward to this epic sight. The rock had inspired famous poets and painters and was a place of legend.

"I'm coming." She hurriedly washed up and dressed herself and went to meet Otto on deck. He was leaning on the railing, staring down the river. A bend was visible and there sat the mighty rock formation that drew artists to it like honey.

"I wonder if we will hear the nymph sing," Otto said with a smirk.

Atalanta stood beside him, watching the morning light play on the stone, turning it from grey to reddish. With the mist rising from the river it was a special, awe-inspiring sight. She could readily understand why people in earlier times had shivered and believed that there was some otherworldly creature involved. Still, her own practical mind searched for rational answers to explain the sounds they heard. "It must be some natural phenomenon," she mused, "that created an effect that people interpreted as singing."

"Isn't it wonderful that a captain can let his ship run

onto the rocks – or whatever happened to cause all the ships to sink in this particular stretch of river – and blame it on some woman singing? If only life were that easy." Otto stared ahead with a tight expression on his face as he spoke. "If only one could say it was all the fault of some influence outside of your own control."

"I guess people often experience life that way. They feel like they are tossed about like they are in a nutshell on an ocean. It is the waves, not their steering, leading the way."

"What do you think of such people? Are they weak? Irresponsible? Unable to lead their own lives?"

Earlier she would have thought he was just making conversation but after Gertrude's revelation about his alleged gambling problems she had a sinking feeling he was testing her.

Her chest grew tight. She could not make light of his situation because she knew all too well what devastating consequences financial troubles could have. Still, she did not want to alienate him with harsh words. "It is not for me to judge," she said finally.

"Oh, come on, Atalanta." He sounded gruff now, almost angry. "You have an opinion. I remember meeting a young woman with opinions about everything who did not hesitate to tell me what they were. You were not intimidated by my name or my money or anything else. You simply spoke your mind and I liked you for it." He looked at her. "I have never forgotten that afternoon."

Atalanta felt her cheeks grow hot. It was true that she had

spoken freely and with passion. The atmosphere had lent itself to such conversation, perhaps also because she had thought she would never see him again. Today it was far different. He was her client and … she found she did care about his opinion of her. She was afraid of what he had ended up in, driven by doubts about his daughter and the pressure his grandmother exerted to have him dance to her tunes.

He said, "Sometimes I feel like there is someone singing this luring melody and I cannot escape its influence. I want to close my ears to it, but no matter how hard I try, I keep hearing it. When I wake up, when I go to sleep. It even haunts my dreams. I cannot…" He clenched his hands into fists. "It all went wrong long ago. With my parents…" His jaw tensed as if he were biting down hard.

Atalanta didn't know what to say or do. She wanted to show him that she was sorry for his losses and his grief, but she also felt like she should not overstep a boundary here. She was conducting an inquiry into his family and … he was also a suspect.

"Gertrude told me they became lost during a walk and it took days for their bodies to be recovered. That must have been dreadful."

"I recall nothing of it." Otto kept his eyes on the rock formation that was getting larger and larger as they closed in. "I was eight at the time so you would think I would remember something. How they said goodbye to us and then left, perhaps looking back as they walked away. I have often wished I had a clear memory of that last goodbye. But

I do not. I remember hardly anything of that entire afternoon."

He met her eyes with a weary smile. "It is as though it has been erased from my memory."

"It is difficult to recall events in detail when they happened long ago," Atalanta heard herself say, and hated how superficial it sounded.

Otto said, "One should recall the day on which one's parents died. It is so momentous. So life changing. I was only eight, and Gertrude two. We…" He fell silent again and his hands formed fists.

Atalanta was not certain whether he was battling emotions he was afraid to show to her – pain, tears even – or whether he was just angry.

"It is almost as though…" His voice was low and sounded as though he were talking to himself. "That day bound Grandmother, Gertrude, and me into some alliance. It is like a blood pact. I am part of an oath I do not remember making and cannot get away from, no matter how hard I try. I just want to be free and happy, but it cannot be, because of the past. Because of some darkness that haunts us."

He stared at the rock. "It is like a siren calling for me. A voice luring me to my destruction."

Atalanta felt a shiver down her spine. It was not so much what he said, but the intensity with which he phrased it. He spoke as though it were the absolute truth, not something he felt or suffered from, but a fact of life he could not escape.

"Have you ever talked to your grandmother about that day? Have you asked her for details of what happened? It might help you work through it."

"She refuses to speak about it. She says it is too painful. But too painful for whom? I sometimes think—"

He stopped with a jerk, as if he were close to an edge and instinctively shied away from it. His breathing grew rapid.

Atalanta stayed still by his side without looking at him. She focused on the rock formation that dominated this stretch of river. She so wanted to say the right thing, but wondered what it might be. She had no real experience with such trauma. And Otto had lived through even more of it when his wife had been fatally shot.

"What do you think?" she asked, attempting to restart the conversation. She didn't really expect an answer but wanted him to know she was there beside him and listening.

"That she knows something she is not telling me."

The words hung in the air, suspended. They did not drift away but instead lingered, gaining size like the Loreley. Towering over them like a sudden threat.

Otto turned his head slowly and looked Atalanta in the eye. "I'm afraid of what she knows. And if she is ever going to tell me. And if she does, what it will mean."

Atalanta held his gaze. "What exactly do you think she may know?"

"I have no idea. But there is something, always present, like a shadow. At first, when I was younger, I believed it was just the grief itself. That it never fades and somehow follows you around. It can be further away for a while, it can keep very quiet until it suddenly springs at you again and overwhelms you." He swallowed hard.

Atalanta nodded. She did know that feeling: a certain instinctive knowledge that one's life could have been different if certain events had never taken place.

Otto carried on: "I believed it was just that and I had to accept it. But for some time now I have come to see it is more. She knows something and she... She enjoys it, her position of power, her silence that somehow keeps us all dancing to her tune. What does she know? What might it mean?" He stood up straight and gave Atalanta a desperate look from his wide-open blue eyes. "I have even started to wonder if ... my parents are really dead."

"Why would you think they are not?" Atalanta queried, overtaken by the suggestion.

"I know it is strange to think so. If they were not dead, they would not have abandoned us, don't you think? They would not have simply vanished." He raised both his hands and rubbed his face. "But I cannot shake the feeling that ... by their deaths she gained complete control of us, and she enjoys that position. I..." He suddenly half laughed. "I must be going insane. Slowly mad because of all the pressure. The problems with the investments, my daughter... Having to decide about many things alone. It must be getting to me. I think that they are still alive, because I want them to be. Because I cannot accept that they died in some senseless accident. I cannot accept that they fell into the depths and ... suffered." His voice broke on the last word.

Atalanta put her hand on his arm. "Do not torture yourself with all these dark thoughts. It happened while you were just a small child. You had no part in it."

"I know but... I just cannot seem to leave it alone." He leaned on the railing again, his shoulders slumping. "I wish she had not asked us to come on this trip. I cannot do much while we are here. I mean, I cannot hide behind all my business arrangements, the meetings and the phone calls. This is time away from my normal life, but while it should be pleasant and relaxing, it feels like I am only getting more and more tense and..." He was silent again before he added, "Afraid."

"Afraid of what?"

"I do not know. That the darkness that snatched my parents in the past is about to strike again? There is something in the air..." He glared at the rock and laughed bitterly. "This whole river region is full of legends about malignant forces threatening human life. Whether they are nymphs or dwarfs or giants, they are never friendly. They are always out to create havoc and destroy human happiness. People come here because they love the stories. My own daughter wants to cut out these paper worlds that celebrate those tales. I wish she would not do that. I wish she would not bring them to life in our family circle. It feels like they are somehow ... taking over. Like the siren's voice is luring the ship to the rocks to ground it and drown everyone on board."

He looked at her again. His eyes were weary now, the fire having died down. Now he just seemed tired. "Do you think I am going mad, Atalanta? Do you think I am finally breaking? Sometimes I feel like I should have broken long ago, but I could always resist it, stand above it, be stronger or smarter. Now it has finally caught up with me."

"You are perhaps under too much strain from your business concerns and your worries for Lisl. You thought she might have frayed that cable and … it started to wear on your calm. You must try and look at facts, not feelings."

She took a deep breath, willing herself to stay clear of the emotion he evoked in her. Forcing herself to engage her logical mind and help him regain control of the situation.

"There is nothing disastrous going to happen. Together we can…"

A piercing scream rent the air. It was an odd echo of the scream at the fort in Koblenz but this time it seemed even wilder and more panicked. It stretched out, resounding across the water towards the rock formation, then came back to them thin and eerie.

"What on earth was that?" Otto asked, pale under his tan. "*Who* is that?"

It was a female voice, that much was certain. They both ran to go and see. The sound came from the left where the cabins for the family were. Atalanta saw Renard rushing from the other side. His expression was grave but his eyes were alert and she knew he would be noticing every detail about the scene they were about to see. She hoped he would notice everything, because her own mind was racing and she felt unable to think coherently. The conversation about impending darkness, some malignant force closing in, and now this…

Frau Rabenhorst stood in the doorway of a cabin looking in. She pointed with a finger, her voice low when she spoke, "It looks like she is just sleeping. It looks like she is just sleeping. But the body is cold. So cold. Too cold. She is dead. She is dead!" With the latter words she began to laugh hysterically.

Otto wrapped an arm around his grandmother's shoulders and pulled her away from the door. Renard entered the room, while Atalanta remained in the doorway. She immediately focused on the female form on the bed. Nurse Sabine Freund lay there as if she were indeed sleeping. Her expression was calm but the arm that hung out of the bed dangled oddly.

Renard put two fingers on her forehead, then against her throat and on her wrist to check for a heartbeat. He looked at Atalanta and shook his head.

Atalanta drew in a breath sharply. Someone in their party had died, but not the old woman. Not the one everyone had believed to be the target. It was instead the nurse. It was so strange. There were also no signs of violence on the body. No blood, no marks on the throat from something like strangulation. Could she have simply died in her sleep?

But someone so young… Was that even likely?

The captain appeared and asked them to stay calm while he called for help. There would be a doctor coming on board at the next stop to share his findings with the police. They would soon know what had happened.

Renard glanced at Atalanta and gave her a silent nod to indicate they must speak. She left the room while the captain took charge. Otto had led his mother away and Gertrude was with them in the salon now, speaking urgently. Renard drew Atalanta aside.

He said in a low voice, "She drank from the flask. The silver flask. Where is it now?"

Atalanta looked at him. "You think the liquid inside contained…?"

"Possibly. We must prevent someone else from drinking it as well."

"Yes, I will see to it at once. I will ask the captain to confiscate it and keep it for the doctor's arrival. He can have the contents analysed." She eyed Renard. "What do you think?"

"I fear that this poor mademoiselle became the unintended victim of a plot against her mistress."

"You mean that … she was poisoned accidentally while someone attempted to murder Frau Rabenhorst?"

"If the killer did not know the nurse liked to treat herself to a little drink, he would have assumed that Frau Rabenhorst was the only one drinking from that flask. It would have been easy to poison the contents and wait for the death to occur."

Atalanta nodded. "I agree. I will talk to the captain at once." She started to leave but then turned back to Renard. "We must receive the information from your contacts as soon as possible. It has become most urgent now that someone has been murdered."

Chapter Eleven

The ship docked in Sankt Goarshausen, a small city nestled against hills. Perched on one of them, an impressive red stone castle with several towers watched over the river. The passengers were ordered to stay on board, while the doctor conducted his first examination. He had arrived with a middle-aged man in a dark blue suit who Atalanta thought was a police chief or other local representative of the law. She had watched through the salon's windows as they had come aboard, speaking to each other with grave expressions. Otto had met them and had accompanied them.

"Do you think we can continue the trip?" Lisl asked. She came to sit beside Atalanta, ignoring her great-grandmother and Gertrude on the other side of the room. "I was looking forward to seeing much more. I think we only did a lot of boring things so far. It was just getting exciting, with the Loreley and all. The river is narrowest and deepest there and ships have gone missing before. I wish I could look at the bottom of the river where they all are. I want to see how much is preserved and investigate if there is treasure buried there. Or just skeletons." She frowned hard. "I do not know if bodies decay in water like they do in the earth. Do you know? Do they even become skeletons? Or do they keep their flesh like mummies?"

Gertrude looked in their direction. "It is not very decent to discuss mummies now, Lisl. Sabine Freund died a few hours ago."

"You are not sad about that," Lisl said. She stuck her chin up in a defiant move. "You never liked her. You were afraid she was stealing your fiancé."

Gertrude laughed uncomfortably. "I was not. She is a mere servant. She has nothing. No money, no connections."

"She was pretty. And he kissed her. I saw them in the botanical garden."

Gertrude's eyes flashed. "No, you did not. You are only making this up to hurt my feelings. You are a nasty little girl like that."

"I am *not* little and I *did* see them. I was in the greenhouse and I saw it through the window. I am old enough to know what they were doing."

Gertrude turned scarlet. "Shut up about this!" she hissed. "You are nothing but a liar and a cheat, just like your mother was."

Lisl's eyes went wide at this unexpected jab.

Frau Rabenhorst scolded, "This is not the time or the place to—"

Lisl jumped to her feet and screamed at Gertrude. "You are the liar! You all want to make me hate my mother, but I loved her. *I loved her!*"

She ran from the room, colliding with her father who grabbed her shoulders to steady her.

"What is the matter now?" he asked but she pulled free by kicking his legs and running away.

Otto looked at Atalanta. "What happened?"

Gertrude was quick to say, "She is just upset because someone died. She finds it scary."

Otto seemed sceptical but his sister forestalled further questions by asking, "What does the doctor think?"

"He thinks she probably died of heart failure. He will examine the body here and then it will be taken away for further investigation. We are allowed to continue our trip as long as there is a policeman with us." Otto gestured at the man clad in a dark blue suit Atalanta had observed before. "This is Herr Georg Schweiger. He will stay with us until it is all cleared up."

It sounded optimistic, as if it were a matter of hours.

Herr Schweiger looked at Atalanta. "I would like to get acquainted with everyone present. You are?"

"Atalanta Ashford. I met Gertrude Rabenhorst in Switzerland and I was asked to come on this trip to spend some time with her and Herr Otto Rabenhorst and his daughter Lisl."

"Her name is Clara Annalise, if you please," Frau Rabenhorst said. She got to her feet and gestured to the new arrival with a grave expression. "I must ask you to be very discreet about how you look into this matter. We are a family with a spotless reputation and we dislike drawing attention to ourselves. I am afraid that…" She waited a moment and added then, "my grandson is to blame for this tragedy."

Otto looked at his grandmother with alarm. "How do you mean?"

"You hired the wrong nurse. She was not capable and terribly frivolous. She was always saying the most inappropriate things. She also liked men a little too much. You should have dismissed her before this trip but you kept telling me how it seemed difficult to find someone else at short notice and … well, I closed my eyes to the problem she posed."

Atalanta felt her spine tighten. The nurse had met a man in the botanical gardens and given him money. What had that meeting been about?

And if Lisl was to be believed, Sabine Freund had also kissed Gertrude's fiancé. Gertrude claimed to have seen her say things to Frau Rabenhorst that seemed to strike her as unpleasant. Renard had confirmed that she was secretly drinking her mistress's liquor. What else had she done? And now Frau Rabenhorst had said she had closed her eyes to the problem the impertinent nurse posed, but what if someone else in the family had not?

If the nurse had been poisoned with something inserted in the flask, who had done this? Gertrude, who had felt threatened by the nurse's flirting with her fiancé? The fiancé himself, who had discovered the nurse was indiscreet and clingy?

Otto, who wanted to protect his sister's reputation?

Or had Lisl inserted the poison believing her great-grandmother would drink it?

Who was to blame here?

Was Sabine Freund even the intended victim?

And if the wrong person had died by mistake, would the killer try again?

———

They stayed docked at Sankt Goarshausen overnight to allow the doctor to complete a first report of his findings. There was still a small hope that the death would prove to be from natural causes and they could continue their journey upstream without having to accept the presence of a police officer in their midst who would be watching them.

Atalanta sat alone on a narrow wooden bench on deck, gazing across the river. Everything was so peaceful. Stars dotted the deep blue night sky. In the distance, an owl called and its mate replied. It seemed so strange and unlikely that there was anything menacing here in this beautiful natural world that breathed its tranquillity straight into her soul.

She lifted the book from her lap and used the lantern she had brought with her to read the lines Goethe had written well over a century earlier. They spoke of this land's wild beauty and the need for human beings to connect with these wonders in order to strengthen themselves against the trials of life.

"I must say," a male voice remarked dryly from nearby, "that I have never worked on a case before where one of the people involved was sitting quietly reading after such a shocking event as a sudden death."

Atalanta looked up to see Herr Schweiger closing in on her and leaning against the railing.

"Goethe would disagree with you," she said. "He would say that it is essential to seek quietude after having experienced a shock. Is poetry not meant to reconnect the soul with everlasting concepts like peace and justice that can take a person far beyond the problems they are facing at that time?"

"Justice?" he said sharply. "Do you think we need justice here?" He eyed her intently, searching her expression for something more than a casual reply to this question.

Atalanta closed her book and rested it on her knee. "I think we always need justice. But to answer your question pertaining to this situation in particular, yes, I think we need justice. Justice for the woman who died. For the family who are suddenly treated with suspicion and expected to explain why someone young and apparently healthy would suddenly die in their midst. There has already been enough tragedy following the Rabenhorsts."

Schweiger nodded gravely. "I am well aware." He stared into the distance. The light that reached them from the windows of the salon where the others were gathered cast a strange glow on his serious features. Atalanta had assumed he was in his forties, but he looked younger now and she realized the weight resting on his shoulders as he came into this strange and complex case. She wished she could discuss some of the interesting elements with him but he was a police officer who was probably not interested in the opinions of some young woman. She was not about to tell him that she was a private detective. Police officers often disliked amateurs, as they called them, meddling in their cases.

Besides, it would be hard to explain why she was here. She could not tell him that Otto Rabenhorst suspected his own daughter of wanting to kill her great-grandmother. That could create a drama when the nurse turned out to have been poisoned, possibly by mistake.

"What do you think happened?" Schweiger asked her. He gave her a quick, assessing look. "You seem an intelligent woman to me. Not prone to hysterics. You are also not a family member. Before this trip began, you had no dealings with Sabine Freund."

"You ought not to simply assume that," Atalanta said, before she was conscious of how it might appear. She hurried to add, "I could have met her earlier in life, before she worked as a companion for the Rabenhorsts."

"That is true. How honest of you to mention it." There was a hint of amusement in his voice. "Or should I say, how professional?"

Atalanta froze a moment. The cool evening air that breathed across her skin seemed suddenly chillier. What did he know? Why had he singled her out for this conversation?

Schweiger said, "You need not worry. I will not give you away. That is, if the Rabenhorsts don't already know who you are and what you do."

Atalanta ran a finger across the edge of her book. "What is it I do? I only help people."

"True. Your grandfather would have said the same thing."

Atalanta jerked upright. "You know him? I mean, *knew* him?"

"We met on several occasions. He solved two murder cases and a burglary. I was just a young policeman then, and I was told by my superiors to ignore him, and when he had success to hate him because he had stolen the moment of glory away from us. But I realised we would never have had a moment of glory without him. The cases would have gone unsolved. Killers would have walked free." His expression was serious and his hand tensed by his side. "I cannot ignore an opportunity for justice when I see one. That, Goethe would approve of."

Atalanta had to smile now. "You should know that my grandfather never wanted to outwit the police. He was simply in a position to notice other things or come to different conclusions."

"I saw that from the very beginning, as I see it now. You are uniquely placed, as a member of this travelling company, to share your impressions with me. I trust that you are yourself not involved in any foul dealings here."

Atalanta felt a small niggle of guilt inside. She had agreed to come along to help Otto. She still wanted to help him – both him and Lisl, to whom she had taken an instinctive liking. She had learned in previous cases that gut feeling could be vital, but it could also lead her astray. Was she involved? Was she more involved than she cared to acknowledge, not to herself and certainly not to this inspector?

Schweiger said, "Otto Rabenhorst spoke very highly of you. It seems he thinks you can work wonders with his daughter who, as an impressionable young girl, needs some female guidance." He waited a moment. "He offered this explanation for your presence very readily. It sounded like a well-rehearsed tale, but why does he need a reason at all other than your friendship with his sister, dating back to the days when you both taught in Switzerland?"

Atalanta felt a new shiver across her spine. This man was very astute and he read between the lines. It would be hard to deceive him.

Did she even want to deceive him?

"I assume that being confronted with sudden death makes people nervous," she said cautiously. "They might feel they would be … scrutinised. Things that are innocent and have no special meaning might suddenly be magnified and twisted to mean something else altogether."

"You mean, I might conclude you are having an affair with him?" Schweiger held her gaze. "A man in his position, an eligible bachelor, an honourable widower from a well-to-do family, must of course guard his reputation with great care." He waited a moment and added, "It would be inconvenient if it was somehow damaged by someone who was not … discreet."

Atalanta slowly drew breath. "Do you mean the nurse Sabine Freund?"

Schweiger shrugged. "It is not uncommon for a man to cast an interested eye on a woman in his employ. He might have believed she would accept his advances, knowing it could never be anything serious. But then she began to make demands on him, asking for money to keep her mouth shut about what had transpired between them. He might have decided that as long as she was alive she would always be a threat to him. He might have wanted to remove the threat."

"That is a lot of assumptions," Atalanta said quietly. "I do not think you climbed the ranks by merely speculating."

"I am not speculating. I am examining possibilities. I am casting my mind over the situation." Schweiger smiled at her. "It is something your grandfather taught me. He was always very cautious not to follow the most obvious lead but keep a broader perspective."

"What would be the most obvious lead?" Atalanta asked softly. She was afraid of his answer but still she wanted to know.

"Assuming the wrong woman died?" Schweiger held her gaze again. "Several people have told me that Frau Rabenhorst drank from a silver flask. They also told me that the nurse often treated herself to a little secret sip from that same bottle. That means it is possible the flask was poisoned with Frau Rabenhorst as the intended target."

Yes, and on top of Otto's confession to her that he suspected an earlier attempt on her life with the frayed cable, it looked very likely. Had Otto lied to her about that attempt to build the suggestion that his grandmother was under threat, all the while really intending to kill the nurse in a way that removed all suspicion from him?

At the very idea, sweat formed on Atalanta's back. If Otto had fabricated all of this, he had also planned for her involvement. What exactly did he expect of her? To go after the wrong clues and make sure he was never suspected?

But Schweiger had snatched at the possibility of an affair between the pretty nurse and her employer at once. If Otto had believed he could deflect suspicion, he was not succeeding.

Schweiger said, "I think you have already accepted this as a possibility. You look so pensive."

"I knew the nurse drank from the flask. My butler had noticed her doing so and mentioned it to me."

"I have seen Renard." Schweiger sounded amused. "I am well aware of what this innocent-looking valet is capable of. He has contacts, does he not? Such a neutral word, *contacts*, hiding an entire world."

Atalanta felt her cheeks heat. This man seemed to know all her secrets. He had worked with her grandfather and seemed to be ahead of her, both in understanding her grandfather's ways and analysing this particular case. It was annoying and at the same time oddly fascinating. She longed to know details about her grandfather's past cases, and here was someone who could tell her more.

Schweiger said, "If the doctor does conclude it was murder, we must work along two lines. One: the nurse was the intended victim. Two: the nurse was not the intended victim and swallowed the poison by mistake. That will make it all much more complicated, especially as I have already established that it was easy to gain access to the flask. Anyone in the party could have done it."

"And the poison used? Not everyone has ready access to something deadly."

Schweiger tilted his head. "Frau Rabenhorst takes heart medication based on digitalis. It was carried by the nurse in the same bag in which she had the flask. Would it have been so difficult to put the digitalis in the alcohol? I think not." He waited a moment. "Again, anyone in the party could have done it. It would not take much time. And they were all aware of her using the medication."

He stared for a moment across the dark river.

"Have you ever been to where the Rhine begins, Fräulein Ashford?"

The sudden change of subject surprised her, but she readily replied, "No. But I know where it is. In Switzerland. I have heard it is an unassuming little stream, a mere trickle, which one cannot even call a brook, let alone a mighty river."

"Indeed. I was there years ago. I realised while I stood there that it was actually the same river, possibly also the same water, that begins as almost nothing and then ends up powerful enough to sink ships." He looked at her again. "It is a good analogy for life. Things that begin so trivial – a little jealousy, a small moment of weakness, a dishonest action – can later grow into monstrous powers that destroy lives and sink ships, as it were, along with everyone aboard."

His jaw tensed. "I am asking myself as I stand here what small thing started the chain of events that led us, perhaps across many kilometres and through different countries, to the death that happened here on this ship. For there is always a moment where it all begins, even if we are not aware of it at the time."

Atalanta clutched her book. The brief moment when she had met Otto Rabenhorst and during which she had enjoyed his company had given rise to an innocent dream about him and about seeing him again, just to make her dull life a little more colourful. But today, she was sitting here on a ship, a young woman had died in her sleep, and a police officer wanted to involve her in solving this death. It had started with a little infatuation – if it could even be called that – as their encounter had been so brief. But however brief, she had felt a connection with Otto which had made her decide to accept his offer to come on this trip. Small beginnings. A single drop of water.

Schweiger said, "When you just said it was all speculations, you sounded almost indignant. I cannot blame you. It is not right to go about suspecting people without evidence, without proof." He moved to stand closer to her and lowered his voice. "There was a lot of money found in her cabin. More than a nurse would earn. *Much* more. She also had some valuable items in her luggage, newly purchased, suggesting she had come into money a short while ago. Is it so ridiculous to assume she was blackmailing someone?"

Atalanta shook her head. "It is a very logical assumption, if you are certain she did not inherit the money or earn it in a prior position."

He shook his head. "She was working as a typist in one of the family's offices before she was hired as a companion for the elderly lady. She is called a nurse but I am not sure she received any formal training. I did not find any references among her things. I made inquiries about her past and should hear back soon."

Schweiger continued after a brief silence. "Having found the money, and concluded that it could be the result of blackmail, it seems obvious why Herr Otto Rabenhorst hired her without her being qualified. She forced him into the arrangement so she was inside the family, so to speak, to ask for more money whenever she liked. She abused her position shamefully."

Atalanta turned her head to where the hoot of the owl resounded again. The night was still peaceful and beautiful, but something very ugly was unfolding in front of her. It made her question everything she had believed so far. Still, she was not certain that the inspector was thinking in the right direction.

"Lisl claimed to have seen the nurse kissing Gertrude Rabenhorst's fiancé Erol. Is it possible that she had a hold on *him* and used that to get into the family?"

Schweiger huffed. "I have not checked the money for

fingerprints so I cannot tell you who handled it. It could have been any one of them."

"Was there anything else in her room that supports a connection between her and Otto?" Atalanta took a deep breath before asking, "Anything to suggest they were indeed … close?"

"Someone in there had been smoking a cigarette. The butt was thrown in the wash basin. She herself did not smoke and the butt was cut to be used in a cigarette holder. That suggests a woman." He looked at her. "Does Gertrude Rabenhorst smoke?"

"I have not seen her do it on this trip, but I know she used to smoke. It was forbidden at the school where we worked. She had to sneak outside to smoke in the garden. She was often caught and punished for it." Atalanta frowned. "But why would Gertrude have been in Sabine's cabin smoking a cigarette? That almost suggests a meeting."

"A friendly relaxed meeting," he agreed. "And that is very odd when compared with the statement of the little girl that Sabine Freund was kissing Gertrude's fiancé."

Atalanta sighed. "I am not certain Lisl told the truth. She enjoys turning people against each other, people she doesn't like."

"Did you notice any tension between the fiancé and the nurse?"

"No, but I have not been watching them closely. I will ask Renard if he has noticed anything. He did see the nurse meet a man while we were in the botanical gardens in

Koblenz. She gave him money, but I do not know who he was or what she paid him for."

Schweiger eyed her with a flicker of interest in his eyes. "That could be very important. You see, I found the cigarette butt while I was checking the wash basin for something else. Traces of ashes. Something was burned in there – papers, I assume. Did the man she paid hand her anything?"

"If he did then Renard did not see that, but I suppose it could have happened before he was watching. You think this unknown man delivered something to her and she paid him for that?"

"I am just curious what was burned in her wash basin."

Atalanta tried to envision the scene: Sabine Freund receiving some documents and paying the man who delivered them to her, then back on the ship she burned them. But why? That made no sense. If they were important to her, she would hang on to them as proof or as material for blackmail.

Had the killer burned them? But when had they had time to do that?

"Are you certain the ashes were from burned papers? Not from the cigarette?"

"I will have it analysed but it will take time." He shrugged with resignation. "It will take more time than we have. The family wants to continue their journey."

"I thought it was already decided that you will accompany us."

He smiled at her with some irony. "I am. But what can

one policeman do in a family full of secrets? They might all know more than they are telling me. They might lie for each other. They might help the guilty party escape. Go scot-free." He held her gaze. "How would you feel about that, Fräulein Ashford?"

"I am just one private detective. I cannot promise you any results, but I can promise you this. If the nurse was murdered, I will help you find out who it was."

"Even if it turns out to be someone you like?"

Atalanta swallowed hard. "Even then. For everything in life has consequences. The river starts somewhere and must run its course. My involvement with the Rabenhorst family began years ago. They came back into my life and I feel like it was for a reason. I would like to find out what that reason is."

Schweiger nodded. "I understand. I will leave you to read on." He passed her quickly and as he did so, dropped something in her lap. It was a small white envelope. She picked it up and with her lantern shone on the handwriting scrawled across.

It was her grandfather's.

Her heart skipped a beat. In every case there had been a letter. One way or another. Handed to her by Renard, or left in her luggage. But now it came to her through the hands of this strange man. Herr Georg Schweiger, who acted both like her opponent and her ally; who had confided in her beyond what was appropriate in a case like this, and yet had also kept his cards close to his chest. She had felt like he was consciously feeding her information he wanted her to know, while he was not revealing all that he had already discovered. What was his purpose? Did he not trust her? Did he fear she would share the information with the family?

Or did he *want* her to share it with the family, because he hoped that certain suggestions would make the killer panic?

We don't even know if there is a killer. She said it to herself without much conviction. With a sigh she tore open the envelope and extracted a note.

My dearest Atalanta,

> *Ah, my heart gladdens at the idea you will ever read this note. If you are, it means you have met Georg Schweiger. He is one of the most interesting people I have ever met. He is extremely cunning and has a lot of psychological insight into human character. It never surprised me that he advanced his career quickly.*

> *But he has a weakness. A flaw, one might call it. Perhaps a fatal one? If you are going to work with him, you should know about it.*

Atalanta turned the note over, eager to read on but the backside was blank. She stared at it in bewilderment. Had Grandfather not finished this note? But why then had he handed it to Schweiger to deliver to her, should they ever meet? That made no sense.

She tilted the lantern to shine on the backside, hoping to discover a secret message but there was nothing there.

Then she noticed something and her heart skipped a beat.

The piece of paper itself! It had at one time been larger. There had been more written on it probably and then someone had cut it very carefully so it would not stand out. But it was obvious when she thought about it. Her grandfather would never leave her hanging like this.

She got up and went into the salon to look for Schweiger. Otto told her he had gone to his cabin. She caught up with him while he was opening his door.

"Herr Schweiger! Where is the rest of the note?"

"The rest of the note?" he asked, without looking at her.

"Yes. You know very well what I mean." Anger rushed through her. "You read a letter that was not meant for you. You invaded my privacy. The privacy of the correspondence between my grandfather and me. You cut off the note so I would not be able to read what he wanted to share with me. That is very serious."

"Serious indeed," he said with an infuriating smile.

"My grandfather always gives me directions. I need to read what he said. Give me the other half of the note."

"I do not know what you are talking about." He straightened up. "I merely delivered the note he entrusted to me shortly before he died. He said he hoped he had found a worthy successor and that I might one day meet her. He said that were I to meet her, I should give her the note, but only after we had spoken about the case at hand. I followed his directions to the letter. If the note is not complete, I am not to blame." He paused and then added,

"If you are indeed a worthy successor to his detective skills, you should be able to work out for yourself what it means. I bid you goodnight." And he entered his cabin and closed the door in her face.

Atalanta stood there, her heart drumming in her ears. Who did he think he was? He obviously didn't care much for female detectives. Doubting she was worthy to succeed her grandfather!

How could he!

This was intolerable.

She wanted to pound on his door and demand he hand over the note. That he give her what was rightfully hers. How could he, a police officer, steal? Withhold?

Despite her anger, she knew that reasoning with him would not work. She would only make a fool of herself. She had to let it go for now. But she would talk to him later. And she would find some way to make him give her the missing half. She would find a way to goad him into it. Prod his ego. Make a suggestion that would elicit a response.

Yes. She would get him to do what she wanted. But she would have to think carefully about it and make her move at the right moment. Take him by surprise.

With a smile on her lips, she walked away.

Chapter Twelve

The next morning over breakfast, Georg Schweiger told them that he had heard from the doctor. They were all in the process of eating, having just cut up toast, or picked up a coffee cup, and they all stared at him, frozen in their movements, caught in a sudden atmosphere of tense anticipation. Atalanta could have sworn that if someone had dropped something, everyone would have shot to their feet as if a gunshot had exploded.

The tension became almost unbearable as Georg Schweiger stretched the silence before finally saying, "Sabine Freund died of a large dose of digitalis medication which she ingested from the silver flask. The contents were laced so heavily it would be fatal."

There was a short silence in which Atalanta scanned their faces intently, trying to determine what they all thought.

Otto looked tense but not surprised.

Lisl was staring at her plate, crumbling a piece of bread with one hand. The other was hidden under the table.

Gertrude stared with an open mouth, as if she did not quite follow.

Erol was pale but grim.

Herr Kaufmann looked tightly at Frau Rabenhorst, as if he expected her to respond first.

And she did. She rose from her seat and cried out dramatically, "I told you I was pushed! At the fort in Koblenz! They are trying to kill me. First there, now here." She stared at the food on her plate. "This could also be poisoned. Take it away! I will not eat or drink anything. At all."

"Don't be silly," Gertrude said sharply. "That way you will certainly be dead soon."

Lisl broke into giggles. Otto turned to her and barked at her to stop it but she kept on going. "I cannot help it," she said between fits of laughter. "I cannot help it."

"She is hysterical," Gertrude said with a look of disgust. "Unfortunately, we no longer have a nurse to give her something to calm herself."

Frau Rabenhorst said in a pitiful tone, "Does no one care that they are trying to kill me?"

Otto said to Gertrude, "I do not need you to tell me what to do about my daughter."

"No, because you are doing so well on your own," Gertrude snapped back.

She paused and then added, "You are right though that I should not have joked about losing a nurse. After all, Sabine

Freund was hardly a nurse. She was a glorified typist who got the position with Grandmother solely because you wanted her close by."

Otto turned scarlet. "I will not tolerate this kind of insult!" he hissed.

Schweiger was watching the exchange with interest. Atalanta realised that he had dropped the bomb and was now glad to see everything explode. She disliked his tactics but she had to agree that it was delivering immediate results.

Lisl had stopped laughing and said in a chill voice, "Father did not want her to be here. She meant nothing to him. I saw her kissing *your* fiancé."

"You saw nothing of the kind. You made it up just because you can't stand—" Gertrude fell suddenly silent, glancing at her grandmother.

Frau Rabenhorst lowered herself to her seat again and gave Otto a stern look. "I will not have such nonsense as someone suggesting that you were interested in that immature vain woman. She claimed to be a doctor's daughter, but I was convinced she was lying. She cannot have been raised by anyone with any sort of education or breeding. She was always looking at new hats and clothes. She could not speak any languages, nor did she play an instrument. A new wife for you, Otto, would have to meet a lot of criteria."

Otto exhaled in a huff. "She was never on my list to become a wife."

Atalanta noticed he didn't say he had never been

interested in her per se. Had he indeed had an affair with her and tried to end it? Had she not accepted that and put pressure on him by asking for money to keep word of their affair under wraps? Had she painted a vivid picture of what might happen, should his grandmother get wind of this?

Frau Rabenhorst leaned back and said, "She was never the intended victim. *I* was. Therefore I want the investigation to focus on people who wanted *me* dead." She looked at Schweiger. "I want you to take this very seriously. Where no one will shed a tear about the death of this silly nurse, *my* demise would have serious consequences." She dropped a meaningful silence. "I want the fullest possible investigation into who is behind this attempt on my life. I want them found and imprisoned as soon as possible. Until that time, I will only eat and drink what others have tried before me."

"Grandmother, you are not a Roman emperor with slaves to taste your food ahead of you," Otto protested. He still seemed to feel mortified.

"You want me to die? You know every bite I take"—she gestured across the table—"could be my last and you even deny me security? What kind of grandson are you? I did everything for you. I protected you. Without me you would have had no life. No life at all."

She seemed to become aware of Schweiger's stare and shrank back against the seat. "I only want to feel safe," she murmured.

Schweiger said, "I think it is reasonable that we all eat

and drink from the same foods and liquids. That way we can prevent another murder."

Atalanta was surprised he was taking this approach as it had seemed obvious last night that he believed the nurse was the intended victim and the killer would be satisfied now. But she was willing to watch what outcomes his choices affected and only act if she thought things were going tragically wrong.

After all, her grandfather had warned her about a fatal flaw in the man. Whatever it might be, she had to guard against it and ensure the solution to the case did not suffer from it.

Frau Rabenhorst exchanged her plate with Gertrude. Gertrude looked at the plate with a sheepish expression and then said, "But wait, does that mean that ... if there is anything in this pork sausage or..." She pushed the plate away. "How can we ever have a journey together when we believe that one among our party is out to kill Grandmother?"

Lisl started laughing again. Otto took her by the shoulder and made her stand up and leave the room with him. Atalanta hesitated a moment and then decided to go after them. She felt the eyes of Schweiger on her as she left the table. He seemed decided that there was something going on between Otto and her and therefore that she was involved – prejudiced, even.

Outside in the cool air that drifted across the river, Otto spoke softly to his daughter. She had stopped laughing and was listening with her head down. As she closed in,

Atalanta could hear him say, "Then you will never be able to do anything anymore, you understand? I cannot help you if you act like this."

"Are you not well?" Atalanta asked.

Lisl looked up at her with a jerk. "I am fine. Great-grandmother is the one who is not well. She is always making people feel bad about themselves. She enjoys seeing us suffer. *She* should have died. Not Sabine." There was something wild in her eyes.

Had Lisl poisoned the flask? Had she believed her great-grandmother would die and disappear from her life? Had she not realised her action would claim another life? Was she now drowning in guilt and despair?

Otto said, "Please, Lisl. You are not making this any better."

Lisl pulled away from him. "You all want to make me look like I am mad but I am not. I am perfectly fine. I only want to be free of her. You want it too. You just don't admit it."

She turned and stormed away, almost colliding with Renard who was approaching them with some newspapers in his hand. He had left the ship earlier to purchase them which had been, Atalanta supposed, a thinly veiled excuse to allow him the means to contact his informants and learn more about the family members.

She was eager to hear what he had to tell her, but something seemed more pressing right now.

As he wanted to give the newspapers to Atalanta she said, "Will you keep an eye on Lisl, Renard? Make sure she doesn't leave the ship or does anything else rash and foolish, that is not helping her? Thank you."

With her mind at ease about the impetuous girl, she could focus on the case. She turned to Otto and said, "We must talk. Can we sit down a moment somewhere we are not overheard?"

Otto seemed to want to protest, then he relented with a sigh and took her to the ship's bow. The crisp morning sunlight caressing the enchanting views seemed at total odds with the dark atmosphere of death that had descended onto the ship.

Otto said, "What is there to talk about, Atalanta? The attempt was made but failed. The wrong woman died. Now we must wait for the next one, which may be successful."

"Do you think Lisl did it?" she asked, looking straight at him.

He avoided her eyes. "I do not know." His features were grey and haggard, as if he had aged considerably during this short trip.

"Do you think she did it?" she insisted. "You cannot know of course for certain, but you must have some instinctive feeling about it."

"I am afraid she might have. I am so afraid I do not know what to do. I want to take her away from here. I want to run, somewhere Schweiger cannot get to us." Otto wrenched his hands together. "I have to protect her. She is my little girl. Grandmother should not have pushed her so and destroyed the things she made. You saw at the hotel in Bonn how badly Lisl reacted to that. She even said out loud that she wanted her to die." His breathing grew rapid. "I have to take her away."

"No. If you run, you will only make it worse. You will make her the main suspect. You have to be strong and wait it out. We might be able to prove it was someone else."

Otto shook his head. "I told you about the frayed cord and seeing her with the scissors. I should have acted then and put her in a boarding school far away. I should have done something, anything, to prevent this outcome. Now it is too late."

"It is only too late if you do something foolish." Atalanta took a deep breath. She didn't feel like she was getting through to him. She had to convince him, somehow, to hold his nerve and trust her to prove that Lisl had not done it. If she even could.

But anything was better than an act of despair that would only make matters worse. To give him confidence that there was still another outcome possible she had to give him a little information.

"I talked to Schweiger last night. He confided in me because he worked with my grandfather. He admired him a lot. He told me that he does not think a mistake was made. He thinks the killer meant to murder Sabine Freund all along."

She held his gaze.

"Do you understand what that means? It means it was not Lisl. She is just upset because everyone is treating her badly. But the killer is someone else. Schweiger asked me to help him find out who did it and why. If I deliver convincing proof…" She let the words hang.

Otto stared at her. "He told you that he thinks…" He ran a hand through his hair. "He trusts you? He wants to work with you?"

"Yes." She put a hand on his arm. "You have to believe me, Otto. Lisl can still be saved. It is *not* too late."

He stared past her. She had no idea if he believed her, but this had to work. It had to buy her time to find out more about the family and the secrets that threatened them. There had to be something in the past, something among the information Renard was collecting about the family members that could provide her with a vital clue.

A small sound made her turn her head to see who was there. Yards away, out of earshot, stood Frau Rabenhorst watching them with a frown. Atalanta was certain she was not happy with the intimacy she witnessed between her grandson and some stranger who had suddenly intruded into their lives. What was Frau Rabenhorst thinking? That one impertinent employee had just passed away and another was taking her place, worming her way into Otto's confidence with ulterior motives? After all, she had lied to Frau Rabenhorst that she had been hired by Otto as a paid worker to look after his daughter. Frau Rabenhorst did not know she was a detective on the case.

And perhaps if she had known, it would not have changed her opinion about Atalanta at all. She was fiercely protective of the family name and their reputation.

It would not be easy to help Otto and Lisl with the

wrath of the matriarch hanging over them like the dominating presence of the Loreley rock…

Atalanta had retreated to her cabin when Renard came to bring her the newspapers. He looked grave and she asked him how Lisl was. He lifted a shoulder and let it fall in a gesture of resignation. "She is a troubled young lady. It would be good for her to have friends her own age and speak about normal things instead of being smothered in this atmosphere of tension and malice."

Atalanta nodded. "I agree with Otto that he should have sent her off to boarding school to remove her from his grandmother's oppressive influence. But he did not and we have to deal with the situation as it is now. How well do you know Georg Schweiger? He mentioned to me that he had met you on prior occasions and he seems to know that you are a man of many talents with contacts among all the right people."

Renard smiled softly. "Ah, yes, Georg Schweiger. Your grandfather worked on several cases when Schweiger was just starting out as a policeman. He did not have much influence at the time so his actions did not really matter to the cases. What I mean is that he was not in a position to decide whether he wanted to work with your grandfather or not."

"So he said. But he must have made an impression on Grandfather. He wrote me this letter and handed it into

Schweiger's care in case we should someday meet." She showed the note to Renard. He read it and did exactly as she had, turning it over to see the other side. His expression was neutral when he looked up at her.

"There was no second sheet of paper?"

"No. The letter continued beyond what is here. Schweiger cut some part off and kept it from me. If you hold the paper up to the light, you can see the cut. It was done expertly. He denies it though." She took a deep breath. "He even challenged me by saying that if I am a good detective, I should be able to work out what it means."

Renard didn't look perturbed. "I trust that you can," he simply said.

Atalanta sighed. "But I don't want to deal with another mystery on top of everything else. My mind is overtaxed as it is. Did you manage to call your informants and learn anything worthwhile?"

"Certainly. Erol Müller has been in prison for a jewel theft. I wonder if his fiancée knows this."

Atalanta pursed her lips. "Gertrude might find it exciting to be engaged to a jewel thief. She tends to glorify anything adventurous."

"But if she did not know, and Sabine Freund did, she might have threatened to tell the truth."

Atalanta looked at Renard, sudden understanding dawning on her.

"The kiss in the botanical gardens! He tried to charm the nurse into keeping the truth about his criminal past to herself... But did Sabine Freund agree to that? Or did she kiss him first and then decide to try another spot of blackmail later? The engagement to Gertrude certainly meant a step up in the world for Erol Müller so I suspect he would want to guard his newly found position at all costs. I will certainly have to keep him on my list of suspects."

She picked up a newspaper and glanced at the headlines, then began leafing through it. The scent of ink rose from the freshly printed pages. Normally she enjoyed her morning routine with the latest news, but today she was in no mood to concentrate on reading and the topics, whether foreign politics or social highlights, did not really interest her, until her gaze fell on a familiar face in a photograph.

"Raoul!"

She breathed his name as her eyes rushed to read what the article was saying about him. He had always been part of the racing team started by the influential Spanish shipping magnate Felipe Santos but he had made an unexpected and sudden move by joining the recently established team owned by Italian businessman Vincenzo Dulce. Dulce was said to have made a fortune in diamonds in Africa and had only recently returned to Europe. He had hired the best mechanics to look after the sports car he had imported from America and fine-tuned to become the fastest car on the continent. With the best driver of the moment behind the wheel, the article closed, the new team was certain to take many wins in the new racing season.

She looked up at Renard. "I heard in Salzburg that there were doubts about whether Raoul could stay with his current team but it seems that he has now found an even bigger opportunity for his career. It is odd that he mentioned nothing about it to me when we met in Bonn to celebrate my birthday. One would expect ... friends to discuss something important like this with each other."

Renard did not respond. He stared at her with a grave frown over his deep-set eyes.

Atalanta's heart skipped a beat. "What is the matter?" she asked. "Do you know more about this? Some detail that this article does not reveal to the general public?"

"Indeed I do." Renard rearranged the other papers on the table. He waited a few moments before he said, "I was not certain you ought to learn this now. Things are already complicated and your mind must not be distracted."

"I don't understand." Her heart rate went up further.

Renard sighed. "This Italian businessman, Vincenzo Dulce, is said to have made a fortune in diamonds in Africa. That cleverly devised story neatly explains two things in his background: his recent years-long absence from society and the origins of his wealth."

"But the truth is different?" Atalanta asked, her heart now pounding painfully against her chest bone. She did not know what to expect but whatever it was, it would be nothing good. And it involved Raoul!

"Very different. Dulce is a member of a family who have long been established as criminals. They deal in stolen arts, jewels, and they undertake murders for other people."

Atalanta drew breath sharply.

Renard continued. "He has not been to Africa. He has

been in prison. And now that he is free again, he wants revenge on his enemies. He will use the racing as a cover to travel and get close to influential people who will all, no doubt, later fall victim to crime."

"And Raoul has been selected, because of his name and reputation, to be part of this cover for his criminal activities?" Atalanta asked, appalled.

Renard nodded. "I am afraid so."

"I wish he had discussed his plans with me before he agreed to this offer to join the new team." Atalanta began to pace the room. "You could have looked into Dulce and then I could have told Raoul to stay away from him. I understand the attraction of a newly imported sports car and testing what it can do but…" She shook her head. "He has always been impulsive but this time he has made a very dangerous mistake. I must ask him to come and see me. I want to tell him what you just told me. He must think of some reason to withdraw from this cooperation."

"That will be very difficult now that it has already become news. Dulce does not look kindly upon people who abandon him."

Atalanta's heart grew cold. What had Raoul done? In his zeal to safeguard his career and prevent loss of face if his old team let him go, he had entered into a new partnership without thinking or checking who he was dealing with. She looked at the wide grin on his face in the grainy newspaper photo and tears burned behind her eyes. He had not even told her when they had met. She had to read it in the papers. Did that not say enough about their relationship? It meant nothing to him. He had decided he could not love her, did not want to love her, and he had moved on. He was building his life apart from her.

And even if he made choices she could not approve of, choices that seemed dangerous and unwise to her, she had to let him go.

"You are welcome to contact him and ask for a meeting," Renard said. "But if you do enlighten him about Dulce's background, you must understand that it will only put him in an impossible position. He will realise that he was used but also that he cannot walk away without endangering himself and the people he loves."

"People he loves?" Atalanta asked, breathlessly.

"Yes, these organised crime gangs have clever ways to keep people committed to them. If you so much as hint at a possible departure, something tragic happens to someone you care for as a little warning to keep you onboard."

Atalanta leaned on the table, her knees full of jelly. "Raoul has become part of some … gang who will hurt him if he ever tries to walk away?" She recalled the gold bracelet he had been wearing, with the bird charm on it, his grave looks, and his sudden decision to turn against her.

Did he already know what he had landed in? Suspected at least? Did it gnaw at his conscience? Did it breathe fear into his usually carefree heart? Had he walked away from her because he had known that he was now a danger to her?

Atalanta straightened up. "I will send a telegram and ask him to meet me. I will pretend I need his help in the murder case because I am in over my head. That will draw him to me. Then I must see how I can address this with him. I need to know … that he is at least aware of the risks." She lifted a hand to stop Renard from protesting. "I know what I am doing. I need to see his face when I discuss it with him. I need to know … if he knew before or if it is news to him."

There was a shadow of hope inside of her that he had walked away from her not because he had been jealous of Otto or because he was too busy to spend more time with her, but because he was worried he was a danger to her. If that were the case, they could still…

Be together? Who was she fooling? If Vincenzo Dulce was a crime boss, a gangster, he would never allow his best driver to have a relationship with a private detective. A woman who served the law. He would be too worried that secrets from within his organisation would end up with her, and would pose a risk to him. He could not tolerate it and Raoul had to know it as well.

Was it even wise to ask him to come over?

But she could not just leave him be. And a sensitive matter like this could not be discussed over the telephone either. There had to be a meeting. There had to be a conversation, face to face.

Even if it would be the last one they could ever have.

Chapter Thirteen

"When will they allow us to leave the ship?" Gertrude asked in a shrill voice. "I only want to go into Sankt Goarshausen to look at some shops and perhaps see Katz Castle."

"Katz?" Atalanta asked, "as in *cat*? What a curious name for a castle."

"Yes, it is a nickname it received at some point in history when there was rivalry with another castle along the river called Maus. A cat and mouse game." Gertrude told the story without gusto. There were shadows under her eyes and she tapped her fingers nervously. "Can't you come with me? Herr Schweiger seems to like you. He will certainly let us go."

Atalanta flushed. "Herr Schweiger does not like me." *He stole part of my grandfather's letter to me.* "He will have his reasons for keeping us here."

"Cooped up here, I feel like I am going mad. I must have

some fresh air and exercise. If you won't go with me, I will go alone. And if it has consequences, so be it."

With a determined nod, Gertrude jumped to her feet and disappeared apparently to go and get her coat and purse. Atalanta was left with a dilemma: to go with her to protect her against the inspector's wrath or let her go alone. As she turned around, she almost bumped into Georg Schweiger. He looked her in the eye.

"In a hurry, Fräulein Ashford?"

She decided to be open to him. "Gertrude wants to leave the ship for a small walk through the city and to do some shopping. She is very tense and almost depressed. I think it will do her a world of good. I am going with her to keep an eye on her. I will make certain she returns to the ship."

"You do that." He seemed to be suppressing a smile. "And there could be an additional benefit besides exercise and diversion. If you come back with something interesting for me, I have something to trade."

"Trade?" Atalanta echoed.

"Yes. I know more about the man whom our murdered nurse met in the botanical garden in Koblenz, but I will only share it with you if you have something for me. That is very fair, is it not?"

"Very," Atalanta said with a sour feeling. Her shopping trip with Gertrude would probably not deliver any new clues in the murder case. She would come back empty-handed and he would tell her exactly nothing about what he had learned.

She had, of course, learned from Renard that Erol Müller

was a convicted jewel thief but she supposed Schweiger already knew this. If there was anyone with access to police records and reports on past crimes, it was a policeman.

With a sigh she went to collect her coat and purse and joined Gertrude as they left the ship and walked through a narrow cobbled street past tall houses with white and yellow fronts. A door stood open and revealed the inside of a blacksmith's forge where a burly man in a leather apron was working the glowing iron with his hammer.

Perhaps he was the craftsman who had created the beautiful metal signs that several shops and workplaces had hanging from their fronts. The signs depicted items sold or gave the name of the establishment in curly lettering. In the window of the bookshop several old editions in leather binding with gold leaf on their spines drew Atalanta's attention. In the centre of the display was a black and white drawing on an easel depicting armed men bearing royal banners as they scaled the Loreley rock formation to kill the nymph responsible for luring the king's son to his death with her singing. On the other side of the rock, the maiden was seen jumping into the Rhine, her impossibly long hair flowing behind her. Perhaps this shop also sold such maps as Atalanta's grandfather had collected. On trips, she liked to find one to buy as an addition for the collection. But Gertrude did not seem to want to browse. She kept looking ahead and pulling Atalanta along.

In the village square stood an octagonal blue stone fountain with a nymph figure on top. At her feet were four amphorae spouting water. Three children in school uniforms were throwing water at each other. Their leather satchels with books stood leaning against the tree trunk of a gnarled old oak.

On a sagging moss-speckled bench under another ancient tree, a few villagers sat chatting. One of the old men was cutting something from wood with a small knife. His crooked fingers handled the tool with precision, turning the wood as he worked. When they drew closer, Atalanta realised it was a small figurine depicting a maiden with long flowing hair. A nymph figure as well. It seemed that the city had quickly caught on to the popular interest in the Loreley saga and offered tourists the opportunity to experience more of it within the city walls.

Gertrude didn't seem interested in their surroundings at all. She was nervously glancing down the street, craning her neck as if trying to spot something. Suddenly her tense features relaxed a little and she turned to Atalanta. "We must go in that direction. I am certain we will find some quaint little bookshop where you will want to look around."

"But we already passed the bookshop."

"Oh, well, a bakery then? You must want to try some local specialty."

"And you? What will you do?" Atalanta asked. Her heartrate sped up at the idea that she and Gertrude would be separated. She had promised Georg Schweiger she would return with his suspect. If Lisl had told the truth about the kiss between Sabine Freund and Gertrude's fiancé, Gertrude had every reason to hate the nurse and want to remove her from the scene. She could not allow someone with an obvious motive for murder to disappear.

It was rather difficult to see a killer in the Gertrude she had known years ago – someone who had been negligent and who had broken rules, but who did not seem to have anything truly evil inside her. But years had passed since then, and Atalanta did not know how Gertrude might have changed. How she had been forced to act on her fears of losing her fiancé to a sordid affair with someone she looked down on. It might not be Erol she cared about, but the freedom he offered her by their arrangement. Freedom to escape her grandmother's matchmaking and the snare of an unhappy marriage.

Gertrude pointed to their left. "Look. A shop with typical German clothes. I am certain you would look fabulous in a hat with a feather or some other nice local touch. Let us have a look inside." She about dragged Atalanta across the street and into the shop she indicated. Once inside, she quickly collected a knitted sweater, a corduroy skirt and several scarves and other accessories and claimed she wanted to try them on.

"At home I will of course have everything delivered to our house where I can see how it looks at my leisure. But here on holiday one has to improvise."

She spoke in rapid German with the proprietress who cast avaricious looks at Gertrude's jewellery. Even though she had left the rubies and diamonds on the ship, the gold necklace she had selected for this day trip was still obviously valuable, and the shop owner had spotted this at once. Here was a potential customer with money to spend and everything had to be done to accommodate her.

Gertrude was invited into the back to try on her selection and Atalanta found herself alone in the shop. She walked about, feeling fabric and looking at the window display that had some of the small wooden nymphs she had seen the elderly man carving as they sat chatting in the square. Should she buy one to take home as a reminder of this strange adventure?

She could readily see herself adding it to her collection of souvenirs, if the case was concluded successfully.

But what if she failed? Or worse, what if it turned out that Otto was involved? Would she really want a keepsake of such a time in her life? If she bought it now, might there come a night when she burned it in the fireplace, making bitter reproaches about her negligence or naivety?

Speaking of which…

She turned her head with a jerk and looked at the door through which Gertrude had vanished. She was taking her time trying on the garments.

It had been about… Atalanta checked her watch. Ten minutes. Enough time to slip into a skirt and sweater and show them off to her friend.

Suddenly a sense of dread surfaced. She went to the door and opened it. In the backroom, the proprietress was counting a stack of bills. When she heard the door open, she looked up with a guilty flush and tried to hide the money. But Atalanta understood.

"*Wo ist sie?*" she asked in a rush. "*Wo ist meine Freundin?*"

"*Weg.*"

The woman gestured towards another door. She added something about an urgent message but Atalanta wasn't listening anymore. She rushed out of the door into a cobbled street much like the one in front of the store. She turned left then right, wondering where Gertrude had gone. Just as she was deciding she had to go left, she saw Gertrude approach her from the right. She was clutching her purse as if it contained something breakable. When she saw Atalanta, her face turned scarlet. Apparently she had intended to come back and act like she had never left at all.

Atalanta didn't know what to say or do. She wanted to know why Gertrude had sneaked away but asking outright would probably not get her any answers.

She feigned a relieved expression and called out, "I knew you would pull some prank on me when you went into the back of the store. It is so like you." She smiled widely, hoping Gertrude would not hear the tremble of her voice. "Come back in here and let me try on that sweater with the deer pattern. I like it a lot."

They tried on clothes and Atalanta decided to buy the brown skirt and a matching scarf with maroon and apricot flowers. She also asked if she could buy one of the wooden nymph figurines. The woman wrapped it in tissue paper and added it to her parcel.

Back in the street, Atalanta gestured ahead to a bakery. "We must try some local sweet treat. Do you have a good suggestion? You must know more about German pastry than I do. Perhaps they have biscuits of some sort? Perhaps even tinned? On a previous trip I bought a really beautiful oval tin with embossed fairytale figures on the lid."

"I don't feel like eating anything," Gertrude said. "I want to go back to the ship."

Atalanta feigned surprise. "Why? We have only just started looking at clothes. You said how on the ship we are just cooped up and cannot do anything. I mean, Lisl might want to play some boardgame but that is boring. I didn't come on this cruise to play games with an eleven-year-old girl."

Gertrude immediately took the bait. "Did you come for Otto?" she asked leaning closer confidentially. "You can tell me the truth. I won't tell."

"Only if you confide in me first." Atalanta tried to look as if she found the reveal both scandalous and exciting. "Did you know that Erol is a convicted jewel thief?"

Gertrude did not seem surprised by the question. She made a dismissive hand gesture as if it were a trivial matter.

"He is innocent, but a friend saddled him with the stones. He was only supposed to keep them temporarily but the police came to his apartment when he was not at home and his landlady let them in. They did a search, which was illegal, as they had nothing against him, and they found the stones hidden in a plant pot. It was all a huge misunderstanding which was never cleared up properly because the police conveniently asked no further questions and simply locked him up." She exhaled with indignation.

"It is not like he did something really criminal. I mean, Erol? He is so bland that at the idea of breaking and entering he would probably faint."

Atalanta doubted the clever Müller was quite that naïve, but she pretended to go along with Gertrude's assessment.

"Still, it seems like an awful risk to me. You agreed to a fake engagement to impress your grandmother, you said. If she hears about this—"

"She won't. And I didn't know at the time of the engagement. Erol told me this morning. He was packing his bags to flee the ship. I convinced him to stay because running away will only make him look suspect."

Atalanta frowned. "Why did he want to flee?"

"Sabine Freund knew about his conviction. She threatened him that she would tell Grandmother, but since she is dead now... You will not tell Grandmother, will you?"

"I suppose once Herr Schweiger finds out about it, he will mention it and—"

"No, he will not, because you will ask him not to. He listens to you." Gertrude threw her a pleading look. "Erol cannot help it that Sabine Freund saw him in prison and recognised him the minute he walked through the door."

"She saw him in prison?" Atalanta echoed, perplexed. "Was she a convict too?"

"No, she worked there as a nurse, assisting her father who was the doctor there." Gertrude grimaced. "Erol told me the doctor was heavily addicted to alcohol and quite an unpleasant and harsh man. All the inmates were afraid of him. Sabine, on the other hand they liked, because she was the only female they got to see while they were imprisoned there. She was nice to them, sneaking them food and things to read."

Atalanta could just imagine how Sabine had vividly recalled handsome Erol because he had probably been one of the nicer-looking men among the rough prison population. She had recognised him straight away in her new job as a companion of Frau Rabenhorst and seen a chance to pressure the man into flirting with her and giving her money. Had Erol Müller put the digitalis in the flask to free himself from the nurse's clutches, hoping her death would be viewed as a case of the wrong victim? If the police had been looking for someone who wanted Frau Rabenhorst dead, Erol would have stayed out of the limelight.

"Now you must tell me about you and Otto." Gertrude wagged a finger at her. "I have been honest with you about Erol, now I want something in return."

Her wording reminded Atalanta that Schweiger expected a trade when she got back and she had nothing much to offer him yet. But Gertrude had of course not sneaked away to pull a prank on her. She had wanted to go ashore for a very good reason.

Atalanta glanced at the purse that Gertrude was still holding close to her with a possessive intensity. Was the reason in there? What secret could the purse contain?

How could she learn? Perhaps by...

She pulled her towards the bakery. "Let us buy some

sweet treats first and then I will tell you all about Otto and me."

"All? I thought there was nothing all that much beside wanting to help Lisl. Now it almost sounds like there is something serious between you." Gertrude sounded half curious, half alarmed.

Atalanta opened the door to the bakery and led her inside. On shelves to their left was a large selection of tinned biscuits and chocolates. Atalanta selected a red tin with white houses on it containing butter biscuits and a dark green one with a river view, full of hazelnut biscuits. "How silly of me. I brought too little money. With what I already spent on the clothes and the souvenir, would you be so kind as to pay for me?"

Gertrude looked at her with wide eyes. "Pay?" she repeated as if the concept were foreign to her.

"Yes, could you please pay for me?" Atalanta stood close to her, determined to see inside her purse the moment she opened it.

Gertrude wet her lips. "I don't have any money on me."

"But you paid the lady in the clothes store to pull that prank on me. You must have some money left to pay for these treats. They are not expensive."

Gertrude looked like a trapped animal. "I really don't have any left. You must ask them to take back the biscuits."

"What is in the purse, Gertrude?" Atalanta asked softly. "You are holding it as though it contains eggs that can break."

"I, uh…" Gertrude's gaze wandered past Atalanta as if

she considered bolting for the door. Then she sighed. "Very well, I will tell you. I am tired of acting so secretive anyway. But not in here." She opened the purse and took out a few coins. Atalanta caught a glimpse of a dark brown glass bottle with a stopper. Her heart skipped a beat. What was that doing in Gertrude's purse? How had she come by it?

Once outside, Gertrude took her arm and said, "I need your help. You were always a friend to me at the boarding school. You helped me when I got into trouble with that terrible director. I need you now. I, uh, have a little problem."

"Yes?" Atalanta encouraged her to go on.

"I have been very nervous lately. I just cannot seem to calm down. A friend advised me to take these drops. They help a lot. I needed to leave the ship today to buy more of them. Fortunately, the apothecary here carries them. I did not want the inspector to know because … well, frankly, no one knows about it. Not in the family anyway."

"I see. Is it a common sedative? I mean, if it is an acceptable medicine prescribed by doctors, there is no need to hide—"

"I don't need you to judge me." Gertrude sounded aggressive now. "I know very well that it is considered a weakness to take drops to calm down. Grandmother would never approve of it so our family physician will never prescribe them to me. But I do need them. I really do."

"I am just curious what they are. I have heard about some kinds of drops that can get people addicted to them very quickly so you have to take larger and larger amounts to make them work. It can be dangerous." Atalanta took a deep breath. "You could even take so much that you die."

Gertrude laughed uncomfortably. "My friend gave me a warning. I count the drops carefully. I never take too much." She fell silent, only staring ahead with a dark look in her eyes.

Atalanta asked softly, "Did your friend warn you about the possible addictive effect before or after you started taking them?"

Gertrude stopped and looked at her. "You think you are so smart," she burst out. "That something like this would never happen to you. Because you are so practical and you never fall victim to feelings. But I lost my parents when I was just a little girl. I was raised by a harsh, unfeeling woman who always wanted to change me. Who can never accept the things I like, the hobbies I want to pursue, or the men I want to be with. It always has to be something grander, bigger, and better for her. I cannot stand the pressure anymore." She gasped for breath.

Atalanta put a hand on her arm. "Calm down. I am not judging you. I am just sorry that you were not aware of the risks when you started taking the drops. Perhaps it would have changed your decision about them?"

"Probably not. I cannot live without them anyway." Gertrude sounded resigned now. "I am too weak to make anything of my life. Grandmother has said it a million times and perhaps she is right. When I met Erol and he suggested the engagement as a way to gain freedom from Grandmother, I saw it as a real solution. I thought he was the one who should count himself lucky to be accepted into my wealthy family. I had no idea he was hiding such a huge secret about his past. I am a fool for letting myself be used to cover for his wrongdoings. And then because of blackmail he has to betray me with this despicable nurse and I have to take every insult…"

She clenched her hands into fists.

"We agreed to the engagement on the condition that we would both be free to do whatever we wanted but in a discreet manner. To keep the illusion alive. And then he kisses my grandmother's nurse in a public park where a spoiled eleven-year-old can see it and snitch on me!" Her fury was tangible, glowing like embers in her face. "I pretend I don't believe her because I know Grandmother would not believe Lisl because she always calls her a little liar, but I know the truth. Erol is a criminal who paid money to the nurse who tended him in prison. How embarrassing is that!"

She fell silent and stared at the ground. Suddenly tears began to spill down her cheeks.

"I did everything wrong. Everything! And now I am lost." She looked at Atalanta, despair in her eyes. "I am sinking fast like those sailors on the Rhine. Lisl asked whether their bodies were mere skeletons or…" She sobbed uncontrollably.

Atalanta put an arm around her shoulders.

"You must not turn all morose. You can always end the engagement. You will survive the ensuing scandal, I am certain. And as for those drops… If you start taking a little less each time, you can wean yourself off them, drop by drop."

"I would have to be strong to do it and I am not. They all told me. Grandmother, Sabine…"

Gertrude fell silent and Atalanta felt her jerk under her touch as if she realised her mistake.

"Sabine?" Atalanta repeated, understanding dawning on her. "*She* provided you with the drops?"

"Yes. Do you see now how this is for me? First she was so nice to me, telling me she knew of a remedy that could help me. She claimed that as a nurse she had easy access to these drops and could get them for me without anyone ever knowing about it. She said such kind things to me and … I believed her. Then she started to ask for more and more money for them. It was outright extortion. But of course I could not resist as I could not risk her telling my family."

And then she had become totally dependent on the substance, Atalanta thought with a pang of sorrow. It was hard to realise that the very people who appeared the most carefree and superficial were dealing with serious issues alone, lacking support to overcome their situation and rise above their troubles.

Gertrude said, "And on top of taking all my money for the drops, she has been taking Erol's money to keep quiet about his time in prison. She also forced herself on him. She was a truly evil person."

All the money Schweiger found in Sabine Freund's cabin could have come from Gertrude and Erol.

Not from Otto… "How much did she make you pay?" Atalanta asked.

"A ridiculous amount. It was not about covering costs for the drops anymore. It was all about her keeping my secret. That is why I call it extortion."

"I would also call it blackmail."

And blackmail is a viable motive for murder.

It gave Atalanta no pleasure to think of her former colleague as a potential killer, but it was better than having to accept that it was Otto or Lisl. They had to be innocent in order to stay together and make something of their lives. She would advise him to take Lisl away from her great-grandmother, and outside of the circle of that malign influence, her condition would improve. Their bond would get stronger and Otto would be able to experience some kind of happiness, a feeling that had been sorely lacking in his life so far.

"Did you go to her cabin at night to give her the money and receive the drops from her? Did you smoke a cigarette in her cabin? There was a stub left in the wash basin."

"I was so nervous whenever I had to go and see her." Gertrude sniffed. "It was terrible to look at her smug face and realise how much power she had over me. I tried to act like I didn't care at all and the money also didn't matter to me, but … I think she knew the truth. That she enjoyed her position and seeing me squirm."

Atalanta squeezed her former colleague's shoulder. "But all that is behind you now. Sabine is no longer alive."

Gertrude nodded with a grateful smile. Then the deeper

implication of the words seemed to sink in and she pulled away from Atalanta as if stung by a scorpion.

"Are you suggesting I have anything to do with that? That *I* put the medication in the silver flask?"

"I am saying nothing of the kind."

Atalanta raised a hand to ward off Gertrude's rising anger but she snapped back, "You *do* think that! You think I might have… Some friend you are!" She narrowed her eyes. "You implied earlier that you came on this trip for Otto. Would you go so far as to accuse me of murder in order to clear him and be with him? We all know Otto hated Sabine because of her smug attitude. He could not stand her condescending behaviour towards Grandmother." Gertrude gasped for breath. "He also knew, like I did, that she was probably putting pressure on Grandmother too with some lies or … secrets. She had her firmly under control too. I just know it."

Atalanta had to admit this was probably true as the woman who forced her wishes on everyone had not been able to get rid of the unwanted nurse either. She had tried to blame it all on Otto who had hired Sabine, but in other matters she had overruled his decisions, so why continue with a companion she didn't like unless there was a compelling reason why she had to?

Otto had said that he feared his grandmother knew something about his parents' accident which she had never shared. Was the key to the whole thing hidden in the past?

She said, "I'm not trying to implicate you in anything, Gertrude. I only want to understand what is going on here.

When we go back to the ship, the inspector might question us as to where we went and what we did so we had better make up a good story."

Gertrude eyed her with distrust. "You talked to him in private before. He must think you are somehow above suspicion."

"I assure you he does not think that at all. In fact, we argued because he is speculating about some elements of the case and I do not agree at all with his approach."

Gertrude took her arm and said in a pleading voice, "Please, Atalanta, don't tell him about my drops. Lie for me that we went shopping. You can show him what you bought." With a hint of her wry humour she added, "You can even treat him to a local biscuit."

Chapter Fourteen

Atalanta was reminded of this remark when she met Georg Schweiger in the ship's salon. She had returned with Gertrude and heard upon arrival that the ship would proceed to their next stop, Bingen. It felt strange to continue a cruise after a death but with Schweiger in their midst they would not be allowed to forget that the investigation was ongoing and suspicions swirled.

They had both gone to their cabins to freshen up. Atalanta expected Gertrude would also administer some of her beloved drops. Her heart still ached for her former colleague's addiction, not so much because she had ever been very close to Gertrude but because it reminded her painfully of others in her life who had been or who were in a desperate position.

Her father.

Raoul.

She had sent him a telegram but not yet received a reply.

Part of her feared he would not reply at all. That he would leave her hanging. That she was on her own solving this case and he was on his own dealing with the criminal connections of the man to whom he had carelessly entrusted his career – his entire life, in fact.

"Did you enjoy your little tour of Sankt Goarshausen?" Schweiger asked. His cool blue eyes surveyed her with a probing look. "Did you buy any souvenirs or is this city too small for your liking? After all, you live in Paris and are used to travelling to the most interesting places. Santorini, Milan, Salzburg."

It seemed that he had informed himself about her latest exploits. But this was certainly not published in the newspapers so who could be his source?

As if guessing her thoughts, Schweiger said, "I had a very interesting conversation with Renard. It seems he was eager to convince me of what a great detective you are. He could not resist giving details of all the cases you have solved since inheriting your grandfather's fortune. I must say, I am impressed."

His tone was clearly ironic and Atalanta flushed, wishing Renard had not felt the need to shine such a favourable light on her abilities. Schweiger would always regard her as an amateur and a woman at that. Renard's attempts at showcasing her abilities only made Schweiger more sceptical as they confirmed to him that she needed this praise.

Schweiger said, "Did you learn anything worth trading?"

"I am sorry but no." Atalanta held his gaze. She was not about to share Gertrude's weakness with him at this point in the investigation. It might prove to be the wrong choice later on, but his attitude did not sit well with her and she reckoned she could not expect any understanding on his part for people who fell into a trap like Gertrude had. She didn't want to hear his opinion about it.

Schweiger's eyes twinkled with amusement.

"Poor Fräulein Ashford. You had to endure being dragged through one shop after another while not even learning the slightest bit of interesting information. Perhaps this will teach you something about what real policework is. Long hours watching a house or following a suspect and then having no result to show for it. You are spoiled, always having the clues falling into your lap."

Atalanta was tempted to say that her life had been in danger on several occasions but it would sound pathetic and even self-congratulatory. If Schweiger was ever to appreciate her capabilities, he would have to find out for himself what she could do.

His amusement died away and he seemed to become a little more approachable. "Well, despite your lack of material for an even trade, I am willing to give you something I have. But only because I want to hear your opinion about it."

He stared at her with a directness that made her feel uncomfortable. She had the distinct impression he was not after an opinion but a heartfelt emotion. Something she would betray when he revealed this bit of information to her.

He said, "You mentioned that Sabine Freund received information from a man in the botanical gardens in Koblenz. Now, I happen to know a man working there as a gardener. He sometimes does jobs for the police force."

"Meaning he is an informant."

Schweiger shrugged. "If you want to use that official term. I contacted him with a physical description of your party and he confirmed he had seen the exchange between the man and Sabine Freund. He even knew the person in question. A somewhat shady character who turns up information to hurt people."

"I see." Atalanta waited for the next revelation. She could sense by the tension in his stance that he was expecting something from her. And not knowing what he was about to spring on her, her own back grew rigid and her hands clenched into fists by her side.

Schweiger said, "My contact talked to the man and put a little pressure on him to reveal what he knew." He made a careless hand gesture. "It is always useful when one has something to use against these people. Force is a language they all understand."

Atalanta still waited.

Schweiger continued, "Our nurse asked this man to look into an old matter: the death of Frau Rabenhorst's son and daughter-in-law."

Atalanta could not quite hide a little shock. She had asked herself whether the key to the whole affair was in the past, but she had not expected to get an answer so quickly. "You mean the accident they had when out walking in the mountains in Bayern?"

Schweiger's eyes lit up and Atalanta knew she had made a mistake.

He said in the deliberate, careful tone of someone bringing a slow pupil up to speed, "You believe that story about it having been an accident while they were out walking in the mountains? Oh, certainly Frau Rabenhorst told that to everyone who wanted to hear. It was so sad and tragic. And especially terrible for the children who were orphaned."

He waited a moment.

"But I learned something quite different. They did not die while they were out walking together. Two coffins returned home from that trip, but rumour has it only one of them contained a body."

Atalanta's jaw grew slack. "I don't follow."

"Only the daughter-in-law died. The son disappeared. He is, as far as we know, still alive."

Atalanta stood and stared at him. Otto's words came back to her that he sometimes believed his parents were still alive. That he sensed his grandmother knew some terrible truth that she would not share with them. Had Frau Rabenhorst not said herself that children were better off not knowing certain things? That they had to be protected?

She took a deep breath. "This piece of explosive information was handed to Sabine Freund in Koblenz?"

"Indeed. And two days later she is dead." Schweiger

held her gaze. "Now I am asking you: who silenced her and why?"

Atalanta's mind was whirling and she could not make sense of her emotions. What was the most likely? To whom would Sabine have turned, to profit the most from her knowledge? The elderly lady who had kept the matter a secret all those years? It seemed more than likely. As soon as Sabine told the truth to someone who had previously not known, the value of her knowledge would decrease. She had to start with the person who stood the most to lose. Frau Rabenhorst.

"I see that you are thinking along the same lines as I am," Schweiger said. "We can conclude with almost complete certainty that Sabine Freund would not have told the truth to the children of old. It would not serve her purpose to put pressure on them to keep the tale hidden. She would go to the person who had created the lie and who was eager to keep it alive. It was extremely clever of Frau Rabenhorst to put the medication in her own flask, thereby suggesting she was the intended victim."

"There was another attempt on her life before I joined the party," Atalanta said softly, more to herself than to Schweiger. "Or did she also orchestrate that herself? But why, if Sabine Freund only learned the truth about the empty coffin in Koblenz? That makes no sense."

"Now *I* am not following," Schweiger said. "But it matters little. We have to talk to Frau Rabenhorst and convince her that confessing is the best way to go about this. She is old and we can assume that Sabine Freund terrorised her with this knowledge."

Atalanta thought of Gertrude telling her that the nurse was always whispering words to the Frau Rabenhorst while leaning down to straighten her collar or help her with something, and that her whispers had struck fear into her charge.

Schweiger continued making his point. "Frau Rabenhorst became desperate and acted under duress. She will of course have to stand trial but perhaps the court will be lenient and not give her a long sentence."

"You seem convinced you have the murderer pinpointed."

Schweiger smiled at her. "I am merely saying that it is all very logical. But we need a confession." He waited a moment and added, "And who knows? Perhaps, under pressure as her own neck is on the line, she will tell us something worthwhile that can help us further."

"So you doubt her involvement?" Atalanta asked. His approach confounded her and she was not certain what to make of it.

Schweiger said, "It would have been very clever of her to put the medication in her own flask, but she would also have realised that the flask would be used by the nurse to offer something to her. She could not very well refuse to drink or she would create suspicion and her plan would fail. She would have to take a big risk to play it out this way. Would she have dared to do it?"

"I think she is a very strong-willed woman who, when she decides to take action, does not turn back."

Schweiger nodded. "I tend to agree. With her old secret about to come into the open she had a lot to lose and she might have accepted the risk as inevitable if she wanted to contain the situation. But we must speak with her now and find out. Come along." And he went ahead of her to the old woman's cabin.

Although it wasn't far, to Atalanta's mind it was a thousand paces. With every step she took closer to what might be a fateful revelation her heart ached for Otto as he would also inevitably learn the truth. One of his parents had not died. He was not a true orphan. His suspicions had been founded and his grandmother was to blame. He had tried to be loyal to her through the years even as she harmed the family by her behaviour, especially hurting Lisl with her rejection. But he had felt he owed her for her care after his parents had died. But once it was proven they had not died and the entire story of his life was shown to be a lie, how would he feel? What would he do? His suspicions of Lisl had already frayed his nerves. This could prove to be the blow that broke him.

When Schweiger knocked at the door, there was a long silence before finally a voice called, "*Herein!*"

Schweiger opened the door and let Atalanta go in first. The cabin was even more luxurious than her own with gilded accents on the bedposts and the dressing table while oil paintings on the walls displayed glorious Rhine views with castles and vineyards.

Frau Rabenhorst sat in a dark blue velvet chair, reading. She rested the book on her lap and regarded them with a blank expression. If she feared that at some point along this murder investigation the past would be revealed, there was no trace of it in her calm features. Atalanta felt, again, that this woman was a force like the Loreley rock formation, not to be moved or conquered.

Schweiger began in a soft, respectful tone. "May we come and sit with you for a moment?"

"There is only one other chair, inspector. Fräulein Ashford will have to stand." Frau Rabenhorst threw Atalanta a condescending look. "She has worked all her life so she is more like a servant to me than a family friend."

"I value her opinion highly," Schweiger said.

Frau Rabenhorst seemed surprised. So was Atalanta. His words were the complete opposite to his behaviour towards her. He acted like he felt superior and was only tolerating her. Now he claimed to value her opinion. Highly, even.

Why was he saying this? Was it some trick to play the old woman?

Despite her dislike of Schweiger because he had stolen half of her grandfather's letter she was fascinated by the psychology behind his approach.

Frau Rabenhorst asked with a frown, "Why would you value her opinion?"

"Your grandson told me that she has great psychological insight."

Immediately Frau Rabenhorst's lips turned up in a mocking smile. "Really? I do not think my grandson is the best judge of that. Otto trusts people too easily. He also hired this nurse who treated me terribly and now has the gall to die during *my* cruise. She has ruined everything."

"Your grandson hired a woman you did not like and did not get along with." Schweiger leaned forwards with his elbows on his knees. "Why did you not dismiss her?"

"Nurses can be hard to find, on short notice. I knew I needed to put up with her, at least for the time being."

"Yes, until you could find the right occasion to murder her?" Schweiger said it in the same pleasant conversational tone he had used before.

Frau Rabenhorst blinked. "If this is intended to upset me, inspector, you will not succeed. I have nothing to hide. I did not poison this woman. I was the intended victim of the murder attempt."

"Really?" Schweiger managed to put a world of disbelief into that one word.

"Yes. I can explain to you—"

"I am not questioning whether you were the intended victim. My 'really?' was geared towards your statement that you have nothing to hide. It seems to me a rather bold assertion. Considering the past."

Frau Rabenhorst's blue eyes were watchful but not alarmed. "I do not understand what you mean, young man."

Schweiger said, "I mean the fact that you have lied to your grandchildren for all their lives. Their mother died, but their father didn't. Your son is still alive and you have always known this."

The blunt words shocked Atalanta, even though she had heard them before. It just seemed so incredible that someone would do this to young children. That someone would pretend their father was dead when he was still alive and could have cared for them.

Frau Rabenhorst did not so much as blink. She sat as still as a statue, her hands calmly resting on the book. Nothing indicated she had even heard or understood Schweiger.

He shifted his weight uncomfortably now that his surprise tactic had failed and the subject was not budging. There was no confession forthcoming. Not even a hint that what he had said was true.

Atalanta would have been amused, had not so much been at stake here. She felt that she must contribute to the good outcome of this interview so she said to Frau Rabenhorst, "You must have known the truth would come out sooner or later. You must have been preparing for this moment all these years."

Frau Rabenhorst still did not reply. Schweiger seemed to search for a fresh load of ammunition to blow her calm apart. He leaned even closer and, staring hard at the suspect with cold eyes, said, "I can prove that the nurse Sabine Freund had uncovered your secret and was blackmailing you with it. You knew she would never stop, so you had to kill her."

Frau Rabenhorst snorted. "She was not blackmailing me. She knew nothing. She was just a very unpleasant character who thought too much of herself."

Schweiger sat up straight. "You do not seem to

understand. I can prove that Sabine Freund learned the truth at the botanical gardens in Koblenz. I can prove that she had plenty of money in her cabin when she died. She was poisoned with *your* heart medication."

"To which everyone had access," Frau Rabenhorst said sharply. It was as though she had already rehearsed this response beforehand. "You are not building a very convincing case, inspector. A good lawyer will be able to take each of your arguments apart in a matter of seconds. The money, for instance, could have come from several other sources."

Schweiger's jaw tensed. Atalanta wished he had thought this through better. Frau Rabenhorst was far too clever to fold under pressure. Perhaps she had even known about Gertrude's addiction to the drops Sabine Freund provided to her? If that was the case, she could rest safely in the knowledge that the money in the cabin could be explained away as payments for the drops. Any excess could be seen as an added inducement for the nurse to keep Gertrude's guilty secret.

Schweiger had played his ace too quickly and now there was no way he was going to win this hand. In fact, it seemed like he was losing his entire case against her and he would be left looking a fool. Despite their tense relationship, she felt a little sorry for him. He was probably a good policeman who was only trying to apprehend a murderer.

"What happened in Bayern?" Atalanta asked. Perhaps they could induce the woman to share her side of the story.

Surely she was also a victim of the circumstances, one way or another.

Frau Rabenhorst did not even look at her. Her lips pulled into a thin stripe.

"You will have to tell us now or be heard at the police headquarters later," Atalanta tried. She had no idea if Schweiger could even take the woman in for questioning, based on so little actual evidence, but perhaps he was willing to try and get a confession that way?

Still there was no response in the woman's demeanour. She seemed to be completely untouched by the idea that others knew of her secret. Probably because there was no way to prove it after all these years.

Unless of course…

Her heart rate sped up as she realised the one weak spot in Frau Rabenhorst's armour. It felt almost cruel to use it, but it might be the only way.

"I think we are wasting our time," she said to Schweiger. "You thought we could save her pain by giving her a chance to share the truth without resorting to drastic measures, but it is impossible. She will not cooperate so you will just have to proceed and send the telegram."

Schweiger glanced at her. The flash in his eyes betrayed how he hated her for taking the lead, but he was also curious where she was going with it.

Atalanta continued calmly, "There is still time before the telegram office closes. That will make it all official. The coffin will be dug up and opened and the truth will come out." Atalanta felt her breathing grow shallow as she said it, realising how incredibly intrusive this was. They were talking about this woman's son's grave. His coffin. But if they were right, there were no remains in it.

Frau Rabenhorst turned to look at her, disgust in her eyes. "There is no need to violate the sanctity of a grave."

"There is no need indeed," Atalanta said standing up straight and facing the woman head-on. There seemed to be only one type of communication Frau Rabenhorst understood. Direct, to the point, with no room for denial. "If you confirm what we already know. Your son never died in Bayern, did he."

Frau Rabenhorst looked down. It was the only change in her; otherwise she sat as before, still and defensive.

Schweiger said to Atalanta, "I have had enough. I will go to the telegram office." He turned on his heel to go to the door. "They will act in the morning and we will have word of the outcome later tomorrow."

"Wait." Frau Rabenhorst's voice was thin. "There is no need. The coffin is empty."

Atalanta felt enormous relief that her tactic had worked and at the same time a new weight settled on her shoulders. Otto's father had not died in Bayern. But why had Frau Rabenhorst pretended that he had? Why present such a monstrous lie to two young children grieving the loss of their parents?

Schweiger said, "I am glad you came to your senses."

"My senses?" Frau Rabenhorst spat at him, her eyes sparking fire. "I must be mad to acknowledge this to you. But the coffin cannot lie. It is empty. If you dig it up…" She took a deep breath. "My son did not die in Bayern. I have known that all along. I lied about it and I will keep lying about it. I request that you both make a promise to me here and now never to reveal the truth. It serves no purpose and can only cause harm."

Atalanta blinked at this sudden request – or demand, rather. Frau Rabenhorst was still in control of the situation and expected everyone to obey her.

Schweiger said, "This truth may be the reason Sabine Freund was killed. We cannot hide it."

"Nonsense. Sabine Freund died because she drank from my flask. I was the intended victim. It has to do with my will or some other thing. But not with the past. Leave it be."

Atalanta said, "What happened in Bayern? You might as well tell us."

"Why would I? I want to forget."

"How can you forget?" Schweiger asked with disbelief in his voice. "You told those children their parents were dead. You made them believe they were orphans while they still had a father."

"No, they have no father. He is dead to them. It is better this way." The old woman turned her head away.

Atalanta stared at her. Slowly, with frightening clarity, the truth dawned upon her. The only credible reason why someone would lie about this. Why someone would believe that this was better for all involved, especially the young children. She said in a low voice, "Your son was involved in your daughter-in-law's death."

"It was an accident." The old woman's eyes sparked at

her. "He did not mean to—" She shook her head. "No one would have believed him. I convinced him to go away. I told him I would make arrangements so it would look as if they had both died."

"He agreed to that?"

"He was in a panic and I was persuasive."

Oh yes, that was all too easy to imagine. This woman, this strong, unemotional woman with a razor-sharp mind and an equally sharp tongue had convinced her son he would be convicted of murder and that it would be better for his children if he disappeared.

Schweiger said, "Where is he now?"

"I have no idea, nor do I wish to know. He is dead to me." She looked up again, her eyes burning with a strange light. "You must promise me that Otto and Gertrude will not hear of this. They will not understand why I kept it from them. I know it was for the best. It still is." She raised a frail hand. "Please make this promise to me. For the sake of the woman who died and the man who had to run. He also did it for his children. To save them from heartbreak. He made that great sacrifice."

Schweiger shook his head. "You can make it sound noble, but I see something different. A man killed his wife and you covered for him, because he was your son. That is not justice. In fact, it is a grave injustice. I must put this right."

She laughed softly. "You are idealistic. You must put it right? How can something like that be put right? It cannot.

Ever. It happened and we must live with the consequences. All of us. In our own way."

Atalanta realised the tragedy of what had been revealed here. How this woman had acted all her life as a loving grandmother to these children, not telling them that they still had a father because it was better not to know that he was a murderer.

Frau Rabenhorst turned her head away again. "Leave me. I am tired and I want to rest. I have done nothing wrong." She repeated it softly, as if to herself. "I have done nothing wrong. I have done … nothing wrong."

Schweiger rose and made for the door. He gestured for Atalanta to follow.

Outside he said, "That does make you think. She can claim all she wants that Sabine Freund's knowledge did not hurt her, but I saw something else in there. She would rather die than let her grandchildren find out about the past. And perhaps her secret was dark enough to convince her she had to kill for it."

Chapter Fifteen

Frau Rabenhorst did not come to dinner. Lisl was not there either.

Otto whispered to Atalanta that Lisl had claimed a headache and he was worried for her. "Could you look in on her?" he asked.

Atalanta nodded and went to the young girl's cabin. She knocked, and when there was a vague reply, she entered. Lisl sat at a small table in the corner cutting figures from paper. Her hands worked quickly and the paper creation took shape in seconds before Atalanta's admiring gaze. It was a mountain landscape with little goats on the slopes and cabins and a pointy church tower in the distance. Then people appeared, little goatherds with feathered hats and a woman walking and...

Atalanta watched with a frown as there also appeared to be a woman who seemed to be falling. Dropping backwards. Was it the nymph from the Loreley? The one she had also seen in the black and white drawing in the bookshop window?

But in Lisl's creation there was no army marching to apprehend her. Just a single man turning away from the falling woman as he prepared to flee.

Her heartbeat sped up. Why was Lisl including this in her scene? It seemed out of place among the other idyllic elements. It also seemed to be a chilling reference to a family secret. One well hidden. Buried deep in the past.

Had she depicted the falling woman before? Was that the reason her great-grandmother had destroyed her creations? Because they revealed something best kept under wraps?

But how could Lisl know the truth? She had not even been born at the time.

"Your headache must be better if you are able to create something so delicate and beautiful."

Atalanta sat down opposite Lisl.

"It is not better. The pain makes me want to hide. I hide in these worlds I create."

"I see." Atalanta was not certain if the pain Lisl referred to was physical or mental. She asked softly, "Did you use the legends along the Rhine to make this scene? Is the woman falling the nymph of the Loreley?"

Lisl shook her head. "That is just a story. Not reality."

"No?" Atalanta queried, keeping her voice low and friendly. "Are you upset because Sabine died?"

"Sabine was not nice." Lisl kept cutting out more mountains with cabins and cows and goats, herded by an impossibly small dog. "She liked to hurt people. She only kissed Gertrude's fiancé to hurt her. Not because she really liked him."

She had probably kissed him because she could. Because he had to endure anything she put him through if he wanted her to keep the secret of his conviction. But Lisl did not know about Erol's past and surely could not understand this.

The girl took a deep breath. "She also kissed my father. Not because she likes him either. Just because she wants to get into money. She always wanted beautiful things. She looked in every window when we were in a city. She always talked about getting furs and diamonds. That is strange when you are just a servant, is it not?"

Atalanta nodded. She did not like the condescending tone Lisl took but she agreed with her in order to keep her talking. "Often when people are in unpleasant circumstances they cling to some sort of fantasy to make it through. Like you creating your paper worlds."

Lisl looked up with a jerk. "I am not at all like her. She was vicious and mean and horrible. She whispered lies to people. She told my father lies about me. She wanted to separate us. She wanted to send me to a boarding school so she could have him all to herself."

"Would it not be nice to go to school? To meet other girls and make friends?"

"I don't need friends. I just want to create." Lisl looked at what she had made and smiled. "This makes me happy but nobody else likes it. Great-grandmother wants me to stop doing this, but if I stop, I won't survive." The words were uttered without melodrama, but with a strong urgency, as if they contained an absolute truth.

Atalanta felt gooseflesh form on her arms. "Nobody is forcing you to stop."

"*She* is. She is so old. So very, very old. Why does she not die? Old people die, don't they? Their hearts just give out."

Atalanta's breath caught. Had Lisl laced the liquor in the flask with the heart medication, thinking that if Frau Rabenhorst died from heart failure, it would simply be ascribed to her age and weak health? That there would be no investigation of the flask?

But Lisl did not know that there had already been suspicions of attempts made on her great-grandmother's life. The frayed cable…

"I don't think he did it," Lisl said in an earnest tone. "She did it herself. And she made it look like he did it and he had to run."

Atalanta eyed her. "I don't follow."

"You should. You know it all." Lisl started to cut out a new scene. "You cornered her and made her admit it. That was clever. I never thought anyone could best her. But she only admitted to part of it. To the death. Not that *she* killed her."

As it dawned on her what Lisl was referring to, Atalanta drew breath sharply. "You know… How?"

Lisl shrugged. "I was in the room. I often sneak into her room when she is not there. I like her books. They are grown-up books, not the silly children's books my father lets me read. Sometimes she comes back unexpectedly and I have to hide. I was in the wardrobe while you and the inspector talked to her. I heard everything."

Atalanta felt her heart sink. If she had ever contemplated honouring Frau Rabenhorst's wishes by keeping quiet about what she and Schweiger had learned, that plan was now worthless. Lisl knew.

A volatile, highly emotional eleven-year-old girl had learned the explosive truth about Otto's parents. Their deaths that had been far from accidental. There had, in fact, not been two deaths at all. Just one, and a desperate escape from the consequences. Now Otto would surely hear of it too. How hurt he would be, not understanding why his father had done it, or why his grandmother had helped cover it up. It would create even more tension and reproaches in this already fractured family.

She straightened up as if to brace herself against what was to come. What chain of events had she set in motion by suggesting they would ask for the coffin to be dug up? Her bold move to assist Schweiger in his questioning of a suspect had worked and they had a confession, but a confession to what exactly? And at what price?

Lisl said, "Great-grandmother killed Grandmother and then made Grandfather take the blame. She forced him to run away and lied that they had both died. That way she could raise Father and Aunt Gertrude the way she wanted. She loves to rule over people." She focused on her paper cutting, the tip of her tongue peeking through her lips. Then she said, "She is a murderer and nobody knows it. Nobody will punish her for it. That is why she is always so smug and self-important. She believes no one can touch her."

"Lisl…" Atalanta stopped and took a deep breath. It felt like she was sinking into quicksand. This girl was difficult to read, let alone influence. Still, she had to try and convince her that this tale should not be told. And that she should refrain from pointless allegations.

Although…

Pointless? Were they totally without foundation? Did anyone know what had happened in Bayern? How the daughter-in-law had died? What part had the husband played in it? What part the mother-in-law?

From the very start, as Atalanta had come into this family and had begun to travel with them, she had sensed that there was darkness surrounding them, a menace hiding below the surface of their privileged lives. Now it reared its ugly head and swept her up in the turmoil with them.

Lisl said, "My father will never believe me when I tell him what I heard. He will say I am making it up because I don't like Great-grandmother. It is true that I don't like her and that I am happy she is a murderer. That means she will be put in prison. She will become the prisoner and we will all be free." Lisl smiled widely, her eyes lighting at the prospect.

Atalanta said, "Lisl, nobody knows exactly what happened. It was many years ago. There are no witnesses to it."

"*She* knows. When the police put pressure on her, she will have to confess. Then we can all be free of her. That would be so much better. Not just for me. For all of us. For Aunt Gertrude, too. She is so sad sometimes. She cries and nobody cares. They all want her to look happy so there will be no gossip."

Atalanta was overtaken by Lisl's sharp insight into the situations of the people around her. She wasn't merely selfish but showed compassion for her fellow prisoners, as she viewed them. Still, her idea about how everything could be solved was simplistic and improbable. Even if Frau Rabenhorst was questioned, she would never confess to a murder. Her son was gone; he wandered the world somewhere. There were no other witnesses to the death. They would probably never know the truth.

"How are things in here?" Otto asked, putting his head around the cabin door. He smiled tenderly at his daughter. "Are you coming to dinner, *Schatzi*?"

The German word for *darling* cut through Atalanta's heart. She could not imagine what it was like to raise a child alone, after your wife had been taken from you, and your parents too, and then to see that beloved child struggle and worry for her…

"Atalanta has to tell you something, Father," Lisl said with an answering smile. "It is very important. She found out because she is such a good detective."

Atalanta froze. How did Lisl know she was a detective? Had she overheard more conversations? Was she everywhere, like a shadow, sneaking around, trying to learn things that were not meant for her ears? Things that were too grown-up for her and should not bother her at her age?

Otto looked at Atalanta with a question in his eyes. Lisl said, "Tell him now. He needs to know."

"It is complicated," Atalanta said quickly, signalling him with her eyes not to ask more questions. But Otto did not take the hint. He looked from Lisl to Atalanta and back in evident bewilderment.

"What is the matter? Do tell me. Don't leave me in the dark."

"Great-grandmother confessed to the police," Lisl said. "Atalanta was there when it happened. She admitted that back in Bayern only Grandmother died, not Grandfather. He had to run away because she accused him of having murdered Grandmother but in truth she had done it herself."

Otto stared at his daughter. His expression was puzzled but then suddenly his features convulsed in pain. There came a distant look in his eyes as if he saw something different than this cabin and the present company. With a groan he lifted his hands to his face.

Alarmed, Atalanta asked, "Otto, what is the matter?"

He made a new sound as of an animal in anguish.

Atalanta closed in on him quickly and touched his arm.

"Otto? Are you unwell?"

Was it poison again? Had he already eaten something? Who was doing this to them? And why?

"I could never remember," he whispered. "It was like that day was erased from my mind. I tried to bring it back, but it was just emptiness. They said it was because I was only eight. Or because I didn't want to remember. Because my subconscious blocked the memories. Blocked the fact that…"

He groaned again and sank to his knees, pressing his hands against his face. Atalanta stared at him in panic. "Are you in pain? Do you need a doctor?"

"I saw it," Otto whispered. "I saw it happen. They argued. He raised a hand to her. She shrank back, cowering, afraid he would hit her. And then she slipped and fell. It happened so fast. But he did it. It was him. He did not fall with her. He survived."

Atalanta's heart was pounding, unsure how to react as Otto relived that fatal day. The shock of hearing Lisl's words had broken a barrier inside him and he could at last remember what he had long suppressed. The terrible thing his father had done. The way his mother had died.

"He went back to the hotel. I don't know what I did. I must have gone back as well. But I cannot remember. It is…" He pushed his hands against his temples. "I want to remember. I want to know. I need to know!" He shouted the last few words with an intensity that made Atalanta step away from him.

Lisl ran to him and said, putting her arms around him, "No, that is not right, Father. Great-grandmother did it. She killed your mother. *She* did it. Not your father. *She* is guilty. She is evil. It was her! It was her!" she shrieked, as if she were under attack.

The door opened and Schweiger rushed in. He looked at Otto's crumpled form on the floor and Lisl shaking him, still screaming, then asked Atalanta sharply, "What has happened here?"

"I am not entirely sure." Atalanta tried to steady her trembling limbs. "Apparently Lisl listened in on our conversation with Frau Rabenhorst. She told her father about it and he is suffering some sort of flashback to the day his parents died. Or rather, the day his mother died and his father had to flee because he was implicated."

Schweiger nodded gravely. "I see. Do we need a doctor here? Someone to look after him? He seems to be out of his mind."

"Where do you want to get a doctor? Our next stop, Bingen, is still quite a few kilometres upstream."

Schweiger ran a hand through his hair. He looked out of his depth and Atalanta again felt a pinch of pity inside her. He might be a little conceited at times but no doubt he took his profession very seriously and wanted to solve this case. But with all the strange twists and turns, it had begun to feel like a maze and they were lost in it.

"I will ask Herr Kaufmann to come and sit with you," Schweiger said to Otto. "He is a very calm and level-headed man. He will not panic." He looked at Atalanta. "You and I must speak with the girl."

"I already said what I wanted," Lisl protested. "I want to stay with my father."

"Your father needs rest." Atalanta tried to put a hand on Lisl's shoulder but the girl pulled away from her. She returned to her table and resumed cutting figures from paper. Her expression was concentrated, emotionless almost.

Schweiger supported Otto to his own cabin while Atalanta fetched Herr Kaufmann. She told him that Otto had suffered a shock and was talking nonsense. That he should just sit with him and ensure he stayed put and didn't do anything rash or foolish. By emphasising that anything he said might be total fantasy, she hoped to contain the story about Otto's parents a little longer. But part of her knew it was in vain as the truth was leaking out on all sides.

Finally, standing on deck with Schweiger, she said, "Lisl should not be alone either."

"Ask her aunt to sit with her."

"No. Gertrude cannot be trusted with her." Atalanta took a deep breath before adding, "I think she is addicted to laudanum or some other sedative. Do not ask me how I know – I cannot go into details now – but she is very volatile and should not be left with a girl who is upset, angry and disappointed."

Schweiger seemed to want to comment on the revelation about Gertrude, perhaps reproach her for having kept this from him, but he refrained and merely said, "I will ask the ship's chambermaid to sit with her."

Atalanta nodded assent and he went to get the girl and instruct her. Atalanta stood on deck watching the peaceful landscape float by. The forests rustled and a group of birds soared overhead looking for a resting place for the night. In the distance, the silhouette of yet another castle stood out against the darkening sky. The square towers betrayed that it had been built for defence and warfare rather than for pleasure.

There was just a trace left of blood-red light tinging the waters of the river. The views were achingly beautiful and at the same time they each carried a hint of menace, the birds' eerie cries echoing across the water and the castle standing there with its ink-black walls like a sentry watching their approach to suddenly unleash deadly arrows on them. Atalanta realised that not once on this trip had she ever felt truly relaxed – always on guard, as if she could never be certain from which direction the danger might be coming.

It seemed that Lisl had been right when she had told Atalanta on that very first night in Bonn that the family was full of secrets. Lethal secrets. The first victim had been claimed and with the chill of evening on her face and arms, Atalanta feared it would not be the last.

Chapter Sixteen

"What do you think now?" Schweiger asked after Atalanta had told him all that had transpired when she had gone to look in on Lisl before dinner. "Did Otto Rabenhorst's mother die in an accident? Was it murder? If so, who is responsible? Can we ever be certain after so much time has passed?"

"I think it will be hard." Atalanta sat on the deck chair and stared into the distance. The stars twinkled above and along the riverbank little lights indicated the presence of houses or cabins. Schweiger had brought her a glass of wine as if to suggest they were sitting here like tourists enjoying the view and chatting about the delights yet to come, but she thought no one was fooled. She turned the stem of the cool glass around and around in her fingers. "Otto thinks he remembers something but I am not sure we can trust such memories. He was only eight at the time. Over time his recollection will have been affected."

"I agree. The only one who has a reliable memory of it is Frau Rabenhorst. But if she was somehow involved in it, she will have every reason to protect her own interests."

Atalanta nodded slowly. "We cannot even be sure that her memory is reliable. She kept repeating *I have done nothing wrong*. If she has rewritten the story to her own liking and repeated it again and again over the years, she may have started to believe it herself. Without the testimony of her son, we cannot know anything."

"Oh, well, I could always try and advertise for him," Schweiger said cynically. "He might just respond and show up to tell us how everything unfolded."

Atalanta could not blame him for feeling disheartened. The past was something they clearly could not hope to unravel. And if the motive for Sabine Freund's murder lay there, they would have a hard time uncovering why she had to die and who had killed her.

"Excuse me?" Herr Kaufmann stood beside them. His tie was undone, as if he had been playing with it and he looked grave.

Schweiger jumped to his feet. "Why have you left Otto Rabenhorst? He must not be alone. He is very unstable."

"He is asleep. I sat with him to make sure he was comfortable." Herr Kaufmann gestured with both hands. "But now I must talk to you. It is very important."

Schweiger looked past him towards the cabins. "Are you certain he is asleep and will not suddenly start raving again? I don't want another casualty on this ship."

"He is asleep. I gave him one of my own sleeping pills. It

is not a very strong medicine, but effective enough. He will not wake for several hours. I will remain with him all night. I am drinking strong coffee to ensure I stay awake."

Schweiger said, "I will check on him and then we can talk outside his door. Just to be on the safe side."

Atalanta followed as the two men went ahead and Schweiger entered the cabin to check on Otto. He looked visibly relieved when he came out. "He is indeed sleeping and looks better. Poor man, he must have had a great shock when he learned the truth about his parents. He has been lied to all his life." Schweiger shook his head. Then he focused on Kaufmann.

"You are the family lawyer. Did you know any of this?"

Kaufmann shifted his weight uncomfortably.

"You did." Schweiger pointed a finger at him. Outrage flitted across his features. "When the nurse died, you should have come forward at once and told me everything. It is illegal to withhold pertinent information after a sudden death."

"Pertinent information? But I don't know *everything*." Kaufmann sounded defensive. Atalanta wished Schweiger would be a little more diplomatic in order to draw the man out. After all, Kaufmann was a lawyer and used to phrasing things with great care and avoiding snares.

She smiled at Kaufmann and said, "You would help us greatly if you just told us what you do know. It will be treated with the greatest confidentiality."

"I am not sure I understand your role in this," Kaufmann said stiffly. "You are not a family member or a close friend. And yet you seem to know more than anyone else and the police are working with you..." He cast Schweiger a reproachful look.

Schweiger flushed and said, "Fräulein Ashford was engaged by Herr Rabenhorst to look after his daughter. To help out with some matters. She is a detective in her own right. A private investigator."

Kaufmann's eyes widened for a moment. It seemed as if he wanted to back away but forced himself to stand his ground and look calm. "I see." He knotted his fingers and stared at the floor.

Schweiger said, "You can tell us now."

Kaufmann cleared his throat. "Yes, well, um... Ahead of this journey, I was contacted by someone over the telephone. Someone who claimed to be Frau Rabenhorst's son."

"Her son?" Schweiger looked at Atalanta with raised brows and then to Kaufmann again. "You mean, the one who allegedly died in Bayern, together with his wife?"

"Yes. I was of course sceptical and thought he was pulling my leg. I asked him politely never to call again but he did and what he told me convinced me that it was indeed her son. I need not go into details now, but suffice to say that he knew certain details about family life that no one else would know. He told me that he had reasons at the time to fake his death but that he was determined now to come forward with the full truth. He wanted me to arrange for a meeting with his mother ... during this Rhine cruise."

Atalanta stared at Kaufmann. "Her son, whom we all

believed to be dead, is alive and coming to meet her during this very trip?" She could not believe it, even as she put it into words.

"Yes. The meeting will take place in Bingen. Among the vineyards."

Atalanta blinked in disbelief. "She is an old woman with a heart condition. Her son cannot possibly have imagined that he would just appear and say *'Hello, Mother.'* She could suffer such a shock that it kills her."

"Yes, he knew that. So he wanted me to prepare things ahead of time. Prepare her."

Atalanta could barely keep her mouth from hanging open. "Have you already informed Frau Rabenhorst that her son is going to appear to meet her on this trip?"

"I was going to tell her but with the death of Fräulein Freund, the shock she had, and the fear she felt over possibly being the intended victim, I did not dare say anything. But we are approaching Bingen now and..." The lawyer's normally calm face was pinched with anxiety. "I do not know what to do."

Schweiger raised a hand as if to cut him off. "I will go to the meeting. I will speak with this man and learn the truth about the past. Then we can decide whether he is allowed to meet with Frau Rabenhorst or not."

Kaufmann shook his head. "I cannot betray him by letting him walk into a trap."

"A trap?" Schweiger was scarlet now. "I am a police officer, not a criminal! I am working on a murder case – two murder cases, if the death of Otto Rabenhorst's mother in

Bayern was murder too. I am *entitled* to information. If he knows relevant things, he must share them with me. Even if they incriminate him. He got away with it years ago. He must now—"

"He must not do anything." Kaufmann was calm again. "I will not let you meet him without assurances. Assurances that he will not be arrested."

"How dare you!" Schweiger hissed. "I will arrest you for obstruction of justice. Then you cannot warn him and he will come to the meeting."

"But you do not know where the meeting is," Atalanta pointed out gently. She glanced at Kaufmann. "If you give him assurances that the meeting will not end in harm for him, he must trust you. Can you go to the meeting and explain that Frau Rabenhorst has had a shock because her nurse died under suspicious circumstances? Let him tell his story to you. You are a lawyer. You can swear to what you heard in court and you will be believed."

Schweiger shook his head. "I will not allow this. I must attend the meeting. I will not let a killer go free."

"We do not know if he is a killer." Atalanta leaned over to Schweiger. "You would never have found this man on your own. Now here is the answer to the ad you said you could not put out. Please give it a chance. We can learn valuable information."

Schweiger protested but she continued, stronger, "If you were there, what could you do that Herr Kaufmann cannot? Pressure him to tell the truth? He is the only one who knows what happened, aside from Frau Rabenhorst. We agreed she might lie or have convinced herself of another truth. With his story, we have comparison material. Please let us try. It can only make things better."

Schweiger sighed. "I guess you do have a point."

"I am trying to weigh all interests." Atalanta turned to Herr Kaufmann. "Once we are in Bingen, you must go and meet Otto's father. Engrave every little detail in your memory and report back to us."

"To *me*," Schweiger said futilely.

Herr Kaufmann nodded his agreement. "And now I will continue to sit with Otto." He turned away and then said, "I am sorry, inspector, that you feel I am not cooperating, but it can only be done this way. Believe me."

As the door to the cabin closed on Kaufmann, Schweiger formed his hands into fists. "I do not understand," he said in a hiss, "how you can simply allow this. The key to the whole situation lies in the past and now we have a chance to meet such an important eyewitness. A potential killer as well. And you let it slip? What kind of detective are you?"

"Someone who lets her common sense prevail," Atalanta bit back. "Kaufmann has a confidential relationship with this man. He may achieve something. If you appear, the other party will be alarmed and might even disappear again. You will learn exactly nothing."

Schweiger huffed in indignation but did not argue anymore. They stood there in the stillness of the night, with the dark skies overhead and the moon glinting on the inky waters, until Renard approached them with a white object in his hand.

He said softly to Atalanta, "There was a telegram delivered for you earlier. I have had no time to give it to you yet."

"Delivered on board?"

"Yes, a small boat came alongside, with food supplies. It had the telegram as well."

Atalanta opened it and read:

Will meet you in Bingen. R.

Raoul. He was coming to meet her. Normally this would light up her day and make her feel more confident that she could solve the case. She would tell him everything and he would have some good idea, some hunch, that would help her. But now his imminent arrival only added to her troubles. They had not parted on the best of terms. She wanted to discuss his dangerous liaison with Vincenzo Dulce. He would not like to hear that, and he might even repeat that he did not want to see her anymore.

How could she suffer such heartbreak on top of the weight of the current case?

Renard asked her softly, "Is it bad news?"

Atalanta shook her head. "Raoul is coming to meet me in Bingen. We are going to see some vineyards. It will be a nice break from the case."

She heard Schweiger huff. He did not take her seriously at all. To him she was an amateur who sleuthed a little on the side, for fun. Who went sightseeing with a friend the first chance she got, leaving him to deal with the hard things. But he had no idea how much she and Raoul had endured together. How they had been in danger together. How Raoul had saved her life.

Yes. He had saved her life and now she was indebted to do the same for him. She had to save him from Vincenzo Dulce's clutches, even if she risked their bond by addressing the matter. Friends had to be honest with each other.

And he was so much more to her than just a friend.

Chapter Seventeen

When they docked in Bingen, Raoul was waiting for her on the jetty. He paced impatiently, his hands folded behind his back. Even from a distance, she could see the gold bracelet he wore. Was it a present from Dulce? A token of Raoul's loyalty to him? Again she felt anger that he had allowed this to happen just to preserve his career.

But then, his career meant everything to him.

"Atalanta!" Raoul came towards her, seeming to want to grab her shoulders and look her over but he stopped himself and gave a formal little bow. "How is the trip going? I understand it has become a case, again? You have no luck with these things."

"I desperately need your help," she said.

He held her gaze and then melted into a smile. "Come on then. My car is waiting."

He helped her get in on the passenger side and walked around to the other side.

He said as he seated himself, "I have arranged for us to see a vineyard and try some wine. This is very good land for several wines. The vineyards lie on the sloping riverbanks and receive a lot of sun. The soil is also very suitable. I do not know all the details, but I enjoy the results!"

Atalanta felt a deep relief when they turned away from the ship and the Rhine and drove through the gorgeous landscape. The sun was shining brightly in a clear blue sky and trees were blossoming in pink and white. Here there seemed to be room to breathe, unlike on the ship where all the secrets seemed to steal the oxygen from the air.

Raoul glanced at her. "You don't look very relaxed. Are you not enjoying your river cruise? I do realise there has been a murder but you should be used to that by now."

"I will never get used to it. It is so momentous. Someone loses their life and will never get it back. I mean, Sabine Freund was a young woman, with her whole life ahead of her. Someone stole away her chances for happiness."

"If she was murdered, she made enemies. Perhaps she was not such a pleasant young woman?"

Atalanta thought of the way Sabine had used her knowledge from her time as a nurse with her father to blackmail the former convict Erol Müller. "I suppose not," she agreed, "but that does not give someone the right to take her life. It is not for them to determine who gets to live or die."

Atalanta frowned hard.

"It feels like the Rabenhorsts are so privileged they

seem to feel entitled to decide matters of life and death like medieval lords of the castle. In any case, the old lady feels that way." She began to tell Raoul everything that had happened since they had parted ways. He listened carefully, asking a question now and then to clarify a point. Simply being with him relaxed Atalanta and reminded her why she liked his company. She had really missed him.

"So right now," she concluded, "Herr Kaufmann is meeting the mysterious long-lost son. He left the ship early, even before breakfast. I am really curious what he will learn."

"Did Herr Schweiger not try to follow him?" Raoul asked.

"I think Kaufmann left so early it was impossible for him to do so." Atalanta had to smile at the inspector's irritation when he had found that Kaufmann had abandoned the sleeping Otto in his cabin and had gone ashore. Still, she supposed Kaufmann would have been watching for someone following him so it would not have been easy to try.

Raoul parked the car and looked at her. "We are going to enjoy our time together without discussing murder. Agreed?"

"Agreed. But I do want your opinion before we get back to the ship."

He nodded. "You can have it right now. I find it very suspicious that the mere mention of how his father supposedly killed his mother triggered such a strong memory in Otto Rabenhorst. I think he only pretended to remember."

"Why would he pretend?"

"For obvious reasons. He has always assumed that his great-grandmother had something to do with his parents' deaths because of her domineering character or her silence about the actual events on the day."

Otto had indeed confided to her that he feared his great-grandmother knew more than she was telling them.

Raoul said, "He suspects her and at the same time he does not want her to be guilty. So by making up this memory in which his absent father is the killer, he can clear her himself."

"That is very insightful."

Raoul shrugged. "People often tell themselves something they want to believe." He rested his hands on the steering wheel and the sunshine hit the golden bracelet on his wrist. Looking at the glinting, Atalanta's throat grew tight. Had Raoul also told himself something he wanted to believe? That joining Vincenzo Dulce's brand-new team could save his career and that without this chance it would all be over? Had he convinced himself that he needed to take this opportunity, even though he knew of Dulce's reputation?

She said softly, "I read in the newspaper about your new team."

Raoul stiffened. He had hoped she had not yet heard of it. It was only putting off the unpleasantness, but he was usually quite good at that. He had hoped they could just have a nice time together. He longed to be with her one more time, without weighty questions or hard conversations. But now it seemed like it was not meant to be.

"And?" he asked without looking at her.

Atalanta said, "I guess I should congratulate you. Your own team, built entirely around you as the main driver. With a new imported car from America. It sounds like a dream come true."

"You don't sound enthusiastic."

She sighed. "You know how afraid I am for you to have an accident. A new car that hasn't been tested yet? You wanting to prove yourself to your new team sponsor?"

Raoul waited for what was to come. Atalanta was extremely intelligent. She might fear for his safety but there was more to her reluctance than that. He just knew it.

"Isn't his name Vincenzo Dulce? I asked Renard about him and he told me that he deals in diamonds from Africa. Sounds quite adventurous."

"Yes, he has travelled a lot and can tell big tales about it. You would like him."

"Would I?" Atalanta's voice was doubtful.

Raoul did not look at her. The chance of a nice day together seemed to evaporate with every passing moment. She knew more than she revealed.

"Why don't you just say what you have to say?" He looked at her then, sudden anger filling his chest. "Did you ask me to come here to discuss your murder case or my choices?"

"Both." Her reply came quickly and without doubt. She eyed him honestly. "Raoul, it is logical that I read about your new team and have questions about it."

"No, it is not logical. You are not my mother nor my guardian."

"Nor your fiancée?" She held his gaze. "In Salzburg I suggested we could get engaged."

"And I told you why it was a bad idea. Those reasons still apply."

"And perhaps there is one more reason added now?"

He took a deep breath. Her question cut through him like an arrow. She was quick to grasp the truth. He had forged a bond with criminals. She was a detective. It was just…

She asked softly, "Why did you do it, Raoul? Did you not know who he was? What he does? How he earns his money?"

"Most of it is just allegations."

"He has been to prison!" Her voice rose in pitch. "He is not a businessman. He enables crimes, including murders."

"That has never been proven." Raoul felt like he was sinking fast and only trying to salvage whatever he could. "The police are sometimes too quick to point a finger. Yes, he has been to prison for a matter of stolen goods being found in his possession. But they could prove nothing else."

"That they could not prove it does not mean he wasn't guilty."

"I know." Raoul eyed her. "I am, however, but a driver on his racing team. I don't work for him in any other capacity."

"There exists something like being complicit by association."

"Look, Atalanta, it is not like I see him often. He travels a lot and he puts money into the racing team. I have only met him twice. I train with my own people. I know I can rely on them. The car is fine. I am confident I can achieve wins this season. I know I can beat the man my old team hired in my place." Pain slashed through him as he recalled the betrayal. How they had cast him aside for someone younger. "I need to do this. Do you understand?"

"I understand you need to race. But I do not understand why you risk getting involved in criminal activities just to be able to keep racing."

"No, of course not, because you have lots of money. You need not worry about paying bills or indeed what to do with your life if everything you love is gone."

Atalanta sat up straighter. "When my father died, I had nothing. Everything I loved, as you put it, was gone. More than that, I was left with a mountain of debts. I had to work hard to pay them off. I was all alone. So do not tell me I don't know what it is like."

"But you are a good person and made all the right choices and I am a villain because I chose to associate with a criminal to get my own racing team." He put it bluntly.

Atalanta shook her head. "It was *not* necessary, Raoul. I

offered to help you. Why turn to this man who now has control over you?"

"He doesn't have control over me!"

"He does. You are wearing that bracelet like a dog wears a collar. He owns you, and you know it."

"Nobody owns me." Raoul got out of the car and slammed the door shut. Atalanta got out on her side and eyed him across the vehicle. "Your anger only proves I am right. You must see what situation you have got yourself into." Her eyes turned worried as she continued. "You must retrace your steps while you still can. Make up some lie to escape from the contract."

"I cannot. I signed an agreement. I will race for him for two years."

"Two years?" Atalanta sounded incredulous. "And not even a trial period or some other legal loophole by which you can escape?"

"Who says I need to escape? You make it all sound so dramatic."

"But I am not a dramatic person." Her eyes were sad now and her pain tore at his heart. "I am a very logical and pragmatic person. You know me, Raoul. I would not tell you this if I were not convinced that you are in great danger."

"I always liked danger. That is why I said no to your generous offer to let you sponsor me. You would wrap me in tissue paper to keep me safe, but I would suffocate. I need room to live."

"Room to crash into a wall?" she asked, half angry, half sad.

He nodded. "If I have to."

Atalanta turned away from him. The tension in her shoulders told him she was fighting her emotions. Perhaps even her tears?

Part of him wanted to rush to her and hold her in his arms and kiss her and tell her it would be alright. That she just had to trust him.

But he knew he could make no promises at all. He had signed away two years of his life, and now he had to do everything possible to survive them. After that, they would see.

Two years suddenly seemed like forever.

Chapter Eighteen

Atalanta smiled perfunctorily at the man who handed her another glass of wine to try. The scent rising from it promised a fruity flavour and everything they had tried so far had been excellent, but she could not enjoy it. She had imagined this meeting with Raoul developing so differently. She had convinced herself that he had signed with Vincenzo Dulce without realising what he was getting into and with some persuasion on her part she would be able to make him see. They would invent something, whatever was needed, to get him out of the agreement and then he would be safe.

But now it seemed he had known from the start and had … accepted the danger? Because he was addicted to it? Or because fame meant more to him than his own life? She wasn't certain. But it was not what she had expected at all, from the man she cared for. She had to rethink everything.

Raoul toasted her with his glass. "This must be the last

one. I still have to drive you back to the ship and you should not arrive less than sober." He winked at her. "Otto thinks you are a nice, prim and proper governess for his daughter."

She knew she should not take the bait but she was tired and the wine gave her a glow in her stomach that spread through her body.

"Who says I am merely a governess in his opinion?"

Raoul immediately stiffened. His eyes narrowed as he studied her. "Does he expect more? I would be careful around him. He is the sort of high-placed character who thinks he can use women and toss them aside when he is tired of them. I would not want to see you hurt."

"You are not my brother, Raoul." It was not kind to echo his words from earlier but she did not feel like being kind. "I can do whatever I want."

"Of course. But Otto is hardly worth your time."

"He has a keen interest in most subjects I enjoy. We have a lot in common."

"He is a suspect in your murder case. To get close to him would hardly be ethical."

Raoul put his glass down and thanked the man for the tasting. He gestured to her. "Shall we go?"

Atalanta emptied her glass and put it aside reluctantly. "Can we not take a walk through the vineyard? It is spring so there aren't any grapes but … the view across the Rhine must be stunning."

Raoul nodded and they entered the vineyard via a small path. They walked for a while without speaking. The sun was warm on Atalanta's head and back and the river views mesmerised her with their blues and greens. Ships went upstream and downstream and the sharp tones of a ship's horn travelled up to them from the distant water.

"I hope you will not throw yourself into another man's arms to prove to me you don't need me." Raoul's voice was low. "You deserve better than that, Atalanta. You ought to find someone who loves and adores you. Someone who would lay down his life for you."

It sounded passionate. She glanced at him and noted the pensive expression on his handsome face. He continued, "You are a woman who would love a man with all her heart. You would be willing to go a very long way to support someone, to forgive his faults and…" His voice faltered. "The other party must not abuse your zeal. Get away with wrongdoings because you are so eager to forgive. You must keep your dignity or you will become very unhappy."

She inhaled the scents of grass and earth. "Is this about Otto in particular or just a general observation?"

"I cannot put my finger on it, but I do not like him. Perhaps because he is so German. So punctual and precise and decent, at least on the outside. I don't know what I can expect from within. Perhaps he is like the river Rhine, one moment flowing smoothly and shining clear blue and the next dragging a ship under and drowning all souls on it in those same deceptively beautiful waters."

"I have never thought Otto was perfect." Atalanta stared ahead. "I even suspected him of having lied to me about the attempt on his grandmother's life. I do not idolise him, nor am I saying that I don't appreciate certain qualities in him. There is something I find attractive about him – his stability or … I don't know. There is something about him that feels familiar, perhaps because he is an orphan like I am. Or perhaps it is the bond I feel with his daughter."

"If it is true that his father never died, he is not an orphan." Raoul sounded gruff. "But if you are looking for an orphan to marry, you should certainly not think of me. I have both parents living – and fighting each other as always."

She had to smile. "Perhaps you should be grateful that they are still there, even though they are not perfect. It can be very lonely when you are all alone in the world."

"You are not alone, Atalanta." Raoul stopped and looked at her. "You have your grandfather's legacy. He left it to you to ground you in something. To anchor you so you do not drift away. He gave you purpose and a connection with the past. He wrote to you to guide you. He put time and energy into your future. He did more for you than my parents will ever do for me. And Renard would do anything for you, you know that."

She nodded, her throat suddenly tight. Raoul had never liked Renard because Renard made him feel he wasn't the right companion for her, and still he acknowledged the place Renard had in her heart and the deep loyalty and commitment he felt towards her.

Raoul hesitated, staring past her at the river view. Then he said, "As for me … you know I will always be there for you. When your telegram came, I dropped everything to travel to meet you."

Her heart grew lighter. "I know."

Raoul smiled at her, a slow smile that lit his dark brown eyes. "Nothing has changed in that respect. I can tell you all I want that I need distance and that it is better if we do not meet, but … I know I cannot stay away." He reached out a hand to tuck a strand of hair behind her ear. "Now who is dangerous for me, Vincenzo Dulce or you?"

Atalanta caught his hand in hers. "Don't…"

They gazed at each other as they stood there, caught in the moment. Atalanta felt the warmth of his skin under her touch. She ached for him to lean down and kiss her. No matter if they could never be together. She wanted to know what it was like to feel his lips on hers. Here and now.

"Fräulein Ashford! Fräulein Ashford!" The urgent voice broke through the haze of her wishful thoughts. Raoul stepped away from her and Georg Schweiger appeared, sweat gushing down his face. He held a sheet of paper in his hand which he thrust at her without speaking. Atalanta accepted it and read:

> *By the time you find this note, I will be long gone. I lied to you about meeting Frau Rabenhorst's son. I will not meet him for I cannot meet myself.*
> *I am her son.*

Atalanta gasped. Blood drained from her face as she continued to read.

I worked my way into her confidence long ago. I had access to all her bank accounts. I have been syphoning off money for years and I put it all in accounts abroad. No one ever noticed. I felt safe. My only mistake was, perhaps, that I wanted more and more. That I didn't take my leave before things turned ugly. Sabine Freund discovered my true identity. She blackmailed me. I had to kill her to safeguard my secret.

Too bad that a detective was on board. But I think that even that little problem doesn't matter much now. You let me go to this meeting. Of course I will not be coming back. I have what I always wanted. And I already know what life on the run is like. Only now I will be living in much more comfort. Thanks to my dear mother and her generosity.

Yours truly, H. Kaufmann.

Schweiger said, "I found this in his cabin. He must have realised I would search it as soon as he left for the meeting or later, when he failed to return. He left most of his belongings behind. He must have sneaked away quietly in the night. I cannot believe I fell for this lie of him going to meet the long-lost son. I should have insisted on going with him."

Atalanta shook her head. "No. He planned this all along. He had some nerve though, offering his help to us like he did. He could have stayed silent and run away." She thought of Kaufmann's appearance last night – the crumpled tie, the worried look. He had played the role of the concerned family lawyer to perfection. The dutiful man who had sat beside the bed of his employer's son all night drinking strong black coffee to stay awake.

She eyed the note that seemed to smirk at her. Both she and Schweiger had been greatly deceived. Sabine Freund's killer had been under their very noses and they had let him get away. He had discussed his escape plan with them and they had agreed to it. What a clever deception.

It made it a little easier to stomach that Schweiger had also been deceived, but still … her grandfather had said he was such a good policeman but for his fatal flaw. It felt like he had expected her to make sure that this fatal flaw did not interfere with their case but she had failed. Schweiger had believed Kaufmann, also on her advice.

She could kick herself!

Raoul said, "Does this mean that our day trip is over? Do you want to go back to the ship to work on the case?"

"What case?" Schweiger said morosely. "The killer has escaped. I can only try to send a description to various police stations to look out for him but with that head start he must be far away by now. Perhaps he has even crossed the border into Switzerland. From there he can go to Italy or France. And I never did think his appearance was very noteworthy – the type of man you easily forget. It will not be hard for him to hide, especially since he has spent his life on the run ever since he killed his wife all those years ago in Bayern." Schweiger ground his teeth. "A double murderer and we let him walk! I can never forgive myself for this." He turned away and walked off.

"The note!" Atalanta called after him but he did not turn back for it. She slowly lowered her hand with the message.

Raoul said, "Well, if the killer got away and there is no way to apprehend him, we might as well take the rest of the day off, and treat ourselves to some more sightseeing. We could visit a castle ruin and have lunch in some little cafe. What do you say?"

Atalanta sighed. "I guess that is the best thing to do. On the ship I would only get frustrated thinking of my own stupidity."

"How could you have known"—Raoul gestured at the note—"that the man who was allegedly killed in Bayern was under your very noses all that time, playing the innocent family lawyer. The man who was going to change the old lady's will. Perhaps he wanted to get more money out of that."

"As the lawyer putting the will together he could hardly benefit from it. I think there are legal procedures to prevent that. At least there should be, else a lawyer could always entice a client to settle money on him."

"Or forge the will." Raoul nodded. "Once the testator was dead, they could not say that the will did not contain their wishes. Clever."

Atalanta nodded as they walked further down the path. "It is very daring that he syphoned off money from the company accounts over a long period of time. But apparently nobody noticed! I wonder that Otto never looked at the books, but I suppose he trusted Kaufmann implicitly."

"To think, her own son worked with her and she didn't recognise him." Raoul shook his head in disbelief.

"She had not seen him in many years." Atalanta pursed her lips. "And like Schweiger said, he does have a very common face. Nothing about him you would remember; no special marks to identify him by."

She slowed her pace.

Raoul looked at her from aside. "What are you thinking?"

"Nothing special. Just that … we simply assume because we have this note claiming he was the long-lost son that he actually was. But of course we don't know for sure. We only have his word for it."

She stopped and looked again at the note.

"Come to think of it, do we even know this is his handwriting?"

Raoul eyed her. "What are you suggesting? That he didn't write this? But he vanished. He wrote the note and then he ran."

"Do we know for certain that he ran?" Atalanta felt a surge of worry in her chest. "Do we know that he actually left the ship?"

Raoul touched her arm. "What is the matter? You are suddenly very pale."

"I was afraid there would be a second murder. And now I fear that it has already taken place."

"What? You think Kaufmann was murdered? And the killer wrote this note to suggest that he left the ship and ran because he was the long-lost son?"

"Yes."

"But why? Just so the case of Sabine Freund's murder would be closed?"

"Or because the killer wanted us to think the son had killed the daughter-in-law. This old matter of the death in Bayern is the key to everything. Someone knows what happened that day. And that someone is desperate to keep the truth hidden."

Raoul eyed her solemnly. "You are saying Frau Rabenhorst did it? That she killed Sabine Freund with her own heart medication and that she also killed Kaufmann and wrote this note to suggest he had run away? I agree she could poison the flask quite easily but how would she have killed a man decades younger than her and much stronger? I do not see how it is even possible as a thought exercise, let alone a real option for solving our case."

That he said "our case" gave Atalanta a little courage.

She clenched the note in her fist and said, "We need to get back to the ship. Schweiger must search it top to bottom. I fear we will find Kaufmann's dead body. And once we know how he died, we might also deduce who killed him and why."

Chapter Nineteen

Once Schweiger had been convinced of the plausibility of Atalanta's theory, he ordered more policemen over to the ship and a thorough search began. Atalanta was in her own cabin, waiting anxiously for the results. It pained her that the stuffy lawyer might have been killed to serve someone else's evil purpose. But her mind was still processing all available information and she was painfully aware that something did not quite fit.

If Kaufmann was not Frau Rabenhorst's son and he had been killed to suggest he had run, why had he told them last night that he was going to meet the son? He had told them himself. It had not been mentioned by someone else who could have lied about it. No, Kaufmann had informed them himself of his contact with the long-lost son, leading to the meeting in Bingen.

Who had suggested this tale to him? The killer? Or was

there really a meeting organised? Was the son in the vicinity? Was his reappearance connected to Sabine Freund's murder or just a distraction?

She could not be certain and it nagged at her. She had somehow started to confuse matters by allowing the killer to play her. To distract her with tricks that only led her further away from the truth. She had been lured in the wrong direction, just like the song of the sirens that trapped ships on the rocks.

The door opened and Otto came in. He carried a tray with cups and plates. Once he put it down, Atalanta saw it was hot chocolate with whipped cream on top and a selection of biscuits. "We Germans are not accustomed to afternoon tea," he said with a smile, "but we can pretend. Here, have some."

He sat down opposite her and eyed her gravely. "I'm so sorry that my outburst last night shocked you. I was not myself. The moment I recalled witnessing my mother's murder I was just … undone. I suppose I should have known it was possible that there had never been an accident because my grandmother was so cautious to speak of it and … there was always an air of secrecy surrounding it but … I never suspected I had actually seen something."

"Well, shock can cause loss of memory, and another shock can bring it back. But are you certain it is a genuine memory?"

Otto gave her a sad smile. "Of course not. It is so long ago. Also, the sedative Kaufmann gave me to calm down … it has made my head feel like lead." He reached up and massaged his temples. "I think he wanted to make sure I would not remember more. Seeing as he is my father. I cannot believe he sat beside my bed through the night, watching over me."

Atalanta felt the incongruity in that scene: the man who had killed his wife and fled, sitting beside his traumatised son. But was it not possible that while Kaufmann had felt that his mother owed him money and he was entitled to take it from her, he had also still felt a bond with his children? The human heart was complicated.

She kept her eyes on Otto as she asked, "Have you never felt anything strange about Kaufmann? That he was somehow close to you or being nice to you and Gertrude, more than you would expect from the family lawyer?"

"Oh, he was always lenient with her. He paid her bills and kept it from Grandmother or gave her money to spend. But nothing that gave me pause." Otto waved a hand in the air. "I don't want to think of him as my father. He killed my mother and then also this other person who had nothing to do with the matter. Sabine Freund. Only because he saw her as a threat."

"Lisl told me that you were close with Sabine."

"Lisl is jealous of everyone I know. She thinks I ignore her. But I will make it up to her. Once all this is over, we will travel together. I want to show her the Italian cities." Otto paused before he added slowly, "Perhaps you can come along."

"No, that would defeat your purpose. If you want to show her she is important to you then you must go alone with her. Just the two of you. Make her feel like she matters. She is a nice girl, when you strip away the anger and resentment."

He nodded. "You are probably right. I will keep that in mind." He offered her the plate with biscuits. "Try the one with the almond. They are the best."

Schweiger put his head around the door. "Ah, there you are, Herr Rabenhorst. I have just received replies to some telegrams I sent. Herr Kaufmann has indeed been syphoning off money from your business accounts – quite a substantial sum over the years – so that part of his confession is true."

Otto nodded with grim satisfaction.

"I am also expecting replies to more telegrams I sent. I have men speaking with the servants who accompanied your grandmother to Bayern when your parents had their accident. I will let you know what I find out as soon as I receive word." He closed the door again.

Otto said, "So he stole money all those years and nobody ever noticed. Sabine must have found out. She worked in one of our offices before she came to work for my grandmother. Perhaps she saw through his financial manipulations?"

"Why did you hire her as a nurse? She has no training."

"No formal training perhaps but she did nurse people before she came to work for us. Her father was a village doctor. He had a large practice and often took her along to assist him. She learned a lot by experience. That seemed more important to me than a book education." He eyed her.

"I love my grandmother, and I would never have left her in the care of someone who was not capable."

"But Sabine Freund lied to you. Her father was no friendly village doctor. He worked in prisons. She assisted him there."

Otto's eyes widened. "Who says so? I cannot believe that."

Atalanta could hardly tell him that his sister was engaged to a convict and she said quickly, "I know it to be true. Did you know she was selling drops to Gertrude?"

Otto stiffened further. "You mean the drops she takes for her nerves? I was aware that she was taking something and that it was not good for her, but no, I was not aware it came via Sabine. I am sorry to hear that."

Atalanta nodded. "So am I. Gertrude is a nice person but she is so unhappy. Her fiancé is just a pawn in some game she plays to keep her freedom." She waited a moment. Was Erol Müller the pawn? Or was Gertrude?

The kiss in the botanical gardens…! All of a sudden it took on another meaning. What if Erol Müller and Sabine Freund had been lovers and they decided to insert themselves into the rich Rabenhorst family? Sabine came to work for Frau Rabenhorst, befriending Gertrude and getting her addicted to drops while Erol, as her fiancé who accompanied her to parties and such, was able to get close to rich people who all owned valuable jewellery. Who was to say he had not been using Gertrude to find new victims for his thefts?

If the two of them had worked together, had Erol Müller

decided that Sabine was overplaying her hand? That she was risking too much by her blackmail practices? Had he killed her to make sure his own secret stayed hidden and he could continue his criminal career without the risk of exposure hanging over it?

Otto said, "You look so deep in thought. What are you thinking?"

Atalanta was not about to share her musings with him and hastily invented another reason for her thoughtfulness. She said, careful to register his response, "I just cannot keep thinking about poor Gertrude's addiction and how she would never have fallen for those sedatives if she had not felt so constricted by your grandmother's demands on her. On all of you, as a matter of fact. I actually understand your daughter's feeling that if your grandmother died, things would be easier. You all seem to be so ... under her control."

Otto sighed. "I wish you would not support Lisl in those views. I know she feels like she is not allowed to be creative and all, but that is nonsense. Her mother was very creative and I loved that about her. I never opposed her sculpting or even exhibiting. I am only sorry that her association with those artists put her in the place where she was shot. She had no part in the argument in that bar and yet..." He was silent for a long moment. "Life can be very unfair that way."

Atalanta nodded. "But if you feel that her creativity led to her untimely death, would you not want your daughter to stay away from artistic pursuits?"

Otto laughed softly. "She is only eleven. Now she loves

to do paper cutting but in a few years she may have other interests. I am confident she will be alright. Thanks to you also, Atalanta. I cannot tell you how grateful I am that you are here on this trip. I do not know what I would have done without you."

Atalanta picked up her cup of hot chocolate and sipped. She did not know quite what to say. She appreciated her friendship with Otto, and she felt a certain obligation to help him with his daughter and the murder case, but having just spent the day with Raoul she knew what she felt for him was incomparable. And even if he wasn't ready to commit to her and he had now fallen in with a dangerous crowd, she was not about to let go of her hopes and dreams that one day they could be together.

Georg Schweiger looked in again. "Fräulein Ashford, can I speak to you for a moment?"

Atalanta rose and went outside. Once they had made certain no one was listening in, Schweiger started in a soft voice, "My men have searched the ship and we have found no body and no evidence that there was any kind of fight or wrongdoing. As I mentioned, Kaufmann was syphoning off money. We have also established that he put pressure on Frau Rabenhorst to make this trip, probably intending to murder Sabine Freund during the cruise. And…" He paused as if he wanted to ensure that she paid special attention to this bit of interesting information. "I had them check all the money found in Sabine Freund's room for fingerprints and compared them with those on the cup from which he drank his black coffee as he sat beside Otto

Rabenhorst's bed all night. Some of the prints on the bills match those of Kaufmann."

"Yes, but Otto just told me that he sometimes gave Gertrude money for her personal use. If she used that money to buy the drops from the nurse…"

Schweiger gestured with both hands. "I think we have enough evidence now to safely assume that what he wrote in the note was the truth. He was the son who disappeared all those years ago and came back to get even with his mother. He wanted his part of the inheritance and devised a clever plan to get it, but in the end he had to face exposure by Sabine Freund and he killed her to keep the thing a secret. It all fits. He is off somewhere now, laughing at us."

Atalanta had to agree that it seemed likely. "I am sorry that the search of the ship was a lot of work for nothing."

Schweiger looked her over. "You were being thorough and I appreciate that. But I do want to know one more thing. If you suspected that Kaufmann had been murdered, who did you think the killer was?"

Atalanta sighed. "Strictly looking at it from a theoretical point of view, it would have had to be Frau Rabenhorst, but I don't think that she would be physically able to kill a man and dispose of the body. So that would be a little difficult to explain."

Schweiger nodded. "Well, it is never easy to go against members of influential families so I am rather pleased it wasn't her." He turned away from her. "I will let you know if something out of the ordinary turns up. But I fully expect the case to be closed."

Atalanta watched him walk away. He greeted the ship's captain who stood smoking a cigarette. His profile was etched sharply by the late afternoon light. It glinted off his gold braid and the buttons of his uniform. He cut an impressive figure standing there like that, staring out over the water.

Atalanta had a feeling that something was niggling at her brain when she looked at him, as if something about his appearance was highly relevant. That it was the missing piece she was looking for in this whole complex puzzle.

But it was over, was it not? The murderer had killed and had fled the scene to enjoy his stolen riches. Sabine Freund had died because she had blackmailed one person too many. Yet some things still did not make sense. Why had Otto claimed his grandmother's life was threatened by someone before the cruise started? Kaufmann had been staying with them the weekend the lamp cord had been frayed but why would he have wanted to kill her then? There was no reason for it.

Who had pushed Frau Rabenhorst at the fort in Koblenz? Her description had been so vivid of this sharp blow between the shoulder blades that had thrown her off balance.

Most of all, what had Atalanta's grandfather written to her in his letter that had been delivered to her by Georg Schweiger? Schweiger had a fatal flaw but what was it? It seemed to be somehow important for the case. As if it could give her a clue as to what she needed to do to reveal a truth that escaped Schweiger.

But she did not have the other half. *He* had it. And he refused to give it to her. He had gone so far as to claim that he did not know what she was talking about.

What was he afraid of? What could she discover if she only had the letter he had denied her?

Chapter Twenty

They walked past white houses with beautiful wood carving in the door posts and along the roof beams, towards a little church on a square. There was a bronze cast statue of a man holding a scroll in the air. Perhaps it celebrated the granting of city rights, long ago? Pigeons landed to peck at scraps between the cobbles. Sunlight shimmered on their feathers, conjuring spots of pink and green across the grey and their cooing drifted to them as they closed in.

It was such a perfect little scene that Atalanta could not quite believe there had been a murder on this trip. Or that the people walking here with her all had troubles in their lives. Gertrude smiled and chatted with her fiancé as if she weren't addicted to sedatives at all. Erol in turn wrapped an arm around her without a sign that he was foreign to these elevated circles and only playing a part.

Lisl pointed out to her father that there was Latin

writing engraved in the statue's base and they stood together, leaning down to decipher it. Nothing indicated that their relationship was often under strain. Indeed, Lisl had never looked so carefree.

Frau Rabenhorst read from a small book she had extracted from her purse. She did not look like someone who feared for her life … because the case was solved, was it not? They need not be watchful anymore. The danger had left their circle and now they could just enjoy themselves.

Atalanta glanced at Renard who carried the large camera again and was photographing the views. She had claimed to need him along to carry the heavy photographic equipment. In truth she wanted him close to her because she was nervous. Something inside her told her that Kaufmann's disappearance was not the end of it and there was still a final act to this family drama to come.

Schweiger seemed to think the same thing, as he had not taken his leave but was accompanying them yet further upstream. Atalanta wished Raoul was also with them, but he had received word from his team that there was to be another test of the new car, in the Alps. He had told her with regret in his eyes that he had to leave but that they would be in touch again soon.

"I do not want to look at a graveyard," Gertrude said as they stopped near the church. "There must be something more cheerful to do in this little village."

"Why don't we ask that man over there with the carriage to drive us around?" Erol suggested. "I'll pay him for his efforts." He took Gertrude's arm and ushered her in the direction of the man with the cart pulled by two dark brown horses.

Otto said to Atalanta with a grin, "It is hardly a carriage. I think Gertrude will find this all very simple and unsophisticated for her taste. She would rather go shopping and have tea in a city like Paris."

"Perhaps when this is all over, I can invite her to come and stay with me for a few days," Atalanta said. She did not really feel like spending more time with Gertrude, but she also felt she ought to try and wean her off the drops. Perhaps some time away would bring an end to this make-believe engagement that only seemed to make her unhappy.

Otto's amusement turned into something softer. He said with a smile. "You are a true friend, Atalanta. You need not care for Gertrude's unhappiness, but you do. I've always known I could count on you." He folded his hands behind his back and gazed up at the church. "It is strange but sometimes when you meet people, you immediately understand them. Who they are, what matters to them, what they are made of. It was like that for me when I met you. I sensed that you were a very kind-hearted person. Someone who truly sees others instead of judging by superficial first impressions. I can't tell you how glad I am that you agreed to accompany us on this journey. You could have found it rather taxing to travel with such, uh … peculiar people."

"On the contrary, I have found it fascinating."

His eyes lit up. "I hoped that. You have good psychological insight and you must have enjoyed seeing our dynamics, even if they are not always perfect..." He leaned closer to her. "I appreciate my grandmother even more now that I know the truth about the past and how my mother died. She chose to send away her own son, the one to whom she was connected by blood, in order to care for us, her grandchildren. She did not try to cover up the murder and keep him near her, although she must have wanted that. Instead she made the difficult choice to send him away to protect us. In a way, she chose to punish the one she loved for what he did to someone who was nothing to her. She must have felt closer to her son than to her daughter-in-law but still she made that choice. I admire her for her bravery in those hard moments."

Atalanta frowned. "Do you not think she should have notified the police?"

"Those were different times. People relied less on authorities and took action for themselves, especially when they came from influential families. They felt more like a law of their own."

"I cannot approve when people place themselves above the law."

Otto shrugged. "That is your opinion, which I value but with which I cannot agree in this instance. My grandmother did the best possible thing."

"You are not angry she hid the truth from you?"

"No. I can understand why. It was a very shocking thing and... I even think it has been better for me not to know while I grew up. It has certainly been better for Gertrude."

Atalanta stared at the church yard's gate that had a

motto engraved on it. A Latin motto just like the fountain. It took her a moment to decipher the curly lettering but then she realised it was a very well-known motto, used on graveyards around the world.

Memento mori.

Remember you must die.

She shivered despite the warm sunshine. Renard came over to her with the camera.

"I saw the caretaker of the graveyard. Shall I ask him whether I can take a few photos inside the church?"

"That would be nice. Let me come with you. I want to see the interior."

The old man who was sweeping the walkways with a broom talked to them with a ready smile and extracted a set of large rusty keys from his pocket. With one of them he unlocked a small door in the church's larger double wooden doors and let them in. He pointed out the wood carving on the pulpit and the beautifully engraved windows and then left them to return to his duties outside.

Renard began to take photographs while Atalanta sat in a pew and inhaled the silence. It reminded her of the church in Santorini where she had sat during her case, wishing that she would see light in the darkness. Here the dark had cleared up but the picture she was seeing made no sense. She wished with all of her heart that her grandfather was still alive so she could call him to discuss the case. Or even better, that he was with her, sitting beside her, and she could ask for his opinion.

Silently, without her lips even moving, she struck up a

conversation with him, imagining herself telling him everything that had happened and he listened to her without interrupting. She imagined him giving her his full attention and his comforting presence.

Perhaps also his confidence that she could solve this case?

She had to admit that her faith in her own abilities had taken a blow during this case because she felt like her decisions had not always been the best. There was, for example, her urge to push Frau Rabenhorst into a confession…

Or perhaps it was just the difficult partnership with Georg Schweiger. She genuinely liked his level-headed approach, and he had treated her with more respect than other policemen she had come across during her cases, but the question of what his fatal flaw could be and how she could counteract it had overshadowed everything.

She took the letter from her purse and looked at the envelope with a sigh.

"Why did you have to be so cryptic, Grandfather?" she said softly to herself. "I mean, why did you have to use these letters to communicate with me?"

She took the sheet from the envelope and turned it over once more as if she expected that there would suddenly be handwriting on the other side. But it was still as blank as it had always been. Then she ran her finger along the edge where the letter had been cut off. Even the successful conclusion of the case had not enticed Schweiger to hand her the other half or to admit to having cut the letter in the first place.

Was it possible that he hadn't?

Was it possible that her grandfather had given her half a letter? But why?

She took the envelope and looked inside it. The light in the church was dim but there was a ray of sunshine falling in through one of the high windows. She held the envelope up in the sunlight and then she saw it. Very small handwriting she hadn't seen before. Two words only.

Ask Renard.

She blinked as if she expected the words to be a trick of her imagination. But they were really there. Why had she not seen them before?

Ask Renard? So he knew more. And he hadn't said anything!

She looked around for him but he was nowhere in sight. Sounds suggested that he had gone down the steps into the crypt under the church. Perhaps there was a memorial plaque there that he wanted to photograph, or the tomb of a well-known citizen?

She went down the steps hurriedly, steadying herself with the brass railing. In the darkness of the tomb she heard a scuffle. "Renard? Are you there?"

"Oui, mademoiselle. I am almost done here. Then we can go out into the sunshine again. It is a little too damp in here for my liking."

Atalanta said, "Do you have a letter from Grandfather for me? He left me a clue that I should ask you."

There was a brief silence. Atalanta feared that Renard would deny knowing anything and she would be left with nothing but her frustration but then he came towards her with something in his hand.

He said with a remorseful expression, "I follow my late master's instructions to the letter because I know he always has some higher plan and I must not interfere with his intentions. But it was hard for me to see you struggle in this case and wonder if you needed the information contained in here." He handed her an envelope.

Atalanta tore it open. In the wavering light of the lantern on the wall she read:

Ah my dearest girl, you found the clue in the envelope. Did the half-letter occupy you? What could it mean that it was cut off? Who had the other half? What was Schweiger's fatal flaw? I am sorry if you feel like I have led you astray. The letter was cut into halves by me personally. Schweiger had nothing to do with it. He is not keeping any secrets from you. But I wanted you to assume that he was.

You see, while working with him in the past I have discovered one thing about him: he likes his independence. He will keep things close to his chest, and not share, and not involve others. That is his prerogative of course, but it does make it difficult at times and it can even frustrate the investigation. I wanted you to treat him as if he might be keeping things from you so you would not simply rely on what he told you but always verify all things.

I have done this not just for your benefit, but also for his, because his tendency to resist cooperation is harming him. He is very intelligent and has a great career ahead of him if he would only learn that he need not do everything by himself. That others also have a valuable contribution.

Most of all, I want you to know – both of you, for that matter – that in a case there is always the risk of incorrect assumptions. Take your own.

"Georg Schweiger had my grandfather's letter. Said letter contains something negative about him. He must have doctored it to ensure the truth about him would remain hidden."

But my dear Atalanta, let us be perfectly honest: if Schweiger had wanted to hide the truth about himself, why would he have given the letter to you at all? He could have read and then burned it and no one would have been the wiser. The fact that he gave it to you, while it mentioned his fatal flaw, must mean that he was never aware of its contents. Even if you are left with the incongruity of a letter that was unfinished. So instead of starting with the question Who took the other half of the letter? you have to reason that Schweiger would have made the entire letter disappear as it served no purpose for him to hand you what he did. Likewise, in a case you must always ask yourself: what was my first assumption? From what angle am I looking at all of this? And what would happen if I took another angle? If I revisited the case with another assumption, a fresh starting point?

Please do not hold it against an old man that he smiled a little at the idea of your incorrect conclusions and how Schweiger would respond to your accusation of him withholding the letter. I was convinced when I wrote it this way that a little tension between you two would benefit the case.

If I was wrong, I apologise.

Yours sincerely,
Clarence Ashford.

Atalanta reread it with a sense of disbelief. Her grandfather had actually wanted her to start off on a bad footing with Schweiger? To teach him the value of cooperation? That seemed to be so counterproductive. And as for incorrect assumptions… How was it even possible to solve a case with a link to an incident thirty years in the past without assumptions? One simply had no solid evidence to go on.

Renard asked, "Does it help any?"

"Not really. In fact, this is the first time I have read one of his letters and actually felt a bit let down." She took a few deep breaths. "I appreciate that he thought ahead to what I might need to hear at any given time, but it is not logical to assume that he could always predict correctly how it would be for me. At the start, perhaps, because I was totally unprepared to do this work, but now that I have more experience, I feel it is inevitable that his advice will not be directly applicable to my current case. How could it be?"

Renard nodded gravely. "I can only tell you this, mademoiselle. He was a man who took his vocation very seriously. And when he chose you as his successor, he was determined to teach you everything he himself had learned. He also had to discover things by trial and error. He wrote those letters to prevent you from making the same painful mistakes he did."

Atalanta put the letter in her purse with the other one. "I feel like he is having a private joke at my expense. He obviously shared a past with Schweiger and it amused him to think we would cross paths."

"You cannot deny him a little amusement as he envisioned your future. He also felt great sadness that he never got to know you."

As Renard said it, Atalanta's eyes suddenly burned with tears. "Then why did he not reach out to me after my father died? There was time to get to know each other then. He had me watched to see whether I was worthy to succeed him but he never contacted me. Why?" She bit her lip to keep herself from crying.

Renard looked at the ground a moment. She saw the tension in his features. Was he struggling with his loyalty to his deceased master?

Then he said, "I can only imagine he was afraid."

"Afraid?" she echoed.

"Yes. That you would reject him like your father had

rejected him all his life. It was a great burden on his shoulders, the bad relationship with his son. Even though he buried himself in cases as a distraction, it never ceased to give him pain. You provided him with some hope for the future. He was, I surmise, too afraid that the hope would be extinguished."

Atalanta felt a tear on her cheek and wiped it away brusquely. "He feared I would reject him, but he never even gave me an opportunity to choose. Speaking of incorrect assumptions…"

She turned away from Renard and left the crypt. Stepping from the dimness in that burial place into the high church flooded with sunshine, she had to stop a moment and narrow her eyes. Her heart ached for her grandfather's fear and reluctance to reach out to her. Why had he not had faith in her that she would not turn him away?

Perhaps because his hope for her was the only thing that kept him warm and he feared that if he lost it, he would have no more reason to go on?

She closed her eyes and vowed to herself that she would somehow get to know him better and make him proud of her as she worked the cases that came her way. To compensate for time lost and chances not taken. To correct incorrect assumptions.

Her eyes flew open and she stared into the blinding sunlight. Incorrect assumptions…

She had started the case with the assumption that Frau Rabenhorst was in danger but it had been the nurse all along. She had investigated the murder with the assumption that Sabine Freund's blackmail had centred on the death of Otto's parents. Everything that had happened afterwards seemed to confirm that. Kaufmann's revelation that the son was still alive and had contacted him, then his flight, and the note explaining what he had done.

But was it not all too neat and perfect? The confession in the note, the reason why Sabine Freund had to die?

Atalanta fetched a notebook from her purse and sat down in a pew again to write a list of names. All the people involved in this case. Then she wrote down what secrets they had or what incidents in their past might have been painful enough for them to react with violence if someone threatened to reveal them. Her eyes went over the written lines, looking for the thing she had missed. The other angle Grandfather had written about.

And suddenly she saw it. It was right there. Now that she focused on it, it suddenly gained meaning. All the other things made sense. The connections. The questions that had previously been unanswered.

A shadow fell over her and she looked up with a gasp. Schweiger stood beside her. He frowned slightly. "Sorry if I startled you. Are you taking notes about the sights here? I heard from the caretaker that this church has a special crypt?"

"Indeed it does. Renard took some photos of it but we can go now. I am all done here." She put the notebook in her purse but Schweiger held her gaze. "I never did anything to your grandfather's letter. I know you suspect me of it, and I suppose it is logical since I had it in my keeping, but I can assure you I never read the contents, let alone tampered with them."

"I know. The matter resolved itself."

"It did?" He tilted his head with a curious gleam in his eyes. "I wonder how."

"That is a little secret I must keep. But I hope on my part that you are not angry with me. That you don't feel like you let me in on the case and I was nothing but a burden to you."

Schweiger's smile deepened. "Are you fishing for a compliment, Fräulein Ashford?"

"Hardly." She took a deep breath. "Because the case is not really solved."

"Excuse me?"

"The case is not solved. Kaufmann is not the murderer of Sabine Freund."

Schweiger held up a hand. "I don't want to hear it. I am satisfied with the results as they stand. Now I am going back outside to where the rest of the company is waiting. It is too beautiful a day to discuss death."

Atalanta stared after him as he walked away. He had not even given her a chance to explain what she meant. Was he not in the least bit interested?

More than that, how was she going to expose the real killer without Schweiger's help? She had no intention of putting herself in danger because she knew now that this killer was extremely cunning and not afraid to remove people who were a risk to them. She had hoped to persuade Schweiger to make an arrest but he was unwilling to reopen the case. Because he was too stubborn for it? Or too afraid she knew something he did not and an amateur would best him?

She sighed. A fatal flaw indeed!

Chapter Twenty-One

Atalanta stared into the hole that had been dug to unearth the remains of a Roman settlement. Those ancient world conquerors had discovered how advantageous it was to dominate the river Rhine and had built their cities and fortresses on its banks. Some of the finds collected here had made their way into museums in large German cities and even across the borders to exhibitions in Rome and London. Here on the site were a few glass cabinets holding bronze daggers and clay cups and coins with the faces of emperors by whose rule the settlement could be dated. But the most interesting parts were the uncovered walls and the grand mosaic of countless fragments of colourful stone depicting bathing nymphs. It seemed fitting along a river inhabited by these mythological creatures, even if the scene had probably been chosen because this had been the bathhouse.

"The others have gone back to the inn. They want hot

food and drinks." Otto came to stand beside her. "It feels like it is going to rain."

Atalanta glanced up at the sky that had clouded over. A chilly breeze breathed across the excavation site. Moments before, she had seen Renard with his camera but he was gone now. They seemed to be all alone here.

Otto said, "You look very pensive. Are you not enjoying the day?"

"Oh I am, but … a lot has happened."

"I know." He stood beside her, his hands folded behind his back. "I wonder if it will ever be the same again, after this." He took a deep breath. "I am making arrangements for the tour of Italy with Lisl. I know you said you will not join us but you could visit us. For a day or two? We could do something enjoyable together. Just for old times' sake."

"That would be nice." Atalanta glanced past him. "Shall we go after the others? I don't want to get all wet."

"It will hold for a few more minutes. I want to show you something over there." He pointed to their left. "Shall we have a look?"

Atalanta kept smiling but the rising wind made her shiver. "I think we had better follow the others. Whatever you want to show me cannot be worth getting soaked."

"I had expected you to be stronger." He said it pleasantly, but there was a cold look in his blue eyes. "You are showing your fear. That is not smart. It has given you away. This morning in the church I still had some hope that you suspected someone else but now I can almost feel you shrink away from me."

Atalanta forced her voice to sound collected. "Is that so strange? Knowing you killed three people?"

"Three?" Otto queried. "I thought you only suspected me of having killed Sabine Freund."

"And Kaufmann?" Atalanta shot back. She stood with her feet planted apart, one hand on her purse, the other beside her.

"He vanished."

"Having written a confession that he had killed Sabine Freund and stole money from the family?"

"I made him write that before he left. I knew of his thefts from the company accounts. I allowed him to get away with the money and live well off it, abroad, if he admitted to having killed Sabine Freund. He agreed."

"No, he did not." Atalanta shook her head. "I do not believe it for one second. You killed him. And I also know how. When Schweiger asked Kaufmann to sit with you after your sudden shock as you recalled how your father had killed your mother, Kaufmann gave you a sedative. You allegedly took it and slept all night but you never swallowed that pill. You pretended you did. You seemed fast asleep when Schweiger checked on you. Then Kaufmann spoke to us outside the cabin door and you listened in. You heard that he had been in touch with your father and that he was going to meet him. You thought up a brilliant plan. You managed to slip him the pill, putting it in the coffee while he was outside talking to us. He drank the coffee to ensure he could stay awake all night but was soon fast asleep. You tied him up and hauled him overboard and he drowned. You wrote the note with his confession and you were used to forging his handwriting because you were the one syphoning money off the company. You made it look like Kaufmann had initiated it all to provide a scapegoat in case it was ever discovered. The money you stole you used to gamble. Gertrude told me of your addiction."

Otto eyed her with a superior smile.

"You are building quite a nice case but you cannot prove anything. You do not have Kaufmann's body." He paused and then continued. "You just claimed that I killed three people. Sabine Freund because she was blackmailing me, Herr Kaufmann to make it look like he had killed Sabine Freund so the case would be closed and no one would be the wiser that I was the real perpetrator. But who is the third?"

He held her gaze as he leaned closer. "You cannot mean to imply that I tried to kill my grandmother? First of all, an attempt hardly counts as a real murder, and secondly, she was never in any danger. She only thought she was."

"Because you made her believe it. You frayed the cable of the bedside lamp. You shot something at her in Koblenz so she was thrown forwards and fell. You told me once how good you were as a boy with a catapult."

Otto kept smiling. "I never intended to kill her. She is no problem for me."

"I know. For all your clever acting that you are under her control, she has always been under yours. You knew the truth about Bayern. That your father killed your mother and that your grandmother covered it up. As you grew up, she suspected that you knew something and she was afraid the truth might come out. She indulged your whims and though she was harsh to your daughter, she was never controlling of you."

"Still you cannot prove a thing," Otto said mockingly. "I suspect you are only developing this thesis to prove to Schweiger you are a better detective than he is. But to him the case is closed. I overheard your conversation in the church. I was in there, eavesdropping when he dismissed your suggestions as nonsense. You have no supporters, Atalanta. You must let it go."

"Why, when I know it is the truth? You have as good as admitted it." She held his gaze. "The very fact that we are standing here, just the two of us, while all the others have gone away, proves it. You intend to silence me because I know too much."

Otto laughed softly. "You presume a lot. You think you pose a threat to me but nobody believes you. You are overreaching. Perhaps you are even suffering from a nervous strain after taking on too many cases in quick succession. You begin to see murderers where there are none."

His face was still remarkably the face of the man she had liked, admired, and even fantasised about. In another lifetime. Here, she knew, with every fibre of her being, who and what he was.

He said, "You still have not told me who the third person is that I supposedly killed. My other victim."

"Your first victim," Atalanta said. "The ultimate cause of all of everything that happened on this trip – the origin of the Rhine, so to speak. The source, which I never truly saw. I was so focused on the accident of your parents, on your mother's murder once it was clear that your father did not die. Not until I made a list today of all the incidents in the past that were potentially harmful did I see the truth. You did not kill Sabine Freund because she knew your father survived in Bayern. She knew something else about you. Something far more dangerous."

Otto's eyes flickered but he said nothing.

Atalanta pushed on. "She knew you killed your wife."

There was a deep silence. The first drops of rain splattered cold on Atalanta's face. The wind that swept past her whistled low.

Otto said, "That is the most ridiculous accusation I have ever heard. My wife was shot in a bar fight. The police investigated and they produced a full report on it. Two painters had some quibble and one of them in a drunken mood pulled a gun and fired at the other. He happened to hit my wife who was also present. It was a tragic accident."

"No, it was not. The man who fired the shot aimed for your wife. He was hired by you. You were tired of her artistic aspirations and of her nights spent in bars with painters and sculptors. She was bad for your reputation. Most of all, she was unfaithful. Or at least you believed so. You were jealous enough to have her killed. The man who shot her and who was arrested and went to prison for the death contracted a fatal lung disease. He was dying. Sabine

Freund assisted her father, who was a prison doctor, and she nursed him. In the delirium he would have experienced before he died, he told her the truth. That he had taken a commission to kill someone and disguise it as an accident.

"She came to work for your family, first at the office, then as your grandmother's nurse, specifically to blackmail you. You paid her piles of money to keep her silent and then used the cruise to kill her. You hired me – allegedly – to look after your grandmother who was under threat to make it look like she was the intended victim and not Sabine Freund. Unfortunately, it didn't really work. Both Georg Schweiger and I immediately concluded that Sabine had been the intended victim, not your grandmother but we were led astray by too many details. The burned papers in the room. The money with Kaufmann's fingerprints on it. Gertrude's addiction to drops Sabine gave her. Sabine kissing Erol. Was she blackmailing him, too? Or were they lovers and working together to drain the family's coffers?"

She shook her head. "You believed that with so many options around, we would never figure it out. Especially after you derailed us with Kaufmann's disappearance and his confession of being the long-lost son. It was so spectacular that you were certain you had us fooled."

"I still have not heard a single shred of proof." Otto's eyes were cold. "You are close to a nervous breakdown, I fear. You are jumping at shadows and connecting incidents that are totally unrelated."

"I will convince Schweiger I am right." Atalanta stood firm. "I will not let you go to Italy with Lisl while you are responsible for three deaths. Moreover, you do not love her and never have. You implicated her in attempted murder. You acted to me as if Lisl was after your grandmother. You claimed you had seen her come out of the old woman's bedroom with scissors. You did not care about accusing your own child as part of your devious plan to kill Sabine Freund and get away with it."

Atalanta paused to allow for a response but there was none in his marble features.

She took a deep breath before adding, "Then again, you need not love her at all because she is not your child. That was your reason for killing your wife. You knew she had a lover and that Lisl was the daughter of this other man. You punished your wife for her infidelity by having her killed and you have been punishing Lisl ever since by making her feel unhappy and unloved. You pretend to care for her, but you never actually protect her from your grandmother's attacks on her creations or her choices. You enjoyed making her look unstable and capable of murder."

"You must admit she is a very unusual child. So unusual that you yourself have wondered at times whether she is normal or perhaps a little … deranged?" He said it without emotion. "I never intended to hurt her or be unfair to her. I have only ever observed her behaviour and wondered how it might be put to good use."

Atalanta felt a chill anger in her bones. "So you implied to me that she was capable of murder and plotting to kill her great-grandmother! That is how you induced me to come along on this cruise."

"And it was a perfect plan. It worked." He didn't sound triumphant, merely stated it as a matter of fact. "You felt sorry for her and you agreed to join us. That was all I wanted."

"Do you have any feelings at all?" Atalanta asked. "Or are you like a machine? You observe, you conclude, you use people for your own gain."

"I do not know if I have any feelings." Otto said it calmly, almost as if it were a nice philosophical problem to think about. "I tried to go back to my childhood and remember whether I had any strong feelings then, but frankly I cannot recall. I have always been good at interpreting other people's emotions and using them to my advantage, but that is not my fault. It is their fault for being so easy to read and so transparent, so simple. They shouldn't allow themselves to be so vulnerable."

"So the fact that they are making themselves vulnerable is an excuse for abusing that vulnerability?"

"They could be smarter about it. They could choose self-preservation."

"Like you do?"

"Exactly." Otto looked her over. "I am at a crossroads now, Atalanta, because everything was fine after Kaufmann disappeared. All the loose ends were neatly tied up. But you had to come and start pulling them apart again and unravelling it all. Now I wonder what poses the greatest risk, letting you live or killing you? You see, Schweiger may be rather shortsighted, but he is not so stupid that he will believe you simply left without saying goodbye or that you left without that manservant of yours with the large camera. He will also find it hard to believe that you had an accident here on this site and fell into a ditch and gained a head wound or something…" His tone was pensive as if he were considering what to have for dinner.

"It is safer for me not to test him too much. But on the other hand, you are a very persuasive young woman who might just convince him that there is something to this theory of yours. In that case, it could get ugly for me. So what shall I do? Let you go back to the others and wait it out, assuming that you will never be able to convince Schweiger to go against me on such shaky foundations, or try to make you disappear and possibly create even more havoc? I am not sure. Normally I decide what to do pretty quickly and I use every chance I get to make it work for me, but you pose a real puzzle."

He smiled at her. "I suppose that is a compliment, Atalanta. That you are making this hard for me. You see, you accused me of having no feelings at all, and perhaps that is true. Did I ever feel anger, pain, or jealousy, like other people do? Or am I just pretending to myself that I feel it?"

"You must feel something. It led you to murder."

He shook his head. "You are mistaken there. The great detective doesn't know it all! You think I killed my wife out of a bitter gall over her unfaithfulness but she was simply in my way. It was a practical consideration. Problems are there to be solved. And you are now my problem. And what a pretty little problem you are." He studied her as if she were an object in a class. "I really enjoyed talking to you that first afternoon when we met and later on this cruise. You are intelligent and your ideas are interesting to ponder but I cannot claim that I ever felt anything particular for you. Or that I very much wanted you to come with me and Lisl to Italy. One has to say certain things, you know, to make conversation. It is expected. It is polite. And it works oh so well."

Atalanta shivered again. He was so logical and cold, but his logic seemed to border on madness. How could she ever have liked this man or been charmed by him? How could she have felt sorry for him?

He said, "I must make up my mind because the opportunity might pass. In fact, perhaps it already has. You are prepared for me to attack you. I know you are clutching sand in that right hand of yours, Atalanta. You want to throw it in my face the moment I pounce at you. But I am not going to do that. I am not going to try and throw you into the ditch. It is too risky. Will the fall kill you? How can I be certain? No."

With one smooth movement he reached under his jacket and extracted something. A pistol. He pointed it right at her heart. "We are going to take a little walk to the back of this excavation site where there is a tool shed. I think I can find a few items there that will aid me in disposing of your body."

Atalanta's teeth were almost chattering. "You will not get away with this. The others are waiting for us. They will notice that we are not there and come looking."

"Which is why we will retreat into the tool shed. They will not come looking there." He raised the pistol higher, aiming between her eyes. "Start walking now or I shoot you right here."

"You would not. The sound will be heard further down the site and someone will come looking."

"No, Atalanta. The bad weather is about to break. Everyone has gone indoors. We are all alone." His eyes darkened. "Now, move!"

Atalanta turned away from him. Her heart pounded with every step she took. Now that her back was turned on him, she was particularly vulnerable. She was certain he would shoot her and run. How could he expect to return to his family, to normality, after this?

But then he had committed murders before and it had worked for him. He might believe he could make it work again because so far his plans had never failed.

"Stop." A male voice resounded loudly and clearly across the open space. "Put your pistol down or I will fire at you."

Atalanta wanted to glance over her shoulder and discover who it was, but Otto warned her, "Keep walking. If you turn around, or even try to look, I will fire at once."

The male voice cried out again, "Turn around, Rabenhorst! I don't want to shoot you in the back, but I will if you don't obey."

"You don't have the nerve. I could fire, too, and kill this charming young lady."

Was it Schweiger? It was not Renard, she thought. He spoke German with a French accent and this sounded different.

"Last warning," the male voice said.

Otto hissed to her, "Keep walking."

Then everything happened suddenly and very fast. There was a shot and Atalanta dropped to the ground. She waited to feel some kind of burning pain but there was none. Aside from the hard impact with the solid earth, there was no sensation of being injured. Behind her she heard an agonised cry. "You will pay for this, you bastard!" Then there was a scuffle.

Atalanta rolled over to see two men wrestling. One of them was Otto, bleeding from a wound in his shoulder. His pistol lay a few feet away. The other was the ship's captain but he was not in his uniform today. He wore a normal suit, which made him look almost unrecognisable. His hat had been knocked from his head in the fight and the sun glinted on his greying hair. As she watched the men, their faces close together as each fought desperately for the upper hand, she suddenly knew what had been niggling at the back of her brain earlier. The truth that had been staring her in the face all the time.

She scrambled to her feet and collected Otto's fallen pistol. She pointed it at him and said to the captain, "You had better tie him up securely. He is a wily one."

The captain looked up at her with a probing look. "Are you injured?"

"No, I am fine. Thank you for saving me."

The captain dismissed it with a hand gesture and secured Otto Rabenhorst with his own belt.

Renard came running across the site with large strides,

his hair ruffled by the strong wind. He halted beside Atalanta and asked gasping for air. "Are you…?"

"Nothing serious. The captain intervened in time."

"I met him on my way off the site…" Renard rested his hands on his knees and tried to regulate his breathing. "I wanted to protect the camera from the approaching rain. I told him you were still out here and asked him to fetch you before the weather broke. He said he would make sure you came to no harm."

Atalanta nodded. "I am certain he meant that." She looked at the captain's face. She saw the silent request in his eyes not to mention what she might have deduced. Not now, not here. Not with Otto present.

She understood and nodded at him with a careful smile. "Thank you again. You did the right thing."

"I knew I had to."

Chapter Twenty-Two

Renard had fetched Schweiger and he had taken Otto in. Otto kept repeating that he had no idea what was happening and claiming that he was the victim of a scam. He asserted that the captain had attacked him and he had only drawn his pistol in self-defence. Schweiger did not bother to reply. At the inn, Otto was locked in the cellar while Atalanta told her story to Schweiger.

After the local police had taken Otto away to their station, the company departed for the ship in low spirits. Frau Rabenhorst refused to believe her grandson was capable of anything evil, let alone multiple murders. Gertrude told Atalanta that she had much preferred the idea that Kaufmann was the perpetrator. Lisl said nothing, but looked as if she was about to burst with anger and despair.

Back on the ship everybody retreated to their cabins and

Atalanta was left alone in the salon. Heavy rain lashed against the large windows and it was almost impossible to see anything outside. It was almost as if the world around them had disappeared and they were locked in with their feelings.

Schweiger came to sit beside her. He folded his hands in his lap. "I must apologise," he said. "At the church I was rude. I was aware we were not alone and I did not want to discuss whatever you wanted to tell me. I believed there would be another time for it but I was not thinking of the danger you might get into as the killer realised you had discovered his identity."

He lowered his head. "I failed. Again." He waited a moment and added, "When I worked with your grandfather, I also made a mistake, and a suspect almost eluded the police because of it. Your grandfather put in a good word for me and later told me I had everything in me to become an excellent detective but I had to be more cautious in my actions. I considered him an intruder, an outsider who had been lucky in his solving of the case. When you and I met, I … I could not look at you without remembering the mistake I made and how gracious your grandfather had been about it. I was certain that his letter to you would make mention of this fact."

"Then you do not know my grandfather at all. He never tried to make himself look better at anyone else's expense."

Schweiger lifted a hand. "I am apologising. I was wrong. I suspected him of things and you, too. I did not want to work with you. I refused to take you seriously. I hoped you would fail where I was successful so I would feel better about myself."

"You don't have to feel better about yourself because you are already a very good detective. I think you have a great future ahead of you. Especially since you caught this triple killer."

Schweiger snorted. "There is the small problem of Kaufmann's body needing to be found. And a few other details regarding evidence to make a solid case. But you have convinced me that Otto Rabenhorst did indeed kill Sabine Freund and Herr Kaufmann, and that he also ordered his wife's murder, and no matter how deep I have to dig to unearth all the proof to sustain these claims, I will do it."

Atalanta nodded and smiled. "I have enjoyed working with you. I, too, was acting from mistaken assumptions for a large portion of the time. And I must admit that I let my appreciation of Otto delude me. I had no idea of the person he truly was." She waited a moment and said, "I am afraid that this detective work will make me cynical about humankind. I keep discovering that people I meet and like and trust are not at all what they seem."

"Then again, you also find that people you meet and don't like and distrust turn out to be allies after all." He rose to his feet. "I have a lot of work to do. If we do not see each other again before you leave for Paris, I wish you a good journey and much success with your detective agency."

"Thank you. I am going to need it with the competition I have."

Atalanta sat and watched the rain. It was true what she had said to Schweiger. She felt like each new case made her a little harder inside. People had hidden agendas. They used others. Otto had consciously involved her to ensure that when Sabine died, she would state to the police that his grandmother's life had been threatened. He had only needed her as part of his cold and calculated plan. She was sorry for his daughter, though, who now had to go through life knowing her father had killed her mother.

There was a sound at the door and as she looked up, the captain stood there. He was back in uniform, a quiet but imposing man. He came over to her and seated himself where Schweiger had sat before. He didn't say anything but just looked at her.

Atalanta said, "I understood very well why you did not want me to say anything while your son was still lying there injured, Herr Rabenhorst."

He winced. "That name has been foreign to me for thirty years. I have built a new existence."

"And still you wanted to meet your mother one more time."

"Yes. She is getting older and might not live much longer. I wanted to see her and reassess what we had decided at the time. Not to save my own skin but…"

He stared at his hands.

Atalanta said, "You contacted Kaufmann and arranged this river cruise. Kaufmann only knew that you were meeting your mother in Bingen. He had no idea you were on board the entire time."

"You are correct. I wanted to see them, all of them."

"Your children whose lives you have missed all those years."

"And my granddaughter. Lisl." His expression softened. "What a sweet little girl she is. But so tragic, too." He waited a moment and added, "Perhaps it should not have surprised me. Tragedy seems to follow this family."

"Can you tell me what really happened in Bayern that day?"

The captain continued to stare at his hands. He seemed reluctant to comply with her request.

She said softly, "I cannot claim a right to know. In fact, you have gone beyond anything reasonably to be expected of a father by shooting your own son to save my life."

"I had to do it. I could not let him commit another murder." The captain met her gaze, his expression bleak. "You think I mean the murders of the nurse and the lawyer. His wife. But I am referring to something else altogether. The only murder I myself witnessed."

Atalanta sucked in air. "*Your* wife. Did Otto…?" She could not complete the sentence with the horrible words kill his own mother.

"Otto was a very difficult child. He was different from other children. He seemed to feel neither pain nor respond to punishment. It was as if nothing really touched him. But he could react suddenly and violently when he felt something was unjust. During that holiday, my wife had just found out she was with child again. She was hopeful it would be a baby boy. She talked to me about it and Otto eavesdropped on our conversation. He ran over and threw himself at her, beating at her and shouting that he would have us all to himself or not at all, and that he did not want a baby brother. Gertrude he considered insignificant because she was a girl and he felt himself superior, but the idea of a baby brother made him furious.

"My wife tried to evade the beating by walking away but he went after her and somehow in the scuffle she fell over the edge. After that, Otto was like a marble statue. I tried to talk to him but he was unresponsive. It was like he was in shock and… I told myself he could not have meant to do it and he was no murderer. Just a scared little boy. My mother coaxed me into pretending that my wife and I had both died in a fatal accident during a walk in the mountains. I would disappear and she would raise the children. I was not happy with the arrangement but I was in shock and there was no time to think it over. I wanted to do what was best for the children.

"I … was perhaps also a coward. I had seen what my son was capable of and it bewildered me. I didn't want to be anywhere near him. Let someone else take care of him, I thought." The captain looked pained. "I saddled my mother with the problem and left. Over the years I followed what happened in their lives. I heard of the accident that killed his wife, and I was sorry for him and the little girl. I wanted to see them all and … somehow make up for lost time. But it was a mistake. I should never have asked Kaufmann to help me arrange the trip. It ended in so much bloodshed."

Atalanta shook her head. "You are not to blame. Sabine Freund blackmailed Otto with the knowledge of the truth behind his wife's death. That had nothing to do with you. He had already decided to kill her before the journey even began. He intentionally invited me along so he would have someone who could support the story of his grandmother being the intended victim. I am certain our meeting at the museum in Bonn was planned, and not the happy coincidence I believed it to be."

She swallowed hard.

"I was completely taken in by his charm for a long time. Although I did ask myself whether he could conspire to kill his grandmother to get her money, I never thought him capable of these other things. I never realised what he was like, deep inside."

The captain said, "When did you know who I was?"

"I guess I had seen a resemblance in your features before but I could not quite put my finger on it. When Kaufmann claimed to know the long-lost son, I did think about who it might be. And then when you fought with Otto, your faces close together... I saw it clearly."

"His face may resemble mine, but his heart does not." The captain sat up straighter. "I was disgusted when he killed my wife, and I feel even worse now. He is not like other human beings. There must be a name for it. If a good doctor looked at him and assessed his condition."

"Does it matter?" Atalanta asked. "Would a name, a complex term, make it better?"

The captain sighed heavily. "No. Nothing can make it better. My son is…" He faltered and looked away, his hands clenched into fists.

"But nobody knows he is your son. To all intents and purposes, you died in Bayern. No one outside the family needs to know. You can disappear again." Atalanta said it cheerfully as if it was a solution or a piece of good advice. She watched him carefully. He appeared stung.

"I will not abandon my mother while she is so troubled. Finally she will have to admit that Otto is too much for her to handle. That she cannot make him better or change him. Whatever she had in mind, it failed. And Gertrude. She needs help, too. She is addicted to those drops and … that fiancé of hers is only betraying her. She must break the engagement."

"I agree." Atalanta smiled at him. "It would be good if you could give her some support. But after all these years I cannot promise you will be welcome in this family. It is a family of prisoners, as Lisl put it. All held captive by secrets."

"Then it is about time the secrets came out in the open and the truth was told. It is time the chains were broken." The captain rose, suddenly determined. "I must also care for the girl, Lisl. She is all alone in the world now. Her mother dead, her father in prison. My mother never liked her but she must be cared for."

"I agree. Perhaps you can think of ways to show her the

world. She is very intelligent and creative and loves to see new places. She is also adventurous and a little daring."

The captain eyed her with a hint of fear in his eyes. "What if she is like her father?"

Atalanta smiled at him. "Otto questioned whether Lisl was his child. He believed his wife was unfaithful to him. That was why he had her killed. If Lisl is indeed not his, then you have nothing to worry about."

The captain scoffed. "Nothing to worry about? That girl has lived through more traumatic events in her short life than another person will in a lifetime. But I will do my very best to make her life more pleasant. Travelling, hmmm… I like that. Something to connect us."

He nodded at Atalanta and walked away. Atalanta stared after him. Here was a man who had abandoned his children in the belief he was doing the right thing, for them and for himself, and who was now, after all those years, back to do what was *really* the right thing. It was a little ray of light in an otherwise very dark affair.

"Mademoiselle…" Renard entered the salon, his expression troubled. "I have just received word that…" He paused, seemingly searching for the right way to phrase it. "Monsieur Lemont… He has had an accident."

"What? Raoul?" Atalanta jumped to her feet. "How serious is it?"

Renard avoided meeting her gaze. "I cannot be certain, of course, as I've only heard it from a connection—"

"Tell me what they said. Straightforward, without sparing me."

Renard waited a moment as if deciding whether to heed her request. Then he sighed before saying, "He is gravely injured. They do not know if he will survive."

The pain slashing through her was unbearable.

No! everything inside of her cried. *No! I cannot bear to lose him. Not him as well. I have already lost everyone I cared for. Let me keep Raoul.*

"Where is he?" she asked. "I must go to him."

Acknowledgments

As always, I'm grateful to all agents, editors, and authors who share online about the writing and publishing process. Special thanks to my fabulous editors Charlotte Ledger and Helen Williams for their thoughtful feedback; to Lucy Bennett and Gary Redford for the gorgeous cover illustration which captures the scenic Rhine view brilliantly, and to the entire One More Chapter and wider HarperCollins teams for their hard work on the series, especially the Rights team taking the series abroad.

When I plotted this story, I wanted Atalanta to face new personal challenges and connect the unfolding story with the folklore surrounding the Rhine, which although it contains many fairytale elements has always had a dark undercurrent. I hope the beautiful sights gave you an escapist experience exploring alongside Atalanta and enchanted you with the many attractions along this great river.

And if you haven't done so already, do check out all the other instalments in the series, which always have Atalanta visiting gorgeous locations where baffling mysteries await her. Happy reading!

Thank you for reading *Death on the Rhine*!

Join Atalanta for her next adventure in *Trouble in the Alps* as she rushes to Raoul's side after his accident, but soon finds herself trapped at a remote hotel in the snow-covered mountains.

Autumn 2025

Have you read the rest of the
Miss Ashford Investigates series?

Miss Atalanta Ashford suddenly finds herself the most eligible young lady in society when she inherits her grandfather's substantial fortune, but with it comes a legacy passed down from her grandfather ... sleuthing discreetly for Europe's elite.

Not one to back down from a challenge, Miss Ashford must depend on her sharp wit and charm to solve her first case, which takes her to the lush lavender fields of Provence and a wedding at the mansion of the Comte de Surmonne.

Miss Atalanta Ashford is sightseeing near Venice when a mysterious veiled lady approaches her with the urgent request to look into her daughter's mysterious death on the idyllic Greek island of Santorini. Whilst working as a companion for the eminent Bucardi family, the unfortunate girl took a plunge from the dramatic cliffs during a walk alone. But is all as it seems?

Sailing to Santorini and going undercover as the new companion, Miss Ashford soon discovers that her client hasn't told her the full truth. Someone is watching her. Now she must unravel the mystery and prevent the breathtaking azure sea views from becoming the last she too will ever see…

When novice detective Atalanta Ashford is whisked away to Italy by her friend, race car driver Raoul Lemont, she anticipates a happy holiday under the Tuscan sun. But a chance meeting on the Orient Express with Italian heiress Catharina Lanetti leads to a party invitation…and front row seats for a mysterious murder!

With their new friend under suspicion Atalanta and Raoul set to work trying to discover who really murdered Catharina's father. But with more than half a dozen suspects – all with compelling motive – Atalanta may just be facing her toughest case yet!

Miss Ashford INVESTIGATES

LAST DANCE in
· SALZBURG ·

· VIVIAN CONROY ·

After accepting an invitation to attend the ballet in snowy Salzburg, Atalanta is shocked when a convicted jewel thief is found dead in the concert hall where the theft occurred a decade ago.

Did he return to the scene of the crime because he wanted to prove his innocence? Is the real culprit among the high-society guests? In her quest for the truth, Atalanta uncovers dangerous secrets about the European elite that put her own life in mortal danger…

The smell of Glühwein and spiced Lebkuchen from the Austrian winter markets fill the air, but for Atalanta there's an intriguing puzzle to be solved.

Books available in paperback, eBook and audio!

ONE MORE CHAPTER

The author and One More Chapter would like to thank everyone who contributed to the publication of this story...

Analytics
James Brackin
Abigail Fryer

Audio
Fionnuala Barrett
Ciara Briggs

Contracts
Laura Amos
Laura Evans

Design
Lucy Bennett
Fiona Greenway
Liane Payne
Dean Russell

Digital Sales
Laura Daley
Lydia Grainge
Hannah Lismore

eCommerce
Laura Carpenter
Madeline ODonovan
Charlotte Stevens
Christina Storey
Jo Surman
Rachel Ward

Editorial
Kara Daniel
Charlotte Ledger
Lydia Mason
Laura McCallen
Ajebowale Roberts
Jennie Rothwell
Caroline Scott-Bowden
Helen Williams

Harper360
Jennifer Dee
Emily Gerbner
Ariana Juarez
Jean Marie Kelly
emma sullivan
Sophia Wilhelm

International Sales
Peter Borcsok
Ruth Burrow
Colleen Simpson
Ben Wright

Inventory
Sarah Callaghan
Kirsty Norman

Marketing & Publicity
Chloe Cummings
Grace Edwards
Emma Petfield

Operations
Melissa Okusanya
Hannah Stamp

Production
Denis Manson
Simon Moore
Francesca Tuzzeo

Rights
Helena Font Brillas
Ashton Mucha
Zoe Shine
Aisling Smyth
Lucy Vanderbilt

Trade Marketing
Ben Hurd
Eleanor Slater

The HarperCollins Distribution Team

The HarperCollins Finance & Royalties Team

The HarperCollins Legal Team

The HarperCollins Technology Team

UK Sales
Isabel Coburn
Jay Cochrane
Sabina Lewis
Holly Martin
Harriet Williams
Leah Woods

And every other essential link in the chain from delivery drivers to booksellers to librarians and beyond!